Also by Joyce Muriel:

Who is My Enemy?

Ellie's Story

Ripeness is All

The End of the Story

Goodbye Chastity

NOT IN OUR STARS

NOT IN OUR STARS

Joyce Muriel

ATHENA PRESS
LONDON

NOT IN OUR STARS
Copyright © Joyce Muriel 2010

ISBN 978 1 84748 789 6

First published 2010 by
ATHENA PRESS
Queen's House, 2 Holly Road
Twickenham TW1 4EG
United Kingdom

Printed for Athena Press

Prologue

It was a beautiful afternoon in late May when the girl walked into the wood. The sky was a silken canopy of startling blue with a few white, fluffy islands drifting across it. The sun, beating down, gilded the trees; a little stream nearby trickled gently over its pebbles. That was the only noticeable sound, for there was no breeze strong enough to stir the leaves of the trees; even the fragile pennants of the willow hanging over the stream were motionless. *Nature is holding its breath, sharing in my joy*, she thought.

The shade provided by the trees was welcome and the path was easy. She knew this way well now, for she had met her lover several times in the little hidden clearing. Even so, she could scarcely believe that it was only six weeks since she first met him at the yacht club ball. Of course, she had noticed him immediately. He was blond, tanned and handsome, immensely popular and an excellent sailor. But she had never expected that he would take any interest in her, even when they were introduced. Why should he? She was just a poor girl staying with a distant relative who was kind enough to give her a holiday in return for looking after the children. A nobody.

But it had been so different! He had looked deep into her blue eyes and she had smiled at him, and suddenly they were dancing together. In fact, they had danced together several times. During the next week they met often, but always in the company of others. Nevertheless, by his look and the few words he addressed to her, he made her understand that she was special to him. When he discovered that she lived nearby, he had suggested a walk in the woods so that they might get to know one another better.

When her relative finally became aware and warned her about him, it was too late. She was already deeply in love and convinced that he felt the same about her. He had never known anyone so beautiful before, she was the girl of his dreams he told her. His marriage had been a disaster, he said, a terrible mistake. He had never loved Rosalind, as he loved her. How could she not believe him? He convinced her that a wonderful future lay before them.

Now, on this perfect day, he had made it possible for them to spend a whole afternoon together in this perfect spot, their favourite meeting place.

She had read about love, sometimes she had dreamed about it but she had never understood that the reality could be so intoxicating, so wonderful. In a few moments she would see him and they would be together for three enchanted hours. As she almost danced along, the last two lines of an old-fashioned song her mother had sometimes sung came into her mind: 'A Garden of Eden just made for two, with nothing to mar our joy.' She had thought it a bit silly and sentimental but now it seemed a perfect description of their secret clearing in the woods, particularly on a day like this. *A Garden of Eden*, she told herself. As she hurried ecstatically towards him, she had no thought of the serpent. His marriage, he said, had been a disaster, a terrible mistake.

Chapter One

Of course, Catherine was the first to be told. Even Philip would not risk disregarding that unwritten family law. It was about 11 p.m. one Sunday evening in late November when she answered the telephone and, to her surprise, found Philip on the other end. 'Is something wrong?' she asked immediately, for a call from him at this hour was so unexpected that she was already afraid.

In his usual calm voice and, without any preamble, he gave his news. 'Magda is in hospital. I'm ringing from there.'

'In hospital?' she interrupted him immediately. 'Oh, my God, what has happened?'

'I'm not really quite sure. St Luke's rang me about an hour ago. Magda had just walked into their A&E and collapsed on the floor.'

'Oh, no! Whatever had happened to her? She was perfectly well when I saw a few days ago!'

'That is still not quite clear. She was bleeding from a scalp wound. Fortunately, they identified her from some letters in her handbag and rang me.'

'I don't understand. Was she unconscious? Had she been mugged?'

'She was only briefly unconscious and it doesn't seem as if she's been robbed, but we can't be sure as yet—'

Before he could say any more Catherine interrupted him. 'You're not making sense, Philip dear. Why did they have to look in her handbag? What on earth was she doing in that rough area anyway, and on her own? Or wasn't she on her own?'

'She was on her own, and I don't know all the answers.' Philip tried to suppress his irritation at Catherine's usual love of sensation; though God knew, Magda had given her plenty of material. *Why, oh, why?* 'I thought you would want to know. But I must go now. I must get back to Magda. I'll ring you later and give you more news.'

'No need.' Catherine had made one of her sudden decisions. 'I'll drive straight over as soon as I've told Adam. It'll only take me about half an hour. Will you meet me in the main entrance hall? Poor, darling Magda! I must see her and do what I can to help. You know how close we've always been. I've always looked after her. I can't let her down now!'

Knowing it would be useless to protest, he agreed readily. 'If you are coming, perhaps you can bring her whatever's necessary. They say that she will have to stay in tonight and perhaps longer. You'll know what to bring, won't you?'

'Of course I will.' Catherine was delighted to have a part to play. 'By the way, have you told Dad or Constance or Sebastien yet?'

'No, I don't feel that there's any point in bothering them at the moment. But, if you want to…'

'No,' Catherine was very decisive. 'Better to tell them tomorrow when we know more.'

Catherine was already waiting in the main entrance hall when he came to find her. Small and somewhat plump, she was wearing the usual dark brown tight-fitting trousers and the matching cosy, fur-trimmed jacket that she always favoured in winter, and was carrying a large bag. Desperate though the situation was, she had taken time, he noticed, to attend to her appearance. Her 'golden' hair was a sleek shining cap, framing an attractive though slightly plump face with discreet eye make-up and vivid lipstick.

It was hard to believe that she was as overwhelmed as her words implied. 'Oh, thank God you've turned up! I've been almost frantic with worry. How is she?'

She looked up at him as he stood tall and straight beside her. He was as well dressed and elegant as always; his dark hair, prematurely streaked with grey, was unruffled. He showed no obvious signs of stress. She tried to look appealingly in to his dark eyes but his gaze appeared to be fixed on some point beyond her. 'Has she seen the doctor yet?'

'Yes, her scalp wound has been sewn up, she has been sent to X-ray and the doctor seemed pretty sure that she has suffered no serious damage. Naturally, they want to keep her in for tonight, at least.'

'Of course. Thank heaven it's not as bad as I imagined. Can I see her?'

'I'll take you straightaway. It's very good of you to come. I've had her moved to a private room. We can go straight there. Let me carry your bag.'

Without waiting for her answer, he took her bag and began to walk swiftly away towards the lift. With difficulty she kept up with him.

As they neared the lift, he stopped. 'I should warn you, I think, that the situation is not as simple as it might at first seem.'

'What do you mean?' A thousand frightening suggestions rushed into her mind but, before she could voice any of them, Philip continued, 'Magda appears to be suffering from a temporary amnesia. She can remember nothing that has happened since Friday afternoon until she came to in the hospital. At first, she couldn't even remember her own name.'

'I see. So that's why they had to look into her handbag before they could even ring you. I was puzzled about that. I was afraid she might be still unconscious.'

'No, she was only unconscious for a short time. Fortunately she was able to recognise me when she saw me and gradually to recall her own identity, but she still can't remember anything about the weekend. She has no idea where she was staying, who she was with or even how she came to be in this part of the world.'

As Catherine followed him into the lift, which had now arrived, she looked thoughtfully at him. Without any of the drama he had dreaded she simply asked him quickly, 'But surely you knew where she was going and who she was staying with?'

'Apparently not,' he answered her, above the sound of the robotic voice assuring them that the doors were about to shut. 'I assumed – wrongly it seems – that Magda was going to stay with a friend she has met once or twice before over the last few years. I thought you might be able to help.' Before Catherine could answer, the robotic voice assured them that they were at the third floor and that the doors were opening.

Philip picked up the bag and she followed him out of the lift. As he was about to turn left, she caught hold of his arm and stopped him. 'I don't understand. Why do you say that you wrongly assumed? How do you know?'

'I rang up the friend I thought she was visiting and she told me that she hadn't seen Magda that weekend and that she'd not even been expecting to see her. In fact, she said that she'd not seen Magda for some time.' It was difficult to guess his feelings, for his manner and voice both were as calm and controlled as always.

Controlling the shock that she felt, Catherine managed to ask quietly, 'Who is this friend? I wasn't aware that Magda had any close friends.'

'Barbara Metcalf. I imagine that you must know her. Do you?'

'Not really. It's ages since I met her. I think that she and Magda were friends at school but I had no idea that they still were. And surely I would have known. Magda and I have always been so close, as you know.'

'I'm no longer sure that they were.' Releasing himself, he began to move towards the door.

Hurrying after him, Catherine caught hold of his arm again. She was obviously very agitated. 'This is terrible! There must be some other explanation. Surely you're not suggesting that Magda has been lying?'

'I don't know. Perhaps I misunderstood her.'

'Have you said anything to anyone else? I mean, have you told Dad or Constance or Sebastien?'

'No. I only called you because you and Magda are so close.'

'Thank God for that! Don't say anything to any of them for the present, please. You know what they're like.'

'I don't know that I really do but I have no wish to tell any of them at present.'

'They don't love her. I do.'

Catherine followed him through the door into the side ward. Without hesitating, she hurried to the bed where her sister lay propped up with pillows. Magda's normally pale complexion seemed almost transparent in its pallor; her blue eyes, normally so bright, were like dim, cloudy pools. Her dark hair, usually so immaculate, hung in tangles to her shoulders. Her head was bandaged. She neither smiled nor moved as Catherine bent to kiss her.

'Oh my dear.' Catherine sat on the chair by the bedside, taking her sister's cold hands in hers and rubbing them gently. 'I was so upset when Philip told me you were here in this place. I love you so much; you know that I can't bear to think of you suffering. I've always felt like that about you. I can't help it. You're always my baby sister, you know. How do you feel now?'

Magda made no answer but it seemed to Catherine that she felt her sister's fingers clutch hers, although her face remained unchanged. She still stared straight ahead, looking neither at her sister nor at her husband, who was still standing as if stranded, in the middle of the room.

This silence was unbearable to Catherine. 'You do know me, don't you? Surely, you haven't forgotten…' Her voice trailed away as Magda's fingers pressed hers more firmly. Was Magda trying to convey a message? She looked desperately towards Philip, but he seemed to be concentrating on the wall above Magda's head. *What an exasperating man he is*, she thought.

Suddenly, Magda turned towards her sister and smiled. It was only a small change but it was definitely a smile. 'Of course, I know you, Cathy. How could I forget you? I'm very glad you've come.' Catherine was tremendously relieved. The use of the name 'Cathy', which only Magda ever used, was even more comforting than the smile.

'Thank heaven! I don't think I could bear it if you forgot me. I think, however, that you'll be even more pleased to see me when you know what I've brought for you.' She turned to Philip who, without a word, passed the travel bag to her. 'You look as if you could do with some TLC.' She was happy now, for this was what she loved doing – cherishing people, especially her beloved Magda, who so rarely gave her the chance now.

'What's in the bag?' Magda was looking better already.

'Well, there's a completely new cream silk nightdress. I bought it for myself but it was too small. You know me,' she was chattering cheerfully now and laughing, 'I can't bear to face the truth about myself. I'm fat!'

'You're just plump,' Magda corrected her as she always did.

'If you say so. But it will fit you perfectly.' Taking the night-dress out of its packet, she spread it on the bed.

'It's lovely!' Magda stroked the silk. 'I can't bear to stay in this horrid hospital gown another minute.'

'Don't worry, we'll soon have you out of it.' Catherine was in her element now. Confidently, she ordered Philip, 'If you can lift her up and support her, I'm sure I can get her into the nightdress.'

He proved to be much more confident than she had expected, as he gently lifted up his wife and supported her. When the exchange had been made, he held Magda gently while Catherine rearranged her pillows. Then he gently lowered her again – all without a word.

'You're wonderful,' Catherine told him. 'Adam would never have done that without a lot of questions and a lot of fuss.' Philip smiled but made no comment.

'Now we can begin your real rehabilitation,' Catherine said, rummaging in the bag. 'I've brought toilet articles, a brush and comb and most important of all – make-up. There is nothing better for restoring a woman's morale.'

'That I think is my cue for making my escape for a few minutes,' Philip said unexpectedly. 'I'll leave you, my darling, in Catherine's competent hands while I go in search of a cup of coffee.'

'At this hour, you'll be lucky,' Catherine retorted, opening her hazel eyes wide.

'No need to worry. I was invited by a friendly nurse to drop in if I needed refreshments.'

'Well, you certainly don't waste any time!' Catherine said laughing. 'You'll have to watch him, Magda!'

Left alone with her sister, Catherine began what was for her an enjoyable task. She loved caring for people and greatly regretted that her two children, now in their mid-teens, seemed no longer to need her.

Magda, however, had always been special. As a delicate child, nearly four years younger, she had been Catherine's special love. Constance, their elder sister, had tried to interfere from time to time, but Catherine had never accepted that Constance could love and understand Magda as she did.

'Would you like me to give you a little wash first?' As she spoke, Catherine took flannel, soap and towel out of a plastic bag.

'It can't be much, I'm afraid, but it should refresh you a little.' She was already running water in the hand basin as she spoke.

'I would love that, but do be careful of the dressing on the right side of my head, won't you?'

'Of course, dearest.' Deftly and gently, Catherine sponged her sister's hands and face, carefully removing any traces of blood that were left.

'That's much better. Thank you.' Magda opened her brilliant blue eyes fully for the first time, then swiftly closed them again as if she were very weary.

She doesn't want me to ask her any questions, Catherine thought but I must try before Philip returns. 'I think I'd better brush your hair a little,' she said aloud. 'Don't worry. I'll be very gentle.'

'I'm sure you will, Cathy.'

As she carefully brushed out the tangles in Magda's long dark hair, Catherine asked her first question. 'Have you really no memory of anything at all since Friday?'

'None at all.' Magda's voice was suddenly firm and decided.

'It must be horrible. I've heard of it happening to people but it's difficult to imagine what it's like.'

'There's just darkness,' Magda shivered as she spoke, 'and a feeling of cold.'

'What's the last thing you remember?'

Magda frowned. 'I seem to remember leaving the house. I think I was in a hurry. The next thing I remember is someone asking me if I was all right. I was very frightened. They told me I was in hospital and they put me in a wheelchair. They asked me my name but I had no idea what it was. It was such a relief when Philip turned up. He was so calm and reassuring about everything, as he always is.'

Catherine gave a final brush to her sister's now smooth hair. 'At least we know where you weren't this weekend.' She remarked as she put down the hairbrush and picked up the make-up bag.

'What do you mean?' Magda stared at her.

'You weren't with Barbara Metcalf.'

'Barbara Metcalf? What on earth are you talking about?

Catherine hesitated but only for a moment. She had never

been considered tactful. *So why should I start now?* she asked herself. As she began to smooth cream delicately over her sister's pale face, she said bluntly, 'I mean that your Barbara Metcalf alibi has been blown – completely. So don't try to wriggle out of it.'

'What do you mean? I don't understand!'

'Well, as soon as Philip had sorted things out a bit and phoned me, he remembered that you'd said you were going to visit her, so he rang her up to tell her what had happened.'

'I see.' Magda waited while her sister applied a little lipstick.

Catherine, standing back, admired her work. 'You look so much better, almost your normal beautiful self.'

Ignoring that, Magda went back to Barbara Metcalf. 'And I suppose that Barbara told Philip that I had not spent the weekend with her and that she had never expected me to do so?'

Catherine sat down on the side of the bed. 'Right, but I think there's even worse.'

'Whatever could that be?'

'I gather from Philip that she told him that she hadn't seen you for years, although you had told him some times that you were visiting her. That's true, isn't it?

'Yes,' Magda replied calmly.

'What the hell have you been getting up to?' Catherine asked. When Magda didn't answer, she continued lovingly, 'You know you can tell me. We've always been best friends, haven't we?' Without answering Magda continued to study her face in the mirror Catherine was holding up before her. 'Would you like a bit of rouge? You're paler than usual.'

'No thanks. You've done a good job, Cathy. I feel much better.'

'Good.' Catherine took the mirror and put it away in the bag with the other articles she had brought. She returned to the attack. 'You can't ignore it, Magda dear. It won't just go away.' When Magda didn't answer, she took her hands in hers. 'You know you can trust me. I suppose it's another man, isn't it? Of course I don't approve but I can understand. Philip is a very formidable person and he is twelve years older than you. I'm right, aren't I?'

'No, you're not right,' Magda said forcibly. 'I'm not having some silly, sordid affair. It's much more serious than that. Please, don't try to interfere, Catherine.'

Catherine was hurt. 'You know that I'm not trying to interfere. It's just that I love you and want to help you. I never thought you would reject me. But you've just got to understand that you must tell Philip now, and I want you to know that I'm always your friend.'

'I know you're right, Cathy, but I can't say anything to anyone now, so please don't try to make me. I promise you I will talk to Philip but I'm not sure about anything at the moment. I'm very tired and my head aches terribly.' Closing her eyes, she leaned back.

'I didn't mean to upset you, dear.'

Catherine stood up as the door opened to admit Philip bearing a cup of coffee and a biscuit which he offered to her. As she gulped the coffee down gratefully, Philip approached his wife. 'I'm sorry, darling,' he said gently, 'but I wasn't allowed to bring you anything. The Sister is just about to come and settle you for the night.' He bent down and kissed her tenderly.

'I must be going.' Catherine put down her empty cup. 'I don't want to risk waking Adam.'

'Doesn't he know you're here?' Philip was surprised.

'Oh, you know Adam! Well, perhaps you don't. He was already asleep when you rang. I shook him until he opened his eyes and told him that I was going to see Magda, who had been taken into hospital. He just said, "Good," and went to sleep again.' She laughed. 'If I'm quiet, he won't wake up until I'm back, but I mustn't leave it too long.' She could tell that Philip thought all this strange but he did not say anything.

After giving Magda a quick kiss, Catherine said, 'I'll ring you tomorrow evening to see how you are.'

'Please do. And thank you once again for all you've done, Cathy.'

'You know I'll do anything for you, love. Just ask me.'

'I'll see you to your car,' Philip said. 'This is not the safest of neighbourhoods.'

'Thanks.' She waved to Magda as they went out of the room. To her surprise, she found herself unable to ask Philip all the questions she had intended to ask him. His reserve was impenetrable, as always.

Only when she was about to leave did she manage to ask him if he was returning home that night. He answered without hesitation, 'No, I intend to spend the night with Magda.'

'Is that necessary? They'll sedate her and you won't get much sleep in the armchair.'

'That hardly matters.' He was quite decided. 'It's obvious she's had a frightening experience and needs comfort. I should be there in case she wakes and wants me. Surely you agree, Catherine?'

'Of course! That's just what I would expect you to do.' She was stupidly annoyed that she had not thought of it. How lucky Magda was to be loved like that! Apparently, no doubts, no questions worried Philip. She waved to him as he turned to return to the hospital.

As he arrived back at the door of Magda's ward, Philip met the nurse who was just coming out. After greeting him, she stopped briefly to tell him that she had just settled Magda for the night and given her a sedative. 'The scalp wound shouldn't give her any more trouble,' she said, 'but she's still very shocked and frightened. I think it might be a good idea for you to stay, as you said. I'm sorry we can't give you a bed but I've left you a spare blanket and a pillow.'

After thanking her warmly, he quietly entered Magda's room. One little light had been left burning. Magda appeared to be sleeping. Carefully, he settled himself into the chair, hoping not to disturb her. A few minutes later, however, a quiet voice asked, 'Is that you, Philip?'

'Yes, it's me, darling. I'm sorry if I disturbed you.'

'You haven't. I was waiting for you. Are you going to stay a little while?' Turning her head, she put out her hand towards him.

Gently, he took her hand in his. 'I've decided to spend the night here. I don't want you to be on your own.'

'Oh, I'm so glad!' Her blue eyes opened wide as he bent over her to kiss her. A sudden thought struck her. 'But won't it be very uncomfortable for you?'

He smiled at her. 'No need to worry about that. I've spent

many far less comfortable nights during my years in the Army. I shall be fine. Now, close your eyes and go to sleep, as you've been told to do.'

She did so, but only to open them again a few moments later. 'You're not angry with me, are you? I was afraid you might be. Catherine said—'

'Don't listen to Catherine,' he cut in before she could say any more. 'She doesn't understand our relationship. I'm certainly not angry now but I shall be if you don't try to sleep.'

'You're always so kind to me,' she told him, smiling.

'I love you, my darling.' There were no words he felt in which he could adequately express his feelings. 'Now, go to sleep, please.'

In a very short time she was asleep. Gently releasing her hand, he settled down in the armchair, tucking the blanket around him. For a long time he lay without moving in the darkened room, listening to Magda's quiet breathing.

It was easy for him to imagine what Catherine had hinted at. Naturally, she had suspected Magda of a secret affair and had probably tried to get her to admit it, believing probably that the memory loss was just a ruse or, at least, a partial one. She could not know, because Magda would never have confided in her, how close was the relationship between himself and Magda; far too close, in fact, for him ever to suspect Magda of infidelity.

That possibility had never crossed his mind but now, alone in the semi-darkness, he had to admit that there had to be some explanation for the strange happenings of the weekend. During the fifteen years of their marriage this was, he thought, the first time that Magda had ever been away for a whole weekend by herself. She had been away for the occasional night but she had always told him why and when. This time it had been sprung on him, together with the not very convincing story of spending it with an old friend – a story which had so easily been proved to be false.

It was clear to him as he looked back that this weekend had not been planned by Magda in advance. It seemed to him that a sudden demand had been made on her to which she had only reluctantly agreed. She had not been very happy about going but had explained this by saying that her friend was ill. Whatever the reason, it was now clear that something very terrifying had happened to her. Even if she were able to, he thought, she did not want to recall the truth.

Suddenly, she stirred and cried out, sitting up a little, as she did so. 'Philip, are you still here?'

'Of course I am, Magda darling,' he replied quickly, taking her hand in his. 'You're safe with me. Go back to sleep again.' Her hand clutched his. Gradually, she relaxed. She was asleep again.

As he lay there he remembered their first meeting fifteen years earlier. He had reluctantly gone to some boring reception and was just about to think of slipping away when he had seen her standing alone, apparently feeling as detached as he was. As he looked across the room, he noticed her leaning gracefully against the mantelpiece – a small, slim girl wearing a simple dress of an unusual and vivid shade of blue. As if drawn by some power of attraction he made his way towards her. As he reached her side she looked up at him and he was surprised to discover that her eyes were the same shade of blue as her dress.

She declined his offer of a drink but seemed willing to talk. Very quickly it occurred to him that he had never before met anyone so easy to talk to. About a quarter of an hour later, he persuaded her to escape with him for a quiet meal. That had been the beginning. After about three more meetings he had definitely decided that she was the woman he intended to marry.

I've fallen in love, he admitted to himself in amazement. At thirty-seven he had long given up such romantic notions, if indeed he had ever had them. Although he had known her for so short a time, he was absolutely sure that he loved her and would always love her. When he asked her to marry him, he told her this. She was surprised, but after a little consideration she refused him. When he persisted, she eventually accepted him but her acceptance was unusual. 'I will marry you,' she told him, 'but I can't say that I love you. I know nothing about love. I like you, however, and I like the life you're offering me. I promise to be a faithful wife. Is that enough?'

He told himself it was enough. Even as he said the words, however, he knew that it was much more than that for both of them. Magda at twenty-five was an unusually mature young woman who had just returned from a two-year world trip on her own. They were both people who had chosen to be solitary but who now chose to be together and share everything.

Not quite everything, however. From the beginning he had known that Magda had a secret. He believed that one day she would share it with him. He had been content to wait. Perhaps the time had now come... Even as he thought that, she began to move restlessly and to cry out for him. Without hesitating, he went to her bed, lay down next to her and took her in his arms, soothing and caressing her until she fell into a deep, quiet sleep.

He stayed with her until it was nearly dawn, when at last he felt it was safe to return to his chair and snatch a brief sleep. He had been absolutely right to stay with her. He knew that, but he still did not know why she was so frightened.

Chapter Two

As soon as the Monday evening meal was over, Catherine decided that she had to ring Magda. Since she wished the conversation to be private, she went to the small bedroom, which was known as her study. Her two children, after reluctantly helping to clear away the evening meal, had retired to their own rooms on the pretext, at least, of doing their homework. Adam, her husband, was as usual, sprawled in his armchair watching some boring sports programme on the television. He would probably soon fall asleep but, in any case, he would certainly not worry about her absence.

She had been worrying about Magda all day and had found it difficult to concentrate on lecturing on geography to college students with an apparently limited concentration capacity. Even with Magda on her mind she could not help thinking as she often did, *If these are the teachers of the future, then God help the poor kids!* But on this day, thoughts about Magda had been always in the forefront of her mind. There was so much she needed to ask her, so much help poor Magda obviously needed. She was quite sure that her sister would be honest with her, if she could get her alone away from her husband.

With this aim in mind, she rang Magda's mobile number but, to her surprise and discomfiture, she found herself being answered by Philip. 'Where is Magda?' she asked him. 'Has something gone wrong? Has she had a relapse?'

In his usual calm manner, he reassured her. 'The doctors say she's fine but she still is exhausted, probably as the result of the shock. I've just seen her into bed and she's already asleep, so I answered her phone.'

'That's a relief. When did the hospital allow her to come home?' At least, she could get some information.

'Not until the middle of the afternoon. She had some more tests and then we had to wait to see the consultant. He simply prescribed rest and quiet for a few days.'

'What about her memory? Has that returned?'

'Not as yet, but the doctors seem to think that it will in time. They emphasised very strongly, however, that she must not be worried about it. Questions might cause stress and make it worse.'

She felt quite sure that these remarks were repeated especially for her benefit. *Has Magda*, she wondered, *told him about her questions and doubts?* It was difficult for her to be sure how close their relationship was. She decided to say nothing on the subject. 'So, I can't speak to her tonight. I did so want to have a word with her to reassure her that I care and want to help.'

'I'm absolutely sure that Magda would never doubt that. When she wakes, I'll certainly give her your love and tell her that you called.'

He's determined to keep me away from her, Catherine told herself, admitting at the same time that she was no match for Philip. Then, just as she was about to ring off, he surprised her. 'Would you and Adam be able to come for an evening meal?' he asked her. 'Magda and I were discussing this possibility before she went to sleep.' Before she could reply, he continued, 'It would be easier, probably, if you both made your way here separately from work. You could be here between six thirty and seven, couldn't you?'

'Of course, it's a lovely idea! Thanks very much.' Catherine was amazed. 'What day do you suggest?'

'Tomorrow, if that's possible. Or the day after, perhaps. It's far too long since we got together. I think it will cheer Magda up. What do you say?'

'Tomorrow would be fine for me but I'd better ask Adam first.'

'Your family won't mind being left, will they? You won't need to get a sitter, will you?'

'If I know them, they'll welcome the chance to be on their own. Lucy's just seventeen, you know and Mark's nearly fifteen.'

He laughed. 'I'm afraid I'm disgustingly out of touch. Shall we fix on tomorrow, then, unless you ring me to say that Adam can't make it?'

'That's fine. If you don't hear from me in the next hour we'll be coming tomorrow.' She was delighted and determined not to allow Adam to make any objections. A sudden thought struck her, however. 'Won't it be a bit much for Magda when she's unwell?'

'Magda won't have to do anything. I shall cook. You may not know it but cooking's always been a hobby of mine. I shall enjoy it. We look forward to seeing you.'

'Have you told Dad or anyone else about Magda?' she asked him before he could ring off.

'No, Magda doesn't want them to be bothered. But I'll leave that to you, if you think it should be done.'

'I'll just mention it to Dad when I ring. He can tell Constance. Sebastien and Vivienne are away at the moment anyway. I know that Magda wouldn't want me to make a fuss. I hope we shall see you tomorrow.'

When she returned to the sitting room she was so jubilant that she switched off the television thereby making sure that Adam woke up fully.

'Why did you do that?' he asked, sitting up, clearly very irritated.

'Because you weren't watching anyway, and I've got some important news. We are having a meal tomorrow evening with Magda and Philip. He has actually invited us.' She sat down opposite him, smiling triumphantly.

'I thought you said this morning that she was ill in hospital,' was his only response.

'Why don't you ever listen?' She found the constant explanations he required so very tedious. 'I told you that she had an accident and was taken to hospital with a scalp wound. They only kept her in for observation and Philip brought her home today. But she still can't remember what happened. She's asleep at the moment and so he spoke to me.'

'And he's invited us to a meal tomorrow and we've agreed, although I haven't actually been asked.'

'It's difficult to ask you anything when you're nearly always asleep, so I have to make decisions for both of us. I don't see why you should object.'

'I don't object.' He stood up and moved towards the kitchen door. 'At least it'll probably be a good meal and I shan't have to cook it.'

She resisted the temptation to rise to that. The fact that she arrived home later than he did and was therefore not expected to cook the evening meal had long been the cause of many disputes. Although he actually enjoyed doing it, he nevertheless wanted it to be regarded as a great benefit that he conferred on the family. Catherine resented this. Tonight, however, she had more important matters to discuss. 'As a matter of fact,' she simply replied, 'Philip is going to cook. He says that he enjoys it.'

'Good for him. But why this honour? It must be the first time in the fifteen years they've been married.'

As he opened the door, she called out, 'Where are you going?'

'To the kitchen, of course.'

'Why? I want to talk to you.'

'I thought I'd make a pot of tea. Do you fancy a cup?'

'Good idea. But don't be too long about it. I must talk to you.'

After few minutes, she decided to follow him and found, as she had expected, that he was only just about to fill the kettle. *What do men do, in these lost minutes?* she wondered, as she laid the mugs on the tray and removed the milk from the refrigerator.

When they were, at last, settled comfortably in the sitting room with their mugs of tea and a plate of biscuits, she made sure of him. 'You have no objection, then, to having a meal with Magda and Philip tomorrow? Because if you have, I'll have to ring him.'

'No, I can't really think of any,' he replied thoughtfully. As she helped herself to a chocolate biscuit, he added, 'You'll never lose weight if you keep on eating those.'

'I'm not trying to lose weight at the moment,' she snapped. 'I'm worried and you know I always eat then. It's all right for you, you can pig it as much as you like without putting a pound on!'

'What are you worried about now?' he asked, wisely ignoring her last remark.

'Magda, of course.'

'But I thought you said that she was at home, getting better.'

'She is, but that doesn't solve the mystery.'

'What mystery?' He seemed puzzled.

She was exasperated again. 'The mystery of where she was at the weekend. Don't you ever listen to anything I say? I told you that she staggered into St Luke's Hospital on Sunday night and collapsed. She was supposed to have been spending the weekend with a friend but she hadn't been.'

'Where had she been, then? I thought that had all been sorted out by now.'

'That's just it, it hasn't been. She's lost her memory, or so she says, and no one knows where she's been.'

Adam considered this for a moment or two while he finished his tea. After putting down his empty mug, he merely said unhelpfully, 'That's more Philip's worry than yours, I should think.'

'How can you say that when you know how much she means to me? I've always loved her. You never do understand how I feel! You don't even want to try.' She was on the verge of tears. 'She's always been my little sister. She was different from the rest of the family and I looked after her. We've always been very close. I suppose the trouble is that you're just *jealous*.' Her hazel eyes were wide and staring. She almost spat the words at him.

Adam held himself in check. He really did not know what to say but he did know that if he said the wrong thing it would result in one of those terrible outbursts of Catherine's, which frightened him because they seemed so irrational. 'I'm sorry,' he said, after a long pause. 'I didn't mean to upset you. I was only trying to say, I suppose, that she's forty now and has been married to Philip for fifteen years. It's his job surely to look after her, if she needs looking after.'

Suddenly and unexpectedly she was deflated. Her eyes filled with tears. 'You're right, I suppose. The trouble is he isn't making a very good job of it, is he?'

'Why on earth do you say that? He earns pots of money in the City and she has everything she wants. Surely she hasn't been complaining to you?

'Of course not. Magda would never do that. You know that.'

'I didn't think she would. So, why do you say that Philip isn't looking after her?'

'I should have thought that would have been clear even to you. She seems to have spent time away from home recently. Perhaps she's seeing someone else… Have you ever noticed how often she does go away?'

'I can't say that I have. It's no business of mine. But do you really think you know? You've been too busy to see much of her yourself recently.'

She laughed. 'You would say that! Well, something obviously went wrong this weekend. As a result Philip has discovered that she wasn't where she was supposed to be. So she says she's lost her memory.'

Adam was suddenly quite angry. 'Do you realise what you're saying? You seem to be telling me that your wonderful Magda is a liar and a cheat. You don't seem to think much of her.'

'*I love her*,' she almost shouted at him. 'She specially needs loving. If she's desperate, she might do something silly.'

'Have you asked her?'

'I tried, but I didn't have much opportunity as Philip was there nearly all the time.'

'Well, you should have the opportunity to talk to her tomorrow. Philip's giving you the chance.'

'If you can keep him occupied, I might manage to talk to her.'

'I don't mind that. I've always found him a pleasant enough bloke. He actually knows something about football, although rugby's really his game.'

Catherine smiled but only said, 'Good. I can rely then on your cooperation.'

'I'll do my best.' Adam stood up. 'Would you like some more tea?'

'Yes, but not out of this pot. It's horribly stewed.'

'That's all right. I'll make a fresh pot.' He was relieved that the threatened storm seemed to have passed over.

'It's my turn.' She was almost gracious. 'You go back to your armchair and I'll bring it in.'

'Suits me fine.' Adam strolled back to his chair and settled himself comfortably.

A few minutes later when she came back with a fresh pot of tea, he surprised her by saying, 'I've never understood your family, you know.'

'Whatever made you think of that?'

'It was what you said just now about nobody really loving Magda. It was never like that in my home. Mum and Dad always seemed to love Jack and me equally. There was no favouritism. Surely you didn't really mean what you said?'

'I'm afraid there was no doubt about it, particularly as far as Mum was concerned. Constance was definitely Mum's favourite, perhaps because she was the first baby and a girl. They were very much alike in looks and character.'

'I never knew your mum,' he reminded her. 'She died soon after we met.'

'Of course, I'd forgotten. Sebastien was the only boy, so Dad naturally made a great fuss of him always. I was the baby for four years until Magda arrived. I suspect she wasn't really intended, and that might explain it.'

'I bet you hated her then,' Adam remarked.

'I don't think so, not for long, anyway.' She tried to remember. Suddenly she had a clear picture of a tiny fragile-looking toddler with dark curls and vivid blue eyes, running towards her with a hopeful smile and arms outstretched. 'Cathy, Cathy, wait for me! Magda wants to come with you.' Cathy encircles the toddler in her arms just before she falls. 'Magda loves Cathy,' the little girl says, holding up her face to be kissed, 'more than anyone.' Cathy holds her little sister fiercely, telling herself that she will always love Magda.

Looking back, she realised for the first time that it was not only Magda that had needed to be loved but that she, Catherine, had also needed to have someone special to herself, and that need still existed. Aware that Adam was waiting for an answer, she tried to speak calmly. 'I suppose I may have done so at first, but it wasn't possible not to love her. She was so lovely and so different from the rest of us. She was quite fragile and often ill before she was five, and I looked after her. No one else seemed to bother much.

'I used to make up stories about her. She was like someone from another world, a changeling, perhaps. We were all big and fair with brownish eyes, while she was small, pale and dark with those amazing blue eyes. I always wanted to protect her. I don't know whether that makes sense to you.'

'You've never said much about it before, but I think it does,' Adam replied. 'But you don't have to feel like that anymore,' he continued, 'that's Philip's job now, and he's being doing it pretty well for fifteen years, I should say. He earns a fortune in the City and she can have everything she wants. What's for you to worry about?' Picking up the remote control, he switched back to the sports programme. The discussion was ended as far as he was concerned.

Somehow, Catherine stopped herself from screaming at him. He wouldn't understand her feelings; he never did. He'd simply be irritated. Why, she asked herself, as she looked at him sprawled in his armchair, had she been so stupid as to marry such an ordinary man? He was so different from the men in her family. 'Mediocre' was the unkind word that came into her mind. She studied him as if for the first time – medium brown hair, now growing a little thin at the front; weak brown eyes masked by strong glasses. His face was so ordinary that it was difficult to describe or even to remember.

He was not exactly lazy but he certainly could not be called ambitious. After obtaining a Chemistry degree he had been lucky enough to get a job in a pharmaceutical laboratory. He worked steadily and got steady rises but he never put himself forward for promotion, making it quite clear, when pressed by her, he that did not want the responsibility.

How different he was from Philip, she thought, as she remembered her brother-in-law standing before her that evening. In spite of the unusual and upsetting circumstances, he had appeared to be perfectly in control both of himself and of the situation. He was still attractive, even at fifty-two, and highly intelligent and successful, as she knew.

She would like to have thought that he didn't greatly love Magda but she was too honest to allow herself to believe that any more. His care for his wife had been obvious, especially in his decision to spend the night in the armchair so that he could be close to her.

Magda had, therefore, every reason to be happy, but Catherine knew that she wasn't. But why wasn't she? She could not really believe that her beloved Magda would be secretly seeing another man. But what else could it be? With a frustrated sigh she decided that it would be more sensible to go to bed and wait until she met Magda again.

At about the same time, Philip in his study decided that he too would be more sensible to go to bed. He was tired after missing a night's sleep. *The truth is,* he told himself, *I'm getting older.* The flat was very quiet. Although the windows were large, giving magnificent views of the Thames and Westminster, the double glazing and the heavy curtains kept out all the sounds of the city.

As he approached the bedroom door he decided that, if Magda were asleep, he would not risk disturbing her. He could easily sleep in the spare room. As soon as he gently pushed open the door a little, however, she was awake. Switching on her bedside lamp, she called out, 'Are you coming to bed, Philip?' She was sitting up. Her dark hair fell loosely to her shoulders and her blue eyes were wide open. 'I'm so glad you've come.' She held out her arms to him.

After hurrying across the room, he sat on the side of the bed and drew her close to him. 'I was thinking I ought to go into the spare room so as not to disturb you.' He felt her trembling slightly as he held her.

'Don't be silly,' she replied immediately. 'I've been waiting for you. I want to go to sleep in your arms as I always do. I shan't feel frightened then. Please hurry, darling, and get into bed.'

'Have you remembered anything yet?' He paused in his hasty undressing to look at her.

'Nothing. I suppose that's what is frightening me. I think Cathy still suspects I was with a lover, but you don't, do you?'

'Of course not. I've already told you that.' He got into bed beside her. 'But I do know that you weren't with Barbara Metcalf.'

Chapter Three

The meal had so far gone surprisingly well, Catherine thought, as she tasted the delicious fruit tart which Philip had produced as a dessert. Everything so far, including the wine, had been as nearly perfect as one could desire. Even Constance, always so critical, would find no fault here, she decided. More importantly, however, the conversation had flowed smoothly; even Adam, usually taciturn with her relatives, had freely taken part.

She had been nervous beforehand and, by arrangement, she and Adam had met in the foyer of the luxurious block of flats, so that they might arrive together. She felt suitably smart in her dark brown velvet skirt and matching jacket with her new rosy-pink silk blouse. Adam had agreed to wear a tie, although he was convinced that it was unnecessary.

Adam had been right. Philip, who opened the door to them, had not been wearing a tie. Ignoring her husband's triumphant grin, Catherine after greeting Philip had hurried into the large sitting room to embrace her sister. Magda, although still pale, looked beautiful in a deep blue velvet housecoat that fell in loose folds to her ankles. Her dark hair had been carefully arranged so as to hide the dressing above her right temple. After kissing her sister warmly, Catherine sat down next to her on the wide comfortable couch in one corner of the room, while Philip served sherry chatting amiably to Adam while he did so.

In response to Catherine's anxious inquiries, Magda assured her that she already felt much better. 'Philip looks after me so very well,' she said. As Magda spoke, Philip approached them. 'I hope I'm getting a good reference?' he asked, smiling.

'Excellent,' Catherine assured him, smiling back. 'I imagine that you haven't been into the office.'

'Good God, no! Magda's far more important. They'll have to manage without me for a day or two. No sherry for you, darling, I'm afraid, just fruit juice,' he said tenderly to his wife.

As Magda accepted this without protest, Catherine found herself envying her younger sister. How wonderful it must be, she thought, to be loved like that. Adam would probably not have taken an hour away from work. In fact, he never had whenever she'd been ill. With a shock she realised that Magda was speaking to her and admiring the pretty colour of her blouse. She quickly responded while Philip moved away to chat with Adam, who was standing near the large windows. The curtains were pulled back so that the lights of London and the traffic on the river could be seen below.

'I'm so glad that you and Adam could come tonight,' Magda said to her.

'I'm so very glad that Philip invited us,' Catherine replied warmly.

'We've let the family keep us apart too much,' Magda said, 'don't you agree?'

Startled Catherine looked at her sister. 'Perhaps you're right. I hadn't thought of it like that before.'

'We mustn't let it happen anymore,' Magda replied firmly.

Now, as she continued to eat her tart, Catherine was quite sure that they must not. As she listened to Philip talking so easily and pleasantly, she felt that, although he had been married to Magda for fifteen years, she had never properly got to know him before. Why had that been? What had changed now? She was shocked to realise how little time she had given to her sister recently. It was necessary now to wait patiently.

Her patience was finally rewarded when, at the end of the meal, Adam went with Philip into the kitchen to stack the dishes in the dishwasher and to make the coffee. 'You look amazingly good, but how are you really feeling?' she asked Magda.

'Much better than I expected,' Magda replied. 'Philip has been very understanding and helpful.'

'I can see that,' Catherine said, anxious to please her sister. 'You know, I don't feel that I've ever really known him until now. You said it was the family that kept us apart. Did you really mean that?'

'Yes. Surely you've noticed it?'

'I'm not sure,' Catherine replied. 'I know we never get to talk freely at family dinner parties. To be honest I always imagined that Philip was closer to Constance and Sebastien than to Adam and me.'

'They intended that you should. They welcomed Philip into the family because he was the head of a successful City bank. He was one of the worshippers of money or so they thought. Sebastien was delighted when I met Philip. He thought that knowing him would help in his career. For the first time they were prepared to tolerate me. And you were very useful because of your friendship with me.'

For a few moments Catherine considered her sister's words. What Magda said was so totally unexpected. It seemed as if she was seeing the last fifteen years in an entirely different way. 'I'm not sure that I understand you,' she ventured at last. 'Do you mean that Philip doesn't like the family? I just thought that he was a very aloof person.'

'Of course he doesn't like them. Do you really think that I would have married him Cathy, if he were like them? He simply doesn't care for money and position as they do.'

'But he earns a lot of money,' Catherine protested.

Magda laughed. 'Without very much effort, I'm afraid. He has inherited a flair for dealing with money, and when his brother died early, he had to leave the Army and take over the family business – reluctantly, I assure you.'

Catherine frowned. 'Why didn't you tell me before?'

'Because you never wanted to know, did you?'

'I suppose not. I actually suspected that he wanted to separate me from you, perhaps because he was jealous.'

'Don't be paranoid, Cathy. If that were true, why did he ring you on Sunday night? He knew that you were the person he must get in touch with, because you cared for me.'

Catherine was pleased. 'He is right,' she declared.

'You didn't think that he understood things so well?'

'I suppose not. To be truthful, I'm probably the jealous one.' That confession seemed to come out almost involuntarily. To prevent further revelations, she said quickly, 'Before the men come back, you must tell me whether you have any memory now about what you were doing at the weekend.'

She wanted to look her sister in the eyes, but it was impossible because Magda was looking down at her hands, apparently examining her sapphire engagement ring. After a few moments she replied softly, 'Not really.'

'What does that mean?'

'It means that pictures flash into my mind. They're not connected, they don't make sense and I'm not even sure that they are real memories. Actually, they're rather frightening.' Reaching for Catherine's hand she squeezed it hard.

'I don't want to frighten you, dear. I only want to help you.' Catherine did not know what more to say.

Suddenly, Magda broke the silence. 'Tell me, Cathy,' she asked, 'have you ever met anyone you would consider really *evil*? I don't mean in the present day frivolous sense of that word but in the old-fashioned sense – someone you might feel was devoid of all good, devilish, perhaps. Someone who might say, "Evil be my good." '

Catherine was so startled that she could not at first think of an answer. At last, she said, 'I don't think so. I have met some people who seem to be pretty unpleasant, but you mean more than that, I imagine.'

'You're right,' Magda shivered. 'I meant much more. I meant—' She stopped abruptly as Adam and Philip returned with the coffee.

'Tell me later,' Catherine just had time to whisper but, even as she spoke, she doubted if this would happen. Philip placed the tray on the coffee table in front of their couch, and he and Adam seated themselves on chairs opposite to them.

Magda poured out the coffee, which was unusually good as Catherine remarked. 'Don't give me any credit,' Adam said. 'Philip made it. I'm not in his class. This is the real stuff, not my usual teaspoon out of a jar concoction.'

Philip laughed. 'Don't be deceived,' he replied, 'I'm only trying to impress you.' He then produced chocolates and brandy. Catherine chose the chocolates, ignoring Adam's frown.

It was all extremely pleasant and friendly. The large, spacious room was dimly lit by a couple of standard lamps and a small lamp standing on a nearby bookcase. To Catherine it seemed civilised and secure. This was the right place for Magda. Surely, she could not feel afraid here, particularly with such a reassuring husband?

Adam was in an unusually talkative mood. 'I never realised before,' he said, turning to Philip, 'that you'd spent so many years in the Army. I always thought of you as a City bloke well insulated from the real world and us more ordinary folk.'

Catherine shuddered but Philip seemed quite unconcerned. 'That's because I'd left the Army just over two years before Magda and I met. Her family never wanted to know about my past.'

'Why did you leave the Army?' Adam asked. 'You must have had quite a career there. You did say, didn't you, that you went to Sandhurst straight from Cambridge.'

'That's right. A couple of my relatives had been Army men and I preferred that to joining my father's bank. Then my elder brother died, my father was ill, so I resigned my commission and took over the bank. Did my duty, as one might say.'

'It must have been a tremendous change,' Catherine remarked.

'It was.' Philip shrugged. 'But fortunately I've always been fascinated by numbers, as Magda knows.' He smiled lovingly at his wife, who was leaning back quietly in the corner of the couch.

'They seem to keep you quiet,' Magda replied, smiling back at him.

'Without you, they wouldn't,' Philip said. Adam wondered privately if he could be so indifferent to the amount of money that Philip was reputed to have made, but to Catherine's relief he remained silent.

'Did you travel much in the Army?' she asked, hoping to distract her husband.

'The usual places – a brief and bloody trip to the Falklands, Cyprus, Germany and finally Northern Ireland, which didn't please me. But that's enough about me.' Philip abruptly changed the subject. 'What about your career, Adam?'

'That's easily told,' Adam replied. 'I'm just a boring bloke who enjoys his job and has no ambitions, except perhaps to see England win the World Cup. Ask Catherine if you don't believe me.'

'That's about it,' Catherine agreed.

Before she could say more, Magda intervened. 'Could we have some more coffee, Philip, and more chocolate? Then Catherine and I can indulge ourselves.'

'Of course.' It was as Philip stood up that the front doorbell rang. It was a long, loud ring of someone who was determined to be heard.

'Who on earth can that be?' Magda asked. 'You're not expecting anyone, are you, Philip?'

'Certainly not. It must be a mistake. I'll go and see who it is.' As he reached the door to the hall, the bell rang again, even more loudly. 'Whoever it is, he's a persistent beggar,' Adam remarked. They listened as Philip opened the door. They heard him speak and another man's voice answering him, but they could not tell what was said.

After a few moments the door from the hall was pushed open and Philip reappeared. 'There is someone here, Magda, who seems to think that you are expecting him.'

'That's impossible!' she exclaimed. Startled, she stood up and turned to face the door. 'I'm not expecting anyone. I'm not well.'

'I explained that,' Philip replied, 'but, I'm afraid, he won't take "no" for an answer.'

'Perhaps I should present myself.' As Philip moved aside the stranger moved forward so that they could all see him. Apparently he was perfectly sure of his reception. There was silence for a moment as they all stared at him. Although he was above medium height, he looked small and slim next to Philip. He was wearing a dark overcoat which was unbuttoned revealing a conventional dark suit. Unexpectedly, the outfit was completed with a sumptuous gold and crimson silk cravat.

Catherine, as she studied him, decided that he must be foreign, partly because of the cravat, but more so because of a slight accent when he spoke and because of his very black hair and slightly olive skin. His face was handsome with clear-cut features, and he was smiling pleasantly as he faced them. Catherine, nevertheless, felt that there was definitely something unpleasant about him. She looked towards Magda, who was so pale that it seemed as if she was about to faint.

Obviously the stranger had expected some recognition from Magda, but when this was not forthcoming, he continued in a slightly mocking tone, 'Perhaps I should introduce myself. I am Conrad Vanderlay.' He bowed to them all. 'I feel I must apologise for interrupting your party. The real fault, however, is Magda's.' He turned directly towards her. 'You must remember, my dear, that, when we met at the weekend, you asked me to visit you tonight.'

Magda met his challenge without faltering. Turning her brilliant blue eyes on him she said coldly, 'I have absolutely no recollection of meeting you at the weekend and, if I had, I'm sure that I would never have invited you to come here.'

Before the stranger could remonstrate, Philip intervened calmly, 'I think I should explain to you, Mr Vanderlay, that my wife had an accident at the weekend, as a result of which she has had a temporary loss of memory.'

'I'm very sorry to hear that,' Conrad Vanderlay addressed Philip. Then, turning towards Magda, he said, 'I hope you will soon recover, Magda my dear.' He looked searchingly at her but her brilliant gaze did not falter. 'I must apologise once more for my intrusion. I hope you will soon be feeling better, Magda. I'll be in touch.'

He moved towards the door, followed by Philip who went after him into the hall. There was a short indistinct conversation, then they heard the closing of the front door. A few moments later, Philip returned and looked at Magda, who was still standing.

For a minute no one spoke. Catherine, who remained seated on the couch, could sense her sister trembling. Catherine was relieved that Conrad Vanderlay had gone so quickly; he was definitely an unpleasant man, she had decided. Unfortunately, however, his departure left many unanswered questions. She said nothing, convinced that it was Philip who should ask the questions instead of staring at poor, pale Magda.

It was Adam, however, unimaginative and ordinary Adam, who broke the silence. 'Thank God he's gone,' he said. 'I can't say I liked the bloke. Sorry, if he's a friend of yours, Magda, but I can only say what I think.'

Magda suddenly smiled at him. 'You're right,' she said, 'I don't disagree.'

'But you know him?' Philip spoke at last.

'I do know him,' Magda admitted. 'But I don't like him,' she added vehemently, 'and I'm sure that I would never have invited him here.' She sat down suddenly as if all her strength had gone. Again, there was silence. Philip still stood motionless.

At last Adam asked the obvious question. 'Have you known the bloke long?'

Magda seemed reluctant to answer but at last she replied, 'It's many years since I first met him, but I haven't seen him for a long time.'

'Except that you apparently saw him this weekend,' Philip said coming back to his place.

Oh, God, Catherine thought, *Philip is suspicious now and who can blame him?* Turning towards her sister, she asked quickly, 'Do you remember anything now?'

'No,' Magda almost whispered. Then, looking directly at Philip, she said clearly, 'I'm quite sure that I did not arrange to meet Conrad this weekend.'

'Then who *did* you arrange to meet?' Philip asked. 'Surely you know that?'

'Is it someone we know?' Catherine asked, almost without thinking.

'No.' Magda felt forced to answer. 'No, none of you know the person. It is someone in my other life – a woman. She said she desperately needed to see me, so I went, although I didn't want to...' Her voice trailed away. She had obviously not intended to say so much.

'Someone in your "other life"?' Catherine was astounded. 'Whatever do you mean, Magda?' It seemed to her that the blow had affected her sister's sanity.

'I'm not mad, Cathy,' Magda replied miserably. 'Sometimes I wish I were. My other life began many years ago – when I was only eight, to be precise. If I remind you, you'll probably remember the day.'

'I don't understand.' Catherine felt as if she had suddenly left reality and walked into a dream.

'It was one day in August when I was eight. We were just about to go away on a sailing holiday. It was very hot, stifling hot, and we were bored. Father was at work, of course. Mother and Constance had gone out somewhere, and Sebastien had decided to swim in the pool. You suggested that we should take our books and read under the trees by the lake. I had left my book in my bedroom, so I said that I'd follow you.'

'I remember that day!' Catherine said suddenly. 'It was the day you got lost, wasn't it? And I blamed myself. I should have waited for you. Instead I became so absorbed in my book that it was ages before I noticed that you hadn't joined me. It didn't worry me particularly because I thought that you'd probably joined Sebastien. But when I went back to the house just before lunch, I found Sebastien sitting on the terrace. I was very upset then and I persuaded him to help me to look for you. I searched the house and he searched the garden but there was no sign of you. Agnes hadn't seen you in the kitchen, where she was getting lunch. Mother and Constance had just returned. Then Dad arrived home, expecting his lunch on time, as always. I didn't know what to do. I just prayed you'd turn up.

'When he realised that you were missing, Dad refused to start lunch until you'd been found. Mother was furious and Constance suggested that you'd gone off to the woods.

' "And why would she do that?" Dad asked. He was very angry.

' "Because she's naturally disobedient," Mother said. "Because she likes to be the centre of attraction," Constance added. Sebastien and I said nothing.

' "May I remind you all," Dad said, "that Magda is the youngest, and that one of you, at least, might be expected to keep an eye on her."

'I felt like bursting into tears. "It's all my fault," I said. "I forgot all about her because I was reading my book." I don't know what would have happened then, if Sebastien hadn't called out that he could see you coming across the lawn.'

'Before anyone could say anything you came slowly through the patio doors. You looked dreadful. Your dress was dirty and torn; your face was grubby and smudged as if you'd wiped away tears with your very dirty hands. It was obvious that you must have been in the woods.'

'Mother was obviously ready to make one of her cutting remarks but, before she could open her mouth, Dad froze her with that look of his. He then turned to me and said very quietly, "Catherine, will you please take your sister to her bedroom and help her to change and wash. Lunch will be in fifteen minutes, time."

'He immediately got up and went to his study while I hurried you to your bedroom. I was afraid to ask you any questions, and nothing else was said as far as I know.'

'Nothing much was,' Magda replied. 'I tried to explain to Father but he didn't want to know. He simply told me that I had probably been punished enough, and that I should be more obedient in the future. I promised I would.'

'You only told me later,' Catherine said, 'that you had gone to the woods, had got lost and had been very frightened. So why is that day so important?'

'Why do you still remember it?' Magda asked.

'Because I was so upset and because you never seemed quite the same afterwards,' Catherine replied.

'I wasn't,' Magda replied very quietly, 'for that was when my other life started. I met someone in the wood.' She stopped suddenly.

Catherine waited for her to continue but, when she didn't, Catherine said, 'You can't leave it like that, Magda. You know how much I love you. You must tell me if it's so important.' She had forgotten Philip and Adam. Her eyes were fixed on her sister, but Magda was looking beseechingly at Philip, who had said nothing during all this time.

Suddenly, Catherine realised how shocking this must all seem to him, how he must be suffering. Or perhaps, she thought, he's very angry.

'There is someone,' Magda said sadly, 'who has a greater right than you, Cathy, to know the truth.' Still, Philip did not speak. The silence frightened Catherine. She looked wildly at Adam and, to her surprise, he rose to the occasion.

'I think it's time we went home, Catherine, it's getting late.' He stood up as he spoke. 'I'll just take the tray into the kitchen, and then we'd better leave.'

Without a word, Philip followed him out. Catherine put her arm round her sister. Magda said softly, 'I don't think you have any idea how much Philip loves me. This will have hurt him dreadfully.'

'I probably didn't realise before, but I've seen a different Philip this weekend.'

'I couldn't bear life without him, Cathy.'

'I'm sure you won't have to, dearest,' Catherine replied, 'but you must tell him the whole truth now.'

'I don't know if I can,' Magda began. 'I'm afraid, Cathy...'

The return of Adam and Philip prevented Catherine from replying. Adam produced their coats. Philip was thanked for his delicious meal. 'I fancied myself as a bit of a cook,' Adam said, 'but you're a master. I shall have to ask you for some lessons.'

'Any time,' Philip replied, smiling.

At the front door they made their farewells. Adam shook Philip's hand and Catherine gave her sister a final hug. As they walked towards the lift, Catherine turned back to wave and, to her immense relief, she saw Philip put his arm round Magda. *Perhaps, everything will be all right*, she told herself, as she offered up a silent prayer for her sister.

Chapter Four

Philip kept his arm round Magda's shoulders as they went through the door. As he turned to double lock the door, he released her and she moved into the sitting room. He found her sitting tautly in one of the upright chairs.

'I'm very sorry,' she said sadly as he came into the room.

He sat down opposite her. 'Which bit are you especially sorry for?' he asked. 'The unexpected guest? Or the revelations regarding your other life?'

She looked at him closely. He seemed completely normal and relaxed. She felt reassured, then frightened. What did he really feel? 'You must be very angry with me. I've ruined a really pleasant evening.'

'If you didn't invite Conrad then I don't see how you can be blamed.'

She tried to remember but there was only darkness. 'I still don't remember anything about the weekend. But I think it is extremely unlikely that I ever invited Conrad to visit me. I don't like him.'

'He's not very likeable,' Philip commented, 'I can believe that. But that still leaves us with one or two problems. Firstly, if you didn't tell him, how did he know this address? Secondly, with whom did you plan to spend this last weekend? You may have forgotten the weekend, but it seems unlikely that you know where and with whom you planned to spend it.' He waited calmly for her to speak.

Her brilliant blue eyes stared back into his dark ones. She did not look away but she seemed unable to answer him. The silence was terrifying. She clasped her hands tightly. Suddenly he took pity on her. 'I suppose this has something to do with that other life of yours that even Catherine was unaware of.'

'Yes,' she whispered, 'it goes back so many years that it's hard to know where to begin.'

Leaning forward, he took her cold, clasped hands firmly in his. 'Don't be afraid, Magda darling,' he told her. 'I'm amazed and a bit shocked, I suppose, but I'm not angry and I haven't stopped loving you.'

'Oh, Philip darling!' she sobbed. He saw the tears on her cheeks. 'I need you and I couldn't bear life without you.'

Standing up, he raised her and took her into his arms, holding her close. 'I suppose most of us have secrets,' he said. 'Many of them trivial but some more important and serious like yours. There are things I haven't told you but they didn't seem to matter at the time,' he added after a moment.

'I know what you mean,' she told him. 'When I first met you, I wanted to forget the past. I thought I'd freed myself but I was wrong – very wrong.'

For a moment he didn't speak but held her close until her sobs had stopped. When she was calmer, he said, 'It's pretty late and you're still not well. I'm going to put you to bed, make us both a hot drink and then we can talk for a little while. Don't try to argue with me because I've decided. Now come along straight to bed.'

She was happy to allow him to take charge. She was so very tired and relieved that he had taken her unexpected revelations so calmly that she had no desire to resist him. It was nearly half an hour later before they were both settled in bed. She waited for him to speak.

'I imagine,' he said, 'that you have a lot to tell me and that it can't all be said at once. Perhaps you should just tell me what happened when you went to the wood that day in August. What do you think?'

'Yes,' she agreed, 'it all began then and that must be told first.' For a moment she hesitated.

'You met someone,' he prompted her, 'someone you didn't expect to meet.'

'That's very true. I didn't expect to meet anyone, but I met my mother.'

'I don't understand… you said your mother was out with Constance that morning.'

'I don't mean Rosalind Lefevre,' she told him. 'I mean my real mother, my birth mother; it was then that I learned that Rosalind was only my adopted mother. At least, that was what I was supposed to learn. It all happened apparently accidentally. I went to the clearing that Catherine and I sometimes went to and there was this woman. She was sitting on the tree trunk that Catherine and I sometimes sat on. As I stared at her, she stood up and said, "Hello, Magda. It is Magda, isn't it?"

'I said, "Yes, I am Magda, but how do you know that?" '

Suddenly Philip recedes and she is there again. It is very hot, even in the woods. The sun is glinting through the trees. A little bird is hopping on the ground looking for food. Another on the branches above is watching it – or is watching everything, perhaps.

The woman smiles. 'I know a lot about you, Magda,' she says. 'Come and sit on the trunk with me and we can talk.'

Magda stares at the woman. She is sure that she has not met her before. She is quite small. Her dark hair falls in curls to her shoulders. She is wearing a long blue summer dress with a pattern of white flowers. Her feet are bare, except for plain, rather shabby sandals. Her eyes are very blue and round her neck there is a silver chain with an attractive blue stone, which matches the blue of her eyes and of her dress. As she stares at the young woman, Magda suddenly feels that she recognises her, although she is equally sure that she has never met her before. Frightened, she holds back.

'Don't be afraid,' the young woman says gently, with an encouraging smile. 'I've wanted to meet you for so long and now we have met, you must talk to me for a little while. I want us to be friends.' Taking Magda's hand, she leads her to the fallen tree trunk. Magda responds to the grasp of the surprisingly cool fingers on arm. As she sits down next to the stranger, she notices that there are tears in the woman's eyes.

'I can't stay long,' she explains, 'because I'm not supposed to come here on my own, and my sister will be looking for me.'

'I won't keep you long,' the young woman replies, 'but I do so want us to have a little friendly chat, at last.'

Although she is puzzled, Magda wants to be helpful. 'I live in Brook House, the big house just at the end of the lane. I live there with my Mummy and Daddy, my two elder sisters and my

brother, who is also older than me. I'm the youngest and that's
why I'm not supposed to come here by myself and why I mustn't
stay long.'

'Don't worry,' the stranger says softly. 'I'll make sure that you
get back safely.' She puts her arm round Magda, who would like
to move away but is afraid of seeming unfriendly.

'What is your name?' she asks the stranger.

'My name is Elizabeth but most people call me Lisa.'

'Do you live here? In this town, I mean.'

No, I live in London but I come down often to see someone I
love.'

Magda does not know what else to say, so she sits silently
watching the little bird, which has obviously now found something to eat. Another bird joins him and snatches some of it away
but they do not fight. Suddenly Magda becomes aware that Lisa is
speaking to her. 'Are you happy, Magda?' she asks.

'Of course,' Magda replies. What else can she say?

'Do your Mummy and Daddy love you a lot? Are they kind to
you?' Lisa sounds strangely agitated and Magda, surprised, turns
to look at her.

'I suppose so,' she replies. 'Daddy works very hard and is away
quite a lot but he often takes us out at the weekends. My brother
Stephen is his favourite. That's because he's the only boy, I
suppose. Mummy is especially fond of Constance. She's the
eldest girl, you see, and they're very much alike.'

'You must be a bit lonely, then. Are you?'

'Oh no, Cathy looks after me. She always has.'

'Cathy? Who is she?'

'She's my other sister. She's four years older than I am.'
Magda tries to move away but Lisa's arm tightens round her
shoulders.

'Since you have so little time to spare, I'm going to tell you a
secret straightaway. Would you like that?'

'Oh, yes,' Magda says quickly. *Secrets are fun*, she thinks.

'But you must promise not to tell anyone, ever.'

'I promise,' Magda says solemnly. She watches the little birds
as they fly away, wanting to escape herself.

Lisa, however, makes her look straight at her. 'I'm very

serious, Magda,' she says firmly. 'You must not tell anyone in your family that you have met me. Nor must you tell anyone the secret I'm now going to tell you, because it will cause terrible trouble if you do. Promise me on your honour.' Her voice is very solemn and her blue eyes are very compelling. 'Will you solemnly promise that?'

'I promise on my honour.' Magda's own brilliant blue eyes are now very serious…

'And then she told me.' Philip was suddenly aware that Magda had come back to him.

'Told you what?' he asked.

'She told me that Rosalind Lefevre, as she called her, was not my real mother but that she, Lisa, was, in fact, my true mother. She said that she loved me passionately and was heartbroken when she was forced to give me up.'

'How had she been forced to give you up?' Philip asked. He was leaning back a little on his pillows, and since Magda was leaning forward he could not see her face but he was aware of the tension in her body. She was hating this but he felt sure that it was necessary. He knew something himself about the power of buried memories. 'Did she give you any reason?' he persisted.

At last Magda replied. 'Not at that first meeting. She was more concerned to show me how much she had suffered and how wickedly cruel my father and Rosalind had been.' Her body shook as she tried to repress her tears. Sitting up, Philip put his arms around her and tried to comfort her.

She was not ready to yield yet. She must tell her story first. It had to be told. 'Whether or not, she intended to do it, Lisa ruined that little child's life,' she said. 'She told me that she was only just eighteen when she met my father. She had just left school and lived with her parents in the Midlands.'

'How on earth did they meet? He never had a practice in the Midlands, did he? Philip asked.

'No, they met at the yacht club near Chichester. My father was a keen sailor and we had a bungalow down there. Sometimes they all went down, but quite often he went by himself, since Rosalind was not very keen on sailing and preferred tennis at the local club. The children often stayed at home with the au pair. That continued sometimes after I was born, so I know about that. It was on one of those solitary weekends that he met Lisa. She said they fell passionately in love. She said that she trusted him completely. Finally, he told her that he was married, but that he loved her more than his wife. Then, she discovered that she was going to have a baby and he was very upset.'

'She actually told you, a child of eight, all this?' Philip was incredulous.

'Yes – and much more which I didn't understand until later. She told me that my father bought me from her and because she was alone and poor, she had to agree. Rosalind hated the idea, but she too was forced to agree. She said that my father was a heartless hypocrite. I wanted to get away but she held me, crying and sobbing most of the time.

'At last I managed to pull myself away from her. I remember that I stamped my feet and shouted, "I don't want to hear any more. I hate you, I hate you!" Then I ran away into the wood. That's how I got lost. I was terrified. I thought I would never get home again. And when I was nearly home, I was frightened again, because I realised I was late for lunch. Everyone would be upset and my father would be furious; he hated unpunctuality and having his routine upset. I had no idea what I was going to say except that it couldn't be the truth.

'To my surprise it was my father who protected me. When Rosalind was obviously about to say something horrid, he stopped her. He told Cathy to help me and seemed to think that, although I'd been naughty, I'd suffered enough by getting lost.

'It was when Cathy was combing my hair that I realised why Lisa had seemed familiar to me. I looked into the mirror and saw her face! I knew then that she must really be my mother. I'd often wondered why I looked so different from the rest of the family. Now I had my answer. It made me very unhappy.'

'Did you say anything to anyone?' Philip asked.

'No, there was nothing I dared to say, even to Cathy. As time passed and I didn't see Lisa again, I began to wonder if any of it was actually true. I even tried to persuade myself that it might have been a dream or something. The damage had been done, however. Nothing seemed to be the same as it had been before. My father was not the good man I had always thought him to be. If Lisa was right he was a hypocrite. Rosalind, too, was different. Before I met Lisa, I was happy. I never felt particularly loved by any of my family, except Cathy, but I felt secure and I trusted my parents, as children naturally do. I was even afraid of saying too much to Cathy now.' Leaning back and closing her eyes, she stopped talking suddenly.

Taking hold of her hand, Philip raised it to his lips and kissed it. He was unsure what to do. Perhaps she was tired and needed to sleep? He was wrong, for suddenly her blue eyes opened wide and she sat up.

'I saw Lisa again several months later. I know it must have been winter because she was wearing a long, dark red coat with fur trimming, leather boots, and a purple and red silk scarf. She looked different. Her clothes were fashionable and expensive, but the eyes and the voice were the same. I was in the town library, so it must have been a Saturday morning. Cathy had brought me; we usually came on Saturday mornings. She had left me in the Juvenile Section while she went off to the Reference Department.

'I was sitting at a table trying to decide between two books. There was no one there except the librarian, who was almost hidden behind the bookshelves. One of the books I was looking at was an art book. I was already interested in art. Suddenly someone came up to me and sat next to me. She spoke to me in a voice, which I remembered clearly. "Hello, Magda darling! I've been longing for a chance to speak to you again!" She spoke very softly so that the Librarian wasn't disturbed. If she noticed at all, she probably thought it was my mother helping me.

'I tried to move away a little. "Cathy's with me," I whispered back. "She's gone to the Reference Room but she won't be very long."

' "Then we mustn't waste a moment of our precious time together." That was Lisa's reply. "I've been longing to see you again, my darling." She looked at the book I was holding. "So you're interested in Art. How wonderful!"

' "Why is it wonderful?" I asked. For some reason I was more fascinated than frightened this time.

' "Because I'm an artist," Lisa replied. "You couldn't know it. You've simply inherited my talent. Don't let your parents stop you. They won't like it." It was true. They didn't like it but I said nothing.

'Suddenly it occurred to me that now that she seemed to be so rich she might have me to live with her. But she turned that notion down immediately. "What a lovely idea," she said and kissed me, "but I'm afraid it's impossible, darling. The Lefevres are your legal parents and, in any case, I have to go abroad for ages and I won't even be able to see you for some time. But I shall always remember your lovely suggestion, and one day perhaps it might be possible. Who knows?" After hugging me, she asked me if I liked the convent school, which I had started to attend in September.

'I told her that I liked it a lot and that the nuns were very kind.

' "I'm sure they are," she said, "Good, kind Catholic virgins. Sadly, however, people are not always what they seem." She paused briefly. "Remember, dearest, your parents are supposed to be good Catholics, and yet your father is a mortal sinner."

' "What do you mean?" I asked. I was very upset as I was preparing for my Confirmation. I knew how terrible a mortal sin was. "How can he be?"

' "Surely, you have learned the Ten Commandments, Magda?"

' "Of course, I know them by heart."

' "Well, don't you remember that there is one that says you must not commit adultery?"

' "Yes, but what's that got to do with my father?"

' "Didn't they tell you what it meant?" She smiled at me.

' "They told me that it was something I need not worry about until I was much older."

' "How very sensible of them. A nice little girl shouldn't be upset." She kissed me again.

' "But," I objected, "shouldn't I know what is wrong?"

' "Cathy, I'm sure, will tell you more, if you ask. But please, don't tell her why you are asking. That is our secret. Remember your promise."

' "I have remembered it," I told her proudly.

' "You're a very good girl. I'm proud of you! I must go now." She gave me a quick kiss. "Don't forget me. One day we'll meet again."

'Did you say anything to Catherine?' Philip asked.

'No, as Catherine came back, they passed each other in the doorway but, of course, Catherine did not realise that Lisa had anything to do with me. And I said nothing.'

'And you've never told anyone until tonight?'

'No. Lisa destroyed my trust in my family, even to some extent in Cathy. She was right when she said I was changed from the day I was lost in the wood. I did change. I had always felt that I was different, but now I knew it was true.'

'You believed Lisa then, completely?'

'I didn't want to, and sometimes I tried to pretend to myself that I didn't, but I looked so like her that I knew we must be closely related.'

'Did you see her often?' Philip's voice did not change but she felt his hand tighten on hers and she realised how much this must affect him.

'Not very often, and only briefly until I became a student. She was pleased I was studying English and Drama. I met her often then and came to know some of her friends.'

'Did that include Conrad?'

'Yes, he was one of them. I broke away completely from all of them when I went on my world trip. That was one of the reasons for going. When I came back and then met you, I felt free for the first time in years.'

'But not free to trust me, even in fifteen years?' He could not hide the hurt he felt.

'Philip, darling, you know how much you mean to me. You must believe that.'

He did not answer immediately, then he said, 'Funnily enough, I do.' Drawing her close to him, he kissed her. 'You are not the first person to have a secret which is hard to share even with a person one truly loves. I think I can understand.'

'I've sometimes suspected, Philip, that there is something you never speak about.'

'You're right, darling, but tonight is not the time for that. We're both very tired now. We can talk more tomorrow.'

Clinging close to him, she seemed to agree. After a few moments, however, she lifted her head and said clearly, 'I think I must have arranged to spend the weekend with Lisa. I'm not sure, but I seem to have a memory that she somehow told me that she desperately needed me.' She appeared to be afraid. 'Oh, God, what do you think happened, Philip?'

'Perhaps the Vanderlay guy came to tell you. If he did, he'll come again.' Feeling her tremble, he tried to console her. 'You needn't be afraid, I'll help you now to deal with it.'

Chapter Five

As Adam pressed the button and the lift doors closed behind them, Catherine exclaimed, 'I don't think that I understand anything anymore, do you?'

Careful as always, he did not answer until they had reached the ground floor and had started to walk towards their cars. Then he said slowly, 'I don't think there is much we can say or do. It's not really our business, is it?'

She knew what that meant. He had found all that had happened very disturbing and was determined not to think about it, hoping it would all go away. That was not surprising; it was his usual first reaction to any problem or upset. But it was not enough for her; it rarely was, and certainly not now. 'I'm shattered by it all,' she said as she took out her key and pressed the button to unlock her car.

Adam's car was parked just behind hers and, as he moved along towards it, he said, 'Well, I can see that it must be upsetting for you.'

She restrained her desire to scream at him or to hit him and merely remarked coldly, 'I hope you're sober enough to drive. You didn't exactly hold back, did you?'

'Neither did you on the chocolates,' was his only reply to that.

'At least they don't make me drunk,' she retorted.

'You're being a bit silly, aren't you? One small sherry, a glass of wine and a sip of brandy are hardly enough to make me drunk.' He got into his car and slammed the door. Catherine had no alternative but to set off.

When they arrived home, chaos met them, so Catherine had no chance to express the tumultuous thoughts that had been buzzing around in her head through the tedious journey home. Lucy and Mark had obviously enjoyed their supper, for their dirty plates and remnants of food still lay scattered all over the living-room table. Half-empty glasses of Coke also stood around. In one corner of the room, their school coats, satchels and books lay in a large untidy heap. They had obvious retreated to their bedrooms to enjoy the TV.

Adam, guessing Catherine's mood, almost felt sorry for them. Catherine, however, did not hesitate. Marching across the room, she flung open the door to the hall and called in her most stentorian tones, 'Lucy and Mark, come down at once!' They obviously gave some excuses, for a minute later she shouted again. 'I don't care what the hell you're doing! Just come down straight-away and clear up this disgusting mess you've left in the living room!'

Some further excuse must have been offered, for Catherine next called firmly, 'Rubbish! You're obviously not doing your homework. Your books are all here and most of them still in your satchels. If I have to come and fetch you, believe me you'll regret it. It's your choice!'

She turned back into the living room. 'They're coming down,' she told Adam. 'Don't you dare to touch anything,' she warned him, as he moved towards the table. 'You always spoil them.'

There was a noise of hasty footsteps coming down the stairs. The door was pushed open again and Mark hurried into the room, followed more slowly by his elder sister, Lucy. Both were in their nightclothes. Both looked cross and definitely rebellious, especially Lucy, who resembled her mother both in looks and temper.

'I don't know what you're making such a fuss about,' Lucy snapped. 'It'll only take a few minutes to clear.'

'Good,' Catherine snapped back, 'then why don't you get on with it?' Lucy reluctantly picked up one plate, but Mark, obsti-nately silent as usual, went towards the kitchen.

'Where are you going?' Catherine asked him sharply.

'I'm going to get a tray. It'll take all night if we do it one plate at a time. He glared at Lucy, who glared back. They were seldom allies.

'Get on with it, then,' Catherine told him. Turning towards Lucy, she said, 'Since Mark apparently knows how to clear the table at least, you'd better get rid of the stuff in the corner. You know where everything goes, get on with it.'

Seeing Lucy's furious face, Adam departed quickly to the kitchen. 'I'll stick the dishes in the dishwasher,' he told Mark, 'if you bring them out, OK?' Mark looked far from pleased but thankfully he said no more.

When Adam finally returned to the now almost tidy living room, Catherine and Lucy were on the edge of one of their many confrontations. 'I trusted you,' Catherine was saying. 'I didn't expect to come home to this mess. Mark, perhaps, but not you.'

'Why did you have to come home so early?' Lucy shouted back. 'We didn't expect you, yet. We were going to come down when our programme finished. But, of course, you *would* think I never intended to do it. Stop treating me like a baby!'

'It's hardly early, is it? And, if you are grown-up as you're always telling me you are, why don't you act like a grown-up. It's not what you say; it's what you do that matters.'

'Why did you come home so soon, anyway?' Lucy demanded. 'Have you even managed to quarrel with your precious sister? I'm not surprised. You're good at quarrelling with people! I expect that even she can't stand you sometimes.'

Seeing the anguish visible in Catherine's face, Adam decided to intervene. 'Why don't you go to bed? It's pretty late.'

'Don't worry. I'm going,' Mark said, as he came back into the living room. 'Goodnight.' And he was gone.

Lucy said, 'I'd better do my homework before she tells me again what a useless failure I am. Not a bit like her wonderful Magda.'

Before Catherine could reply, Adam intervened again. 'Go to bed, Lucy,' he ordered her. 'You'll have to do your homework tomorrow.' He was very afraid that Catherine might completely lose her control and say things that she'd bitterly regret later. Taking his daughter's arm, he forced her out of the room.

Jerking her arm away, she asked angrily, 'What's bothering you, Dad? You know I'm right! Mum's always telling me that I can never live up to her precious Magda. And now she's just had an evening with her pet, she comes back in one of her worst moods and starts taking it out on all of us – especially me.'

Adam sighed. 'You were wrong, you know that. You should have cleared up.'

Lucy shrugged. 'Perhaps I should have, but it's no great deal, is it? You know what Mark's like. He just couldn't be bothered. I didn't see why I should do the lot, so I left it. I did mean to come down and shove it in the kitchen before you got back, but you came back earlier than I expected. Why? Did she really actually manage to quarrel with her darling? What fun!'

There was a malicious glee in her voice which irritated Adam. 'Do you always have to behave like a spoiled brat?' he asked her. 'Your aunt Magda's had a nasty accident. Apparently someone attacked her... she had concussion and she's lost her memory. It was worse than your mum expected and she's upset. The mess you two left was the last straw. Can't you just for once see someone else's point of view?

Lucy stopped halfway up the stairs. 'I didn't know,' she said. 'I'm sorry. I hope Aunt Magda will soon be better. Actually I think she's quite nice. It isn't her fault that Mum's obsessed with her. Shall I go and tell Mum I'm sorry?'

Adam hesitated. 'Better not,' he decided finally. 'You go to bed. I'll tell her.'

When he returned to the living room he found Catherine slumped in an armchair. She had obviously been crying. He gave her Lucy's message, which did not seem to affect her greatly. 'I suppose I was a bit hard on her,' she said indifferently, 'but she's always the same and tonight it just seemed too much. Oh, Adam!' she exclaimed suddenly, in obvious anguish, 'I just don't know what to believe!'

Surprised, he stared at her. 'I know it's upsetting, but surely you're not saying that Magda's lying, are you?'

'Well, what do you think about that weird story about meeting someone in the woods, which was apparently the start of another life? Does that seem true to you? The more I think about it, the less I'm inclined to believe it. If it happened, why didn't she tell me, since we were always so close?'

'Perhaps she thought you wouldn't believe it, just as you don't now. If it isn't true, why should she make it up? Tell me that.'

'I don't know!' she replied with increasing irritation. 'Perhaps it was meant to explain away that horrible Conrad. He's probably been her lover for years, for all I know.'

Adam simply stared at her. 'Do you really believe,' he asked after a few moments, 'that Magda is such an accomplished liar that she could invent a story like that just on the spur of the moment? You can say what you like, but I think better of her. I don't agree with you. She was speaking the truth. That's what I think anyway.' Catherine stared at him but said nothing. 'Shall I make us a cup of tea?' he suggested hopefully. 'It might make you feel better.'

Suddenly furious, Catherine almost spat at him. 'For God's sake! Not another cup of tea! That's your remedy for everything, isn't it? "Let's have a cup of tea and pretend it never happened." It never works and it certainly won't work now! You don't understand at all, do you?' She began to cry again, burying her face in her hands.

Adam wanted to comfort her but was afraid of saying the wrong thing. He stood awkwardly by, longing, as she suspected, to get away.

'But how can you understand?' she sobbed. 'You've never loved anyone as I've loved Magda.'

'Perhaps you love her too much and expect too much of her,' he suggested almost timidly.

She looked up at him, her eyes flooded with tears. 'Perhaps you're right,' she agreed bitterly. 'I always love people too much and expect they'll love me in the same way. They never do, of course. They just take from me. They like to have me looking after them, but when it comes to giving something back, that's different.' She laughed bitterly. 'I've always been a fool.'

He knew that her remarks, at that moment, were really directed at him and his inadequacy; that was a familiar accusation. He restrained his usual retorts, however, because he could see that Magda's revelation had wounded her deeply.

'I really did think that Magda was different.' The tears began to roll down her cheeks again. 'I thought that we were so close that we shared everything, even when we weren't able to see each other very often. But, apparently, we didn't really share anything after she was eight. She had another life. You heard her say that, didn't you?' she challenged him. 'I'm not making it up, am I?'

'No, you're not making it up,' he told her. 'But you can't

judge her without knowing a lot more. All you know is that she met someone in the wood and meeting that person changed her life. You don't even know who it was.'

'It must have been that horrible man, Conrad,' she replied angrily. 'She must have known him ever since.' She shuddered. 'Apparently, she spent the weekend with him and asked him to call on her. Perhaps she'd decided to tell Philip, at last.'

'What you seem to be suggesting is horrible,' Adam said quickly. 'But, even if it were true, why did she behave as she did? She didn't want to talk to him. She sent him away.'

'Perhaps it was because she'd lost her memory. But I'm no longer sure if that's true. Oh, Adam, I don't know what to believe about anything or anybody! It seems as if my whole life has been destroyed. I thought that things were going so well tonight, that Philip wanted us to be friends at last and that Magda and I would get really close again. It had never really been the same since she married Philip. But we still kept in touch, and she was very special to me and I was special to her – or so I thought. And now I don't know what to think. What shall I do, Adam?'

'I'm afraid you can't do anything now. Just wait until Magda tells you more.'

'That's what I wanted to do tonight. But you made us leave. Why?'

'Because I thought that Philip should be the first to hear it all from her. He's her husband.'

'She's my sister, and I've loved her longer than he has. I've got rights, too.'

'Philip has the first right,' he replied stubbornly. 'You'll just have to wait.' He hoped that she would give way. It was late and he was tired.

She didn't say anything for a few minutes. At last she stood up. 'You're right. It's too late now to do anything. I think I'll go to bed. We still have to get up early.'

As she turned towards the door, he asked once more, 'Are you sure you wouldn't like a cup of tea first?'

Knowing that he meant to be kind, she struggled to hide her irritation. Why didn't he just give her a comforting hug, she wondered, as she had done many times before? 'No thanks, but you have one if you want it.'

He hesitated. 'I think I will,' he said finally.

'Good night, then. Don't disturb me when you come up.' As she wearily mounted the stairs she told herself that he couldn't possibly understand what it was like to have your whole past life changed. She must talk to Magda and she would not let Philip stop her.

Throughout the following day, Catherine struggled to teach and to put aside her worries about her sister. In every free moment, however, they surfaced. She must do something. But what? She wanted to telephone her, but would that be any use? she asked herself. Her problem was solved just as she was packing up to return home. Her mobile rang and to her surprise she recognised Philip's voice.

'Has Magda been in touch with you?' he asked her.

'No, why should she be? Has something happened?' When he seemed to hesitate, she asked urgently, 'Can I speak to her?' She felt frightened. 'I'm afraid not,' he replied after a pause. 'She isn't here. She's gone. That's why I was wondering if she had been in touch with you.'

'Are you telling me that you don't know where she is?'

'I'm afraid so.'

'Oh God! What the hell do you mean?' Then, as someone knocked on her door, she continued quickly, 'I can't talk here, but I'll be leaving in few minutes. Can I come and see you?'

'I was hoping you would,' he replied. 'Magda wants you to know all she has told me, and I would like to talk to you.'

She had never thought to hear Philip say that. 'I'll be there as soon as I can,' she promised him. 'I'll let Adam know I shall be late.'

The traffic seemed to be worse than usual, and it was not until almost an hour later that Philip opened the door to her.

They had hardly entered the hall before she assailed him with her questions. 'For heaven's sake tell me what has happened! I could hardly sleep last night and I've been worrying all day! At least I thought she was safe with you! Now you say she's gone. What has happened? What do you mean?'

'She's left!' After shutting the door, he gently edged her into the sitting room.

'When?' She stood glaring at him.

'Some time this afternoon. She packed her overnight bag and left.'

'I don't understand. How could she? You were supposed to be here all day, weren't you?'

'I intended to be.' Philip sounded weary, 'but, just after lunch, there were several urgent calls from my office.'

'So, like all men,' Catherine said bitterly, 'you put work first. I actually thought you were different.' She advanced a step towards him, as if she was going to hit him, but instead she began to cry.

'Do sit down,' he begged her, 'and let me explain.'

Sinking into the nearest armchair, she waited, wiping her eyes with the handkerchief he handed her.

'I said I wouldn't go,' he told her, 'but Magda insisted, telling me I was being stupid. She promised that she would lie down with a book and wouldn't answer the telephone or the door. She refused to take no for an answer so, in the end, I went. I came back about two and a half hours later to find this note.'

'Can I see it?'

'Of course.' Taking the note out of his pocket, he handed it to her. It was surprisingly short.

My dearest Philip, I'm sorry to do this but I must go away for a time. There is something I must do and someone I must find. The truth is tremendously important. It's taken a long time for me to realise this but now I do. Please show this to Cathy and tell her what I have told you. She is the only other person who cares, and I want her to know that I appreciate that. I will be back, I promise you.

All my love, Magda

Catherine read the note twice, then, after folding it carefully, she handed it back to Philip. 'Do you understand this?' she asked him.

'Not entirely,' he admitted. He looked weary and it seemed to her that he had aged overnight. She was unexpectedly filled with pity for him, and instead of blaming him, as he half expected, she said gently, 'Perhaps you'd better tell me what Magda has told you. It might help.'

Sitting down, he agreed. As he spoke, Catherine listened with growing incredulity and anger, but she forced herself go remain quiet until he stopped at the point where Magda had told him that she had seen much more of Lisa when she was a student.

'And then what?' she demanded.

'Nothing more. That's where Magda ended the story, except to say that it was then that she met Conrad and other friends of Lisa's.'

'Don't tell me that you actually *believe* this fantastic yarn?' Catherine asked him furiously.

'What other option do we have? I don't suppose it's the whole truth, but I imagine it's basically true.'

'Well, I don't.' Catherine jumped up and walked over to the window. For a moment she stood there, as if seeking inspiration from the lights of London, then she turned towards Philip. It was obvious that she was very angry. 'I think it's utterly incredible. Magda was always good at inventing stories for getting us out of trouble. But this is different. I can't stand by and let her make our father seem like a lying hypocrite and our mother an idiot who never objected to his cruel actions. Surely you must understand that? It destroys my whole life.'

'I understand what you're saying. But people are not always what they seem, Catherine.'

'Couldn't that be true of Magda?' she asked him.

'It could, I suppose. But why do you suggest that she has invented this story?'

'Isn't it obvious? She wants to explain away her relationship with Conrad. They've probably been lovers for years. When he unexpectedly turned up—'

'No!' he interrupted her firmly. 'I simply cannot accept that. I don't know the whole truth, but I do know that she has suffered and is still suffering. I hoped that you might help.'

'I'm sorry, Philip', she replied. 'I know that you must be suffering but I simply can't help you. Please try to forgive me.' Picking up her coat and bag, she moved towards the door. 'I must go home now. I'll tell Adam. He may be more sensible than I am.'

When Philip failed to answer, she asked, 'What are you going to do?'

'I don't know. Just wait, I suppose. Thank you for coming.' As he opened the door for her, she impulsively kissed him on the cheek. Tears filled her eyes again. 'I'll be in touch.'

The door closed behind her and he was alone.

Chapter Six

'Is that all you could find to say to the poor devil?' Adam stared at Catherine, amazed.

'What do you mean?' She glared back at him belligerently.

'I should have thought that it was obvious. His wife's just left him without any proper explanation. He must be really upset and all that you can do apparently is to tell him that Magda's a liar and how upset you are! Anyone would think that it was you who had lost a partner. What on earth's is the matter with you? Can't you ever think of anyone but yourself?'

'What a foul thing to say! But then you always love to criticise me whenever you can.'

'That's nonsense,' he snapped at her, 'and you know it.'

'I know nothing of the sort. You can't imagine how I feel and you never want to try. I've always loved Magda and I thought we were really close. Now, it seems that I haven't known her properly for years. She was pretending all the time. She didn't care at all! And now she's just walked off with that ghastly Conrad. I thought you might sympathise with me for once.'

It has obviously never occurred to her, Adam thought, *that she might have failed Magda.* 'Why should I sympathise with you? And how?'

'You wouldn't know, would you?' She almost spat at him. 'You don't know anything about love. If you did, you'd just give me a hug and a kiss.'

'It's not easy,' he tried to answer mildly, 'when you're in this mood.'

'You could try but you don't bother. You never do. I'm going to bed. If you care so much, you might ring up Philip yourself.'

'I might just do that.'

She laughed scornfully. 'What a hope!' Gathering together the bag and jacket which she had thrown down on her arrival, she moved towards the door. 'You'd better sleep in the spare room, I don't want to be disturbed.'

'Fine. Oh, by the way,' he added as she was about to leave the room, 'I almost forgot to tell you that Constance rang up while you were out.'

She wheeled round swiftly. '*Constance*? What on earth did she want?'

He shrugged. 'I'm not exactly sure but I think it's something to do with your family's great annual event, your honoured father's birthday party.'

'Why me? Sebastien and Vivienne usually help to organise that. I'm not considered good enough for such matters.'

'She didn't exactly say. And I didn't ask—'

'Of course, you wouldn't.'

'—but,' he continued, ignoring her interruption, 'she wants you to ring her as soon as possible and meet her for a chat.'

Catherine was worried. 'You don't think she's heard anything about Magda, do you? Did she sound upset?'

'Not a bit. She was just her usual charming, condescending self. I assured her that, if you didn't ring her tonight, you certainly would do so by tomorrow.'

Catherine looked at her watch. 'It's too late tonight. You might have told me sooner. I'll do it tomorrow.' The door closed behind her.

It was two days later on the Friday evening that Catherine found herself driving up the familiar drive to the somewhat imposing Georgian residence which had been her home for many years. The grounds were screened from the road by several trees, behind which was the small lake where she and Magda had intended to read on that fateful day.

Behind the lake was a large lawn sloping up towards the house. At the top, before the patio doors which led straight into the drawing room was the swimming pool where Sebastien had liked to spend his time.

As she drove round the side of the house to park her car, she wondered, not for the first time, exactly how her father had supported all this magnificence – and the sailing too, which had been his passion. Of course until his retirement five years before he had been a successful and very popular doctor in the comfortable middle-class town in Surrey where they lived. The wealthy patronised him. Her mother, too, she believed had had some money of her own, but even so… She dismissed such irrelevant thoughts as she prepared, somewhat reluctantly, to meet her elder sister.

Before going into the house she sat for a few moments in the car. It was not quite eight thirty, the time at which she had promised to arrive. She had refused Constance's offer of dinner on the grounds that she needed to be at home with the family. The truth was that she had not wanted to leave Adam with the children on Friday night. She had insisted that they all ate together, and had made it quite clear to them and to Adam that she expected them to spend the evening doing their homework.

But, as she drove away, she felt pretty sure that her efforts had been futile. Lucy had made it quite clear that she intended to go out with her friends and Mark, although not so openly rebellious, would most likely do the same. Adam, she was sure, being glad to have an evening to himself, would do nothing to stop them. As she walked slowly towards the front door it occurred to her that Adam might even visit Philip, or at least, telephone him. He had refused to discuss the matter further on the grounds that there was nothing more to be said.

As she walked up the steps, the light in the hall went on. The door opened and Constance was waiting to greet her. They embraced as always and Constance murmured, 'Catherine dear, how good to see you! It's so kind of you to make the effort.'

As she took off her jacket and followed Constance into her small sitting room Catherine felt, not for the first time, that although she and Constance closely resembled each other, her elder sister was a better-finished version of the same model. Constance was well built, but taller and not at all plump. Her blonde hair was perfectly blonde and beautifully cut in the latest loosely swinging bob. Catherine had chosen her best outfit for the occasion. It was good, but Constance's was more expensive and perfectly cut to reveal her still small waist and firm breasts.

The small sitting room, which was always regarded as Constance's own domain, looked very welcoming after the cold night outside. The electric fire with its false logs was burning brightly. Two comfortable armchairs and a trolley had been drawn up near to it. 'I know you've already eaten,' Constance said, 'but I thought you might be grateful for a little snack with your coffee, particularly after such a long, cold drive.' She had certainly gone to some trouble, and somewhat to her surprise, Catherine found herself happily settling down with a cup of coffee and a plate of food. It was pleasantly civilised after the chaos of her home.

'I suppose you've realised why I want to talk to you,' Catherine began after a few minutes. 'It's Dad's birthday soon, and I was hoping that you might be able to help me to arrange the party.'

'Of course I will, if you want me to, but don't Sebastien and Vivienne usually do that? Vivienne's more used to these things than I am.'

'Nonsense, darling,' Constance smiled her sweetest smile. 'You're always too modest. I think it's time you showed what you can do, don't you?'

Catherine made an effort to smile back. 'I'll do my best,' she replied, but privately she decided that Constance and Vivienne must have had a row and she was needed to step in.

It soon became clear that most of the plans had already been made by Constance and that there was little for her to do except to give unqualified support to her elder sister. This improvement of her family status was quite a pleasant thought and, in the meantime, the coffee and snacks were very comforting.

Her peace of mind was, however, shattered when Constance suddenly said, 'Of course I'm planning everything on the basis that there will be twelve of us, as usual. I assume that Magda will be fit again by then. I sent some flowers but I decided not to ring her up before the weekend.' When Catherine didn't immediately reply, her sister asked, 'It will be all right to ring her this weekend, won't it? I thought I'd ask your advice because you and Magda have always been so close.'

Catherine simply did not know what to say. Her first thought was that she should tell Constance the whole truth. But then, what was that? She hadn't even been in touch with Philip for two days – everything might have changed. In any case, she couldn't possibly repeat to Constance the nonsense that Magda had been talking. It would be too upsetting. Aware that Constance was waiting for an answer, she quickly said, 'I should leave it for a day or two. I think they may have gone away to their place in Chichester. Would you like me to find out?'

'If you don't mind, that would be helpful.' Constance seemed to be relieved. 'I'm sure that I can assume that they will be coming as they always have, but I do like things to be settled, especially as Father would be particularly disappointed if they couldn't make it.'

'Why?' Catherine asked suddenly annoyed.

'Why, what?' Constance was puzzled.

'Why would it be particularly disappointing to Father if Magda and Philip didn't come? That's a bit insulting to the rest of us, isn't it?' She knew that her tone was becoming belligerent but she felt unable to hide it.

Constance laughed gently, her cool silvery laugh. She was slightly amused but otherwise completely unmoved. 'You haven't changed a bit, Catherine dear. You're still looking for insults.' Before Catherine could explode, she continued. 'You know perfectly well, darling, that Father is always attracted by success, particularly financial success, and Philip is so obviously successful and very wealthy. I suppose we're all impressed, really, although we don't like to admit it.' Catherine tried to interrupt but Constance smoothly continued, 'Whether or not you agree, our father is impressed.'

'I suppose so,' Catherine reluctantly agreed as she accepted another cup of coffee and a tiny brandy.

'It's strange, isn't it,' Constance observed, 'Magda is a bit like the ugly duckling that became a swan.'

'What do you mean?'

'Surely that's obvious.' Constance sipped her own much larger brandy. 'When she was young, she was always the odd one out. She looked completely different from any of us – rather ugly, I used to think. She was four years younger than you and obviously a mistake.'

'No one was ever horrid enough to say that,' Catherine said quickly.

'Of course not, but they thought so – at least I did as I grew older. Sebastien did, too. She was lucky that you became her champion. You really did look after her.'

'She was my baby sister. I loved her and she needed me.' Catherine seemed to be on the verge of tears.

'And then she didn't. She married Philip. That's natural but it's always hard to accept. But you've got Adam and your own children. You are better off than I was when Richard left me five years ago. I thought I'd never get over it, especially as the children were just ready to leave the nest.'

'That must have been terrible.' As she spoke Catherine realised remorsefully that she had never really given much thought to Constance being unhappy. From Constance's smile she also understood that Constance knew this.

Constance, however, did not make any comment but came back to Magda. 'You've always been so close to her that I don't suppose you've noticed that she really has become a swan. I mean, she's beautiful. You and I are good-looking but there's no doubt that, as she grew up, Magda became truly beautiful and very desirable.'

'Philip obvious agrees with you,' Catherine said.

'I suppose that's why he married her. What do you think?'

Catherine considered this. 'I don't know,' she said finally. 'It was very sudden but it has lasted.'

'And we all hope that it will,' Constance said smoothly. 'Did you know,' she asked suddenly, 'that he's been offered some kind of post, if that's the right term, as some sort of financial adviser to the Government?'

'No!' Catherine was startled. 'Magda hasn't said anything.'

'Perhaps her accident got in the way.'

'Perhaps. Who told you?'

'Sebastien. He thought it was brilliant. Of course, it's possible I got him wrong or misunderstood him.'

'I don't see what Philip would want to do with the Government. He doesn't support them.'

'I believe it's very specialised – something to do with helping Third World economies. That's the popular thing these days, isn't it? We must all do our bit for Africa, etc. I've been helping to organise a fundraising effort at church myself. It looks good and satisfies one's conscience.'

Catherine was shocked by the flippancy underlying Constance's words. 'Don't you care about people starving and dying?' she asked vehemently.

'Of course I do. Every good Catholic should, but there's not much one can do, is there? I'm sure I care more than the millions of idiotic young people flocking hysterically to these ridiculous pop concerts. You surely know as well as I do that most of them would go to *any* pop concert, even if it were to save the snails or something.'

'I don't know. Perhaps you're right.' Catherine was suddenly feeling very much the inferior younger sister. Constance's imperturbable self-confidence overcame her as it had done so often in the past. Constance had always been their mother's friend and confidante who had always seemed to know the right thing to do or to say. Now again, she represented the ultra-respectable and respected Catholic family they had always been. Magda's story seemed to be even more unlikely.

'You'll found out that I'm right in about a year. My Kit went, even though he's nearly twenty-six and much too old for such childish capers. But, of course, he's joined the Peter Pan movement – the young people who think they'll never grow old. Poor devils!'

'Lucy was furious when I refused to let her go,' Catherine admitted.

Constance smiled. 'You're doing your best but I'm afraid you may be doomed to failure. I think that Father has begun to feel that he may not have much pride in his grandchildren. That's probably why he's so proud of Magda's marriage to Philip, who seems about to become a pillar of the Establishment.'

'Surely he isn't as dreary as that makes him sound?' Catherine protested.

'Maybe not, but that doesn't sound dreary to Father, it sounds highly successful.'

'Perhaps Mother would have been pleased if she had lived to see it?'

'I'm afraid not – definitely not.' Constance answered without hesitation.

'How can you be so sure? After all, she died just before Magda came back. Don't you think you should have asked Magda to come home then? Might they not have had a reconciliation?'

'Certainly not.' Constance's answer was both firm and decided. 'I know it for a fact. I knew that you knew how to get in touch with Magda, so I suggested to mother that I should send for her but she said, "No." '

'Really?' Catherine stared at her sister. 'Did she say why?'

'Not exactly.' Constance hesitated before she spoke more. 'What she actually said was, "Don't dream of doing that, Constance. It would not do any good. I've wronged that child enough. I don't want to hurt her any more." '

'What a strange thing to say.' Catherine was afraid of what Constance might reveal. 'Did she ever say anything else? Surely, before she died...?' It seemed impossible that her mother, whom she had always regarded as an exemplary Catholic, should die without repenting.

'I'm afraid she didn't change her mind. In fact, the day before she died she said quite clearly that Magda had ruined her life, although she hadn't meant to, and that she could not repent of her feelings towards Magda. She said very firmly that if I wanted the truth I should ask my father, although it would do no good except to reveal his hypocrisy. She had already said goodbye to us, so these were practically her last words.'

For a moment Catherine could not speak. Then she asked slowly, 'What could she have possibly meant? You must have wondered.'

Constance shrugged, 'I decided that it was best to let it be. She was in such pain. She might have exaggerated. People like to find someone to blame, don't they?'

'But that was a bit more serious, surely? It was hardly fair to Magda. It affected her a lot.'

'Oh God, Catherine, don't start to make one of your scenes! Magda's happy now. I know she was your pet and still is in a way, but it's all over now. Personally, I believe that Mother was dead set against having another baby. She was ill, in fact. I don't suppose you remember that she was in some sort of private hospital before Magda was born. She couldn't bond with the baby and blamed Father. At least, that's what I think. It can happen, you know.'

'But it worries me,' Catherine persisted. 'I want to know the truth. I thought we were a really happy Catholic family, and we weren't.'

Although she was irritated, Constance 'kept her cool', as Lucy might say. 'It's time you grew up, darling, and stopped being so intense about everything. No one is perfect. It would be boring if they were. But "all's well that ends well", as Shakespeare put it. It's all over now and forgotten. I was silly to mention it. We shall now be the perfect family party, with Philip and Magda as the stars.'

Catherine felt almost triumphant. 'No, the trouble is that we might not.'

'What do you mean? What are you talking about?' For the first time Constance was ruffled.

'Because Magda's gone!'

'Gone? What the hell do you mean?'

'She's gone. She left Philip two days ago.'

Constance was obviously shocked. 'You're not making sense! Why ever would she do that?'

'Because it isn't over. The past has come back to haunt us, as they say. Something happened when she had that accident at the weekend. She started to tell us…'

'What happened?' Constance interrupted her.

'I don't exactly know. I behaved terribly. I didn't believe her. I didn't want to believe her.'

'Believe *what*?'

'What she said about Mother and Father. I was horrid to Philip, too.' She stood up suddenly. 'I'm sorry, Constance. I must go.'

She hurried towards the door and was just about to leave the room when Constance caught hold of her arm. 'You can't go like this. You must tell me more. What about the party?'

'*Damn the bloody party!*' Catherine shouted. 'There's no chance of one unless we can find Magda. I must talk to Philip. You see, Magda wants the truth, even if you don't. It matters to some people.' Shaking off her sister's arm, she said firmly, 'I'm going and you can't stop me. It's the only way your precious party will be saved, so you'd better pray I do the right thing – if you haven't forgotten how to pray.'

Before Constance could answer her, she was gone, only pausing to pick up her bag and jacket in the hall.

Chapter Seven

Philip put down his phone slowly, staring into space. He could scarcely believe what he had just been told. Incredible though it was, however, he knew that it had to be true. Julia Masters, the senior therapist at St Austin's Hospital, and Magda's colleague for the last three years, could have no possible reason for lying.

Even before he could give her his message that Magda would probably not be back at work this week, she had greeted him by asking how Magda was. 'I hope your ringing doesn't mean that there is something wrong?' she had asked.

'Magda was mugged on Sunday night and she was injured, but not seriously,' he told her.

'Oh God, how terrible!' she exclaimed before he could say more. 'Give her my love, won't you? I feel so guilty. It's nearly three months since she left and I've never been in touch as I promised. The trouble is we've been so busy. It took ages to find even a barely possible substitute for Magda; she's so brilliant with people. It's such a pity she left. I realised she must have a compelling reason, though I didn't like to press her. There isn't anything especially wrong, is there?'

'Not really,' he hastened to reassure her. 'The mugging's depressed her a bit and I thought it might cheer her up to talk to an old colleague.'

'Of course I'd love to. We all wish she was back – the place isn't the same without her. I'm afraid I can't talk now, as my next client's arrived. Please tell her I'll ring this evening, and give her my love, won't you?'

As he put down the phone he reflected on how incredible this conversation had been. For three months Magda had not been working and she hadn't said a word to him. Looking back, he realised that she must have given up her job just before they left on their last holiday. It had been a longer holiday than usual. When he had questioned her about that, she had merely said that she had an extra couple of weeks owing to her, and he had thought no more about it.

He remembered it now as an especially happy holiday. Having more time than usual, they had wandered into various remote parts of Europe. He had found it a very satisfying time and he had thought that they had been even closer than usual. And yet she had hidden the truth from him. Why?

He had never objected to her working, although he had pointed out that it was unnecessary and had suggested voluntary work, but she had brushed that aside. She had been trained as a teacher of English and Drama before she had spent two years travelling overseas. She had gone back to teaching, choosing always the more difficult jobs, or so it had seemed to him.

About five years ago, however, she had announced that she wished to train as a therapist and counsellor. Her training had taken about two years and she appeared to enjoy it, although she did not say much about it. Suddenly, for the first time, it occurred to him that she might have told him little because he had never asked much.

He looked at the tidy desk in front of him with its neat pile of folders. So much had happened in the last few days, and in the last forty-eight hours he had learned much that had been hidden from him. It all seemed too much for his mind to accept.

Picking up her photograph, which always stood on his desk, he looked closely at it as if seeking an answer. Her brilliant blue eyes looked straight into his; there was no guile there. She did not seem to be hiding anything. Her mouth was curved into her gentle, tantalising smile. It was those eyes and that smile which had first attracted him so powerfully, and still did. The shining waves of black hair framed her face. He put out his hand as if to stroke it as he had so often done. Then, realising the futility of his action, he almost threw the photograph down. His pain was so great that he could not think any more. In her note she had said that she still loved him and would be back. But could he any longer believe that?

Catherine, who had always been her sister's loving supporter, had in her normal impetuous way quickly decided that Magda was a liar. She was a cruel liar who had destroyed their family by inventing this crazy story to cover up her long-standing relationship with Conrad. Finding that no longer possible, she had now, Catherine declared, gone off with him. Catherine had even been angry with Philip himself, as if he were somehow to blame.

Her judgment had seemed harsh and cruel but he couldn't blame her because she was so obviously deeply hurt. He had occasionally been amused and even irritated by Catherine's possessive devotion for her younger sister, but he had said little because he knew that Magda would never reject or criticise her sibling. On that miserable Sunday night he had been quite sure that Catherine needed to be told before anyone else.

Now he wondered if Catherine had perhaps been right. Did some of the blame truly belong to him? He had fallen passionately in love with Magda from the moment when he had first met her, and delighted that she seemed to feel the same. Three weeks later he had actually asked her to marry him. He had known that at the age of thirty-seven he was truly in love for the first time in his life. She had tried to slow things down at first but three months later they had been married. For fifteen years he had told himself that she had been as happy as he had been.

But which Magda had he married? Had there always been another Magda who had chosen to remain hidden, but who now had suddenly reasserted herself and wanted her freedom? Should he have suspected this – after all, she was twenty-five when he met her – and asked more questions? As he looked back he was amazed to remember how few questions he had asked.

Sitting down, he asked himself once again what had really happened that last weekend. Why had Magda been in that part of London? Had she really lost her memory? It seemed possible that Conrad might have the answer but he too had disappeared, possibly with Magda.

Unable to remain still any longer, he stood up and walked across the room, looking down at the busy Thames below. They had stayed in this flat partly because Magda loved the view. As she could not have a child, there was simply no reason for them to buy a bigger and more expensive place simply because he could afford it. She had always said that this was an interesting place in which to live and, since they were comfortable there, they had no reason to move. He had accepted her point of view as he had accepted most things about her: without question. But now he wondered. Had she never really been settled? Why had he never asked these questions? Watching a pleasure boat full of Japanese tourists making its way towards Westminster, he felt utterly remote from life and from other people. He felt intensely lonely and isolated as he had for much of his life, now almost as cut off from everyone, as he had when he resigned from the Army.

Quickly he turned away from that too painful memory and walked across the room to the drinks cabinet. Taking out a bottle of malt whisky, he poured himself a double measure and gulped it down. As he was about to pour himself a second, he stopped. *Not that way again, please, God!*

That was partly why he had so rarely disputed Magda's point of view or asked questions. His loneliness seemed to have ended when he had looked into those apparently candid, brilliant blue eyes. Her beguiling smile had enfolded him in its warmth. For the first time in his life he had fallen in love, and the feeling had been mutual – or so he had always thought. They had been accepted by everyone as a truly happy couple.

Now Magda had gone. Had she ever really loved him? he wondered. Suddenly an unexpected thought struck him. Had he ever truly loved Magda? Or had she simply been an escape? What did he know about love anyway? There had been little love for him in his early life. When his favoured elder brother had been killed in an accident, it had suited him to leave the Army and take his place to help his elderly father. It had been no sacrifice.

Pouring out a second whisky, he sipped it slowly as he tried to sort out his thoughts. He could not deny that he had been happy for the first time in his life with Magda. They had lived harmoniously together. And why not? They were both intelligent and shared similar tastes in food and entertainment, and both enjoyed discussing ideas.

Even as he told himself this, he knew it was superficial and had little to do with the truth. It was a passionate physical attraction that had brought them together and had held them together. Magda had proved to be a wonderful lover, and with her he had, for the first time, fully enjoyed the delights of sex. And this enjoyment had continued unalloyed.

Does this have anything to do with love, or is it simply lust? he asked himself. This was not a question he felt able to answer. It seemed possible to him, however, that love implied trust based on honesty and understanding. It seemed that Magda had not been honest with him; nor had she trusted him.

And what about me? he asked himself. *I don't come out of this very well, do I?* He couldn't truly pretend that he had been honest and trusting himself. Guilt and fear had prevented that. He drew back as always. He was determined not to go along that dark path.

The only way to escape was to work. He had discovered that before he met Magda and began to live. Numbers fascinated him. That his use of them often made a lot of money was only of secondary importance. Strange, he reflected, Magda too had never given much importance to that; she had certainly not married him for his money. So why had she married him? For the moment, there was no answer. Resolutely, he returned to his laptop and to the work which awaited him.

It was early evening when Conrad returned. As soon as Philip heard the resolute peal of the bell he was sure who it was. All day, subconsciously, he had been waiting for him.

For a moment they regarded each other in the open doorway until Philip, moving back wordlessly, led him into the lounge. Conrad looked much the same as he had done on his first appearance. His black hair was smooth; his lean face with its hawk-like nose and high cheekbones was as expressionless as before. Only the very dark eyes glinted. His dark suit was elegantly expensive but he no longer wore a challenging cravat, merely an orthodox tie with a diamond-studded tiepin. On the little finger of his left hand he wore a ring with a large red cornelian stone in it.

For a moment they faced each other; then Conrad spoke. 'I must apologise once again for my intrusion.'

'Not at all,' Philip replied. 'You said you would come again and so I was expecting you some time. But, if you're hoping to speak to Magda, I'm afraid you'll be disappointed.'

'I was indeed hoping for that. I trust she's not ill.' His English was just too perfect to be natural.

'Not ill, exactly…' Philip hesitated. 'But do sit down and have a drink, if you have the time.'

'Thank you. I have the time.' Conrad sat down and watched Philip as he poured generous helpings of malt into two glasses. After handing a glass to his guest, Philip sat down with his. While he sipped his drink slowly, Conrad calmly waited. Finally, Philip decided to speak freely. He knew scarcely anything about this man and he did not inspire liking; nevertheless he had a strange conviction that he might obtain some help from him. He might even be able to suggest some way of finding Magda.

'When I said that Magda wasn't ill,' he began, 'I wasn't telling you the entire truth.' He paused.

'I was sure that you were not. That was why I stayed.' Conrad's crisp enunciation was so perfect that he had to be a well-educated foreigner, but his nationality was not obvious.

'I'm pretty sure,' Philip continued, 'that she has recovered herself physically, but she doesn't appear to have regained the memory of last weekend. And your appearance created a further difficulty for her, since neither her sister nor I had heard of you before.'

Conrad's expression remained impassive but it was clear to Philip that he had been affected by what had just been said. 'Am I to understand, then,' he asked, 'that before last night that you, her husband, knew nothing about her past life? Pardon me, but that seems astonishing.'

'It is surprising, I admit but it's the truth. It was only after you had gone that Magda told us a little about her "other life", as she called it.'

'She told you about Lisa?' Conrad could not hide his interest now. 'And you had never heard of her before?'

'That's right, incredible though it may seem. Magda and I met fifteen years ago. Three months later we were married. And we have been very happy.' He ended almost belligerently.

'I have no intention of disputing with you about that,' Conrad replied calmly.

'Then why in God's name did you come here?' Philip demanded fiercely. 'You distressed Magda and you forced her into revealing something she obviously did not want to reveal, especially in front of her sister, who was very upset to hear about Lisa.'

'Ah yes, the respectable, the possessive Catherine! She would, of course, be upset.'

His mocking tone irritated Philip more. 'It's easy to laugh at Catherine, but harder apparently to answer my question. Why did you come?'

'That was, I thought, made quite clear by me. I came because Magda had invited me and I was pleased to believe that our friendship might be renewed, that the long estrangement between us might now be over.'

'But Magda denied inviting you!'

'Presumably that was because the concussion she had suffered had caused her to lose her memory.'

'She also said,' Philip reminded him, 'that she not invited you and that she never wanted to see you again.'

'That is true.' Sipping his whisky, Conrad seemed to consider the matter. 'That I could not understand,' he said finally. 'Perhaps she explained that to you later when you talked, as I presume you would have done once you were alone.'

'We talked, but I'm afraid Magda did not explain you.'

'She did not tell you very much, then. May I ask what you know?'

For moment Philip hesitated again. It seemed absurd to allow this stranger to probe into his intimate life. But what choice did he have? Conrad seemed his only possible link now with Magda. 'She only told me about her first meetings with Lisa from the time she was eight until she was about sixteen. By then we were both very tired and I decided that we should go to sleep. I didn't want Magda to get overtired.'

'Naturally not.' Conrad agreed. Philip looked suspiciously at him, sensing a hint of mockery but there was nothing to be learned from his expression. 'I presume,' Conrad continued, 'that you expected to resume your conversation the next day? I have a feeling, however, that it didn't happen. Am I right? For example, you learned nothing that could explain my visit. Am I right?'

'That's true. In the morning, Magda was still tired, and then I was called away to an important conference. I didn't want to go, but she persuaded me and promised that we would talk when I came back.' He paused. Sudden doubts about Magda's motives had come into his mind.

'But it seems you didn't.' Conrad prompted him. 'Why not?'

'Because, when I returned, Magda had gone. She had packed a few clothes and left a note saying that she loved me and would be back.'

'If she said she will be back, then she will,' Conrad said firmly. 'Magda always keeps her promises. I can say that because I knew her very well for several years – before she met you, of course.'

'In that case, perhaps you can help me to find her, since you obviously want to meet her, too!'

It was several moments before Conrad was ready to speak. Finally he said coldly, 'I have no idea where Magda might be. Surely you don't believe that I'm playing some ridiculous and childish game with you. Magda has not left you to come to me.'

'I never really believed that,' Philip answered quickly, 'although Catherine seems to, and is angry not only with Magda but with me also for being such a credulous fool.'

Unexpectedly, Conrad laughed. 'How typical of the righteous Catherine! Like many Christians she finds it easier to hate than to love! I sometimes warned Magda, but she was always a little obstinate about Catherine. You must have noticed that surely?' After emptying his glass, he held it out to Philip, who refilled both their glasses.

'That may be true,' he replied, 'but I'm not concerned with that. It seems to me that you are the only person who must know where Magda spent her weekend.'

'I do know that. I know that she spent it in Lisa's flat, because I was summoned to meet Magda there, on the grounds that, after many years she actually wanted to see me again.'

'Then you do, at least, know more than I do.'

'That appears to be true.' After gazing thoughtfully at the golden liquid in his glass, Conrad looked up and replied slowly, 'Unfortunately, knowing Lisa's address does not help much.'

'What do you mean?'

It seemed for a moment that Conrad had decided not to answer. Instead he sipped his malt appreciatively while Philip waited. Finally, putting down his glass, he laughed mockingly. 'I see no sensible reason why I should not tell you. After I had been here, I went to Lisa's flat, but she was apparently no longer there. I have tried to ring her several times but there has been no response. She appears to have vanished – like her daughter!'

'Are you suggesting that Magda has actually gone away with Lisa?'

'I think that is highly unlikely for many reasons. The most compelling being that they seemed to be quarrelling bitterly when I arrived at the suggested time. Knowing Lisa's violent temper, I tried to intervene but neither was ready to listen to me. I could see that Magda was greatly upset but Lisa ordered me to go. As I was leaving, Magda gave me her address, because she said she needed to speak to me. Before she could say more, Lisa pulled her away and the door was slammed in my face. I have no idea what happened next, but I am afraid that it may have been Lisa who attacked Magda that night.' He seemed disinclined to say any more.

'And is that all you have come to say? Don't you care what has happened?' Philip asked, irritated by the other man's apparent indifference.

'My principal reason for coming was to see Magda, as I had promised.'

'And now you know you can't, you might as well go... Is that what you mean?' Philip could scarcely contain his unreasoning antagonism to this unpleasant foreigner.

'Mr Peters, there is no need for you to be rude. If you want my help, you must try harder.'

'Why should I want your help?' Philip stood up as if preparing to dismiss his unwelcome guest, but to his surprise Conrad waved his hand slightly as of to indicate that he should sit down again. 'Apart from our wealth and the power it inevitably brings,' he continued in his soft, smooth voice, 'you and I would seem to have little in common. You are a product of the British Establishment – public school, Cambridge and Sandhurst – who was even fortunate at a time convenient to himself to be able to take over the control of one of the country's few last independent banks.

'Whereas I have even had to discard my name to hide the fact that I was once a stateless Arab, who after escaping the squalor of a refugee camp, decided to obtain wealth and power by any means available to him.' He paused for a moment and then continued with a slight smile. 'I can see from your expression that you have already decided how unpleasant these means probably were. Well, you are right. Drugs, women – whatever commodity makes money – I dealt in it. You see, although I may admire them, I can't afford to have the moral scruples of a man like you.'

Philip sat down suddenly, wondering what he did not want to express how such a man could have been close to Magda. Instead he replied, 'I've no desire to judge you.'

'Good. Which brings me to my one good point. Depraved though I may be, I never lied to Magda. And that, in turn, leads to the one important characteristic we have in common, you and I.'

'Which is?' Philip asked, unable to turn away from those penetrating eyes.

'Magda. Or to be specific, I should say our love for Magda. When I first saw you with her, I realised that you are as devoted to her as I am. Seventeen years' absence has made no difference to me. There were other women before her, there have been other women since, but she is still the only woman I have ever loved. I am right, am I not, in believing that you feel the same?' As he clasped his hands and leaned forward, the cornelian gleamed a fiery red in the light, a gleam that seemed to be reflected in those dark eyes.

Suddenly Philip felt that he had moved into an alien world, but it was a world Magda now inhabited. 'You're right,' he agreed, 'and I'm afraid for her.'

'You're right to be afraid,' Conrad said firmly. 'That is why we must forget our differences and work together to try to find her. Together we may be able to discover the key. Are you willing to try?'

Philip nodded his agreement. There was no alternative.

Chapter Eight

Magda looked round her hotel room with satisfaction. It was exactly what she wanted – a completely anonymous room, decorated in beige and tastefully toning pastels. There was nothing to distract or jar. Perhaps, if she could sit alone here and think undisturbed, her memory would return.

After she had left home, she had spent several hours looking for the right place, and now she had luckily found it and had just moved in. The Alexandria was a respectable private hotel in one of those quiet squares vaguely west of central. She looked through the window across the square of green towards the Georgian terrace house opposite. Although they were a little shabby, like middle-class ladies fallen on hard times, they still retained their original air of respectability.

The Alexandria had attracted partly because the paint was brighter but mainly because of the sign saying 'Vacancies'. The owner/manageress who came to the desk in response to her ring was a vigorous Scot in her early sixties. Her sparkling unnaturally white hair was arranged in the swirls and curls so much favoured by elderly middle-class ladies. The well-cut beige suit was in the same fashion. Magda wondered if she, with her obvious air of wealth, would be acceptable, but she was encouraged by the Scots accent, the lively hazel eyes and the natural friendly smile. It had all been very easy when she had offered a week's rent in cash and mentioned the possibility of staying longer.

She had given the impression that she was thinking of moving down from the Midlands because of a possible change of job, and had casually signed the register 'Mary Lefevre'.

She had not removed her wedding ring so it was obviously Mrs Lefevre. It was growing dark as she quickly unpacked her few clothes and arranged her toilet articles in the bathroom. A couple of books and notebooks on the bedside table, and all was done. By the light of the two reading lamps the room looked satisfyingly spacious and bare.

It was almost time for dinner, so after a few minor adjustments to her toilet she descended to the dining room, hoping that the food would be bearable.

It was over an hour before she came back to her room. The food had been unexciting but satisfactory; the other guests pleasantly friendly but not intrusive. Now, however, as she sat down in the one armchair that the room offered, reality struck her. Up to now it had been as if she was playing a kind of game. Looking back, it seemed as if she had acted entirely on a sudden impulse to flee. But why?

Why am I here? she asked herself. *What am I hoping to achieve?* For no clear reason she had run away from a kind husband who was willing to listen and to try to understand. Cathy might have been difficult but Cathy could always be relied on to come round in the end. In any case, Cathy was unimportant compared with Philip.

Why, therefore, was she now in this empty room, completely alone? There was nothing she had to do; the phone would not ring.

She told herself that she had come to discover the truth; to find out what had happened during that lost weekend. Then why, if she cared for him as she had said she did, was it necessary to leave Philip, her friend and protector? *Of course I care for him,* she told herself. *I've been happily married to him for fifteen years. But is that real love?* Even as she asked herself, however, she knew the answer. It was not her love for Philip that mattered but her fear that, if the true Magda were revealed, Philip might feel that he had loved a false idol, a woman who had never actually existed.

One of her reasons for running away had been this fear but there was another, even greater dread that terrible things had been said and revealed during that weekend. She had convinced herself that she would be better able to face these on her own. It was now clear, however, that she had not thought any further than running away. She had accomplished that. Now she faced a blank. What should she do next?

The answer had been there all the time, of course. The one she most dreaded to face. She must get in touch with Conrad. His arrival at her home had horrified her, but it was clear from what he had said that he must have seen her that weekend. He alone could confirm her vague impression that she had spent it with Lisa. He might be able to tell her more. Seventeen years ago she had declared that she despised him and had sworn that she would never see him again. It was to be as if he had never existed. Now, she had to forget that, humiliating though it was. She needed him.

She had found his card in her purse, although she could no longer remember how she had obtained it. Not wanting to be traced by him, she decided to use the phone in her bedroom and withhold the number.

With trembling fingers she dialled Conrad's number and listened anxiously while it rang out. It took a long time and she had to resist the temptation to ring off. Finally, he answered.

'Hello, Conrad,' she replied, 'it's Magda here.'

'Magda, my dear!' He sounded really pleased. 'I'm very relieved to hear your voice. How are you?'

'Much better,' she replied coldly. She hated having to approach him.

'And where are you?'

'Why do you ask that?' She was surprised.

'Because when I called at your flat earlier this evening your husband invited me in and told me that you had left and that he didn't know where you were. At least I was able to reassure him that you had not run away with me.'

'Philip would never think that.'

'Why not?' His tone was mocking. 'You have told the poor man so little of the truth about yourself that he could have no idea how distasteful that course of action would be to you. You have no need to play games with me, Magda; I know too much. But since Philip apparently loves you and believes that you love him, you should not be so brutal. Ring him. Tell him that you are safe and well and will soon be back.'

'Why should you, of all people, tell me to do that?'

'I am a more complicated character than you imagine, my dear. You need not worry, however. If you don't tell him, then I shall.'

'Why on earth should you do that?'

'Because I promised to tell him if I had any news. We became quite friendly.'

'You'll be telling me next that you're a reformed character!'

'Perhaps I am. But now I suggest that you stop wasting time and tell me why you really rang me.'

Mastering the irritation she felt, she asked her question calmly. 'Did you really meet me at Lisa's flat last Sunday? I have a faint feeling that is where I went, but nothing is clear.'

'I certainly saw you there that Sunday evening.'

'Where is the flat?'

'You really don't know?'

'I'm afraid not.'

'It's on the second floor of the newly refurbished block near St Luke's Hospital, Number 22. She told me that she had invited you and that you had agreed to come.'

'But why were you there?'

'Because,' he laughed, 'I was foolish enough to believe something that I wanted to believe! She told me that your marriage was not as successful as it seemed, and that you were ready to see me again.'

'She was up to her old tricks, then?'

'Yes, it seems so; but if none of that was true, how did she get you there?'

Magda tried hard to remember. 'I'm not even sure about that,' she admitted, 'but I have this feeling that she told me she was ill, perhaps terminally, and as she was my mother, she wanted to see me before she died.'

'That sounds a likely Lisa story, so I think we can accept your recollections as likely to be true.'

'It must be something like that,' she agreed, 'if I really was there…'

'I can certainly confirm that. I arrived about seven, as Lisa had suggested. We were to have a drink and perhaps a meal before you left. Do you want to hear all these details?'

'Of course, since I remember nothing.' A sudden unpleasant thought struck her. She was putting herself into a position where she had to depend on him. Was that wise? But then she had no alternative. 'You will tell me the truth, won't you?' she asked. Almost immediately she wished she could take the words back. She waited fearfully for his reply. Why had she shown herself to be so vulnerable?

'It makes me sad,' he replied, 'that you seem to understand me so little, Magda. I have lied and cheated in business. That means nothing to me. But I have never lied to you because I love you, although you don't believe it.'

'I'm sorry, but will you please tell me what happened. I'm so afraid that something very bad was said or done.'

'I'm afraid that may be true. As soon as Lisa opened the door to me, I realised that I had arrived at an inopportune moment. Although at first she tried to hide it, it soon became clear that Lisa was violently angry, and that you too were angry and very distressed. Lisa went to get some drinks, which gave you an opportunity to tell me that I should go. Then, to my surprise, you added that you nevertheless needed to speak to me. Before Lisa came back I just had time to slip my card into your purse. I hoped that I might be able to help but there was no chance. Almost as soon as she had given us our drinks, Lisa's anger exploded. She said that she was sorry that she had invited me and that, if I had any thought that I might be reconciled with you, I should forget it. She said you were a faithless, heartless bitch, incapable of loving anyone. I thought she was going to hit you, so I intervened. Lisa then turned on me and said I was a fucking fool if I expected to get any return from a heartless slut like you.

'You then told me that it would be better if I went, as I could do no good. Nevertheless, just as Lisa was practically pushing me through the door, you said, "I would like to talk to you, Conrad." The door was slammed in my face and I have no idea of what happened after that.'

'Thank you,' she said. After a brief pause she asked, 'Why did you call on me?'

'When you didn't get in touch as you'd promised, I was concerned. It was easy to find your address.'

'When you saw Philip today, did you tell him all you have just told me?'

'No, only an outline. He obviously knew very little and it was not up to me to enlighten him.'

'Thank you.' She was impressed by his calm manner and lack of malice. 'Do you think,' she asked finally, 'that it could have been Lisa who attacked me?'

'I think it is very possible although we can't rule out the stray mugger.'

'No, I suppose not. Do you think I should go and confront her?'

'Perhaps, although it might be risky. But it's not possible for you to do that.'

'What do you mean?'

'She seems to have vanished. I have rung her several times and have visited her flat twice. I've had no reply to my calls and the flat seems to be empty.'

A frightening though struck Magda. 'Do you think it's possible, Conrad, that I could have struck her, and she's lying there injured or perhaps dead?'

To her relief, Conrad immediately laughed. 'I think that is so highly unlike you that you should even think of it! Lisa has several times been violent, but you have never been. She's also always been good at vanishing. She's most likely gone off with her latest lover. Forget it.'

'Thanks. I will try to.'

'What are you going to do now?'

'Try to remember what was said and done that Sunday. I think I may be able to do so now. If I need your help, I'll ring you again. I need to be alone now to think.'

'I see. I hope you will remember, however, that you are in one way closer to me than to anyone.' Before she could answer he had put down the receiver.

Suddenly she felt very alone. The room, which had seemed like a comforting refuge, now seemed like a prison. For a moment she longed for Philip's calm kindness. Moving back to her chair, she told herself she must not be foolish. She had come here to think without disturbance.

Now, thanks to Conrad, who had been kinder than she had expected, she had a framework on which to concentrate. She was now convinced that if she refused to give in to her fear, her memory would gradually return. If it were something very unpleasant, she would have to face it. Even that would be better than trying to run away from a nameless dread.

Adam was roused from his comfortable doze before the television by Catherine's early return. He had expected her to be spending two or three hours with her elder sister for, although she pretended to be indifferent, she was always flattered by being summoned to the 'Presence'.

As Catherine came quickly into the living room, slamming the door behind her and flinging her bag and jacket onto the settee, he realised that she was very angry. As escape was impossible, he pretended to greet here cheerfully. 'Hello, you're back early. Can I get you anything?'

'Well, you can turn that rubbish off for a start!'

Marching across the room, she switched off the television. Adam, controlling his useless irritation, consoled himself with the thought that he would be able to see the results later and that it had been a pretty boring game anyway.

'That woman is a bloody bitch!' Catherine announced, flinging herself into an armchair. 'I don't believe she's ever cared for anyone except herself and what people think of her and our "wonderful" family.' She paused, obviously waiting for him to respond.

Adam was at a loss. When Catherine started swearing, it was time to tread carefully. Something had gone wrong – but what? 'I thought you went to discuss arrangements for your father's birthday party,' he ventured at last. 'What happened?'

Catherine laughed bitterly. 'I was only there to agree with everything; to praise her wonderful planning and to accept my usual menial tasks.'

'What about Vivienne?'

'How the hell should I know? She's out of favour for some reason.'

'What happened then?'

'Well, when I realised that Magda and Philip were to be the stars of the show...' She broke off for a moment, then asked abruptly, 'Did you know that Philip has been asked to be some financial adviser to the Treasury, or something like that?'

Adam shifted uneasily. For some reason he felt guilty, although God knew why. 'I did see something in the paper about it, but when he didn't mention it the other evening, I decided it must be one of those silly rumours.'

'Constance does not agree with you. She was positively purring about it. This really puts our family in the news, she thought, and Magda, the ugly duckling, has truly become a swan.'

'I suppose you found that irritating?'

'Yes, but worse than that she made it clear that the only reason that Magda was important was because she had managed to marry a rich man who was now even richer and more important. In the end, of course, I had to tell her that Magda and Philip might not be coming. It was awful. I told her that Magda still wasn't well and that they'd gone away for a bit.'

'I suppose that upset her?'

'Not really. She simply didn't want to believe that they would miss the party and so, of course, she didn't.'

'Is that why you're so angry?'

'Not really. It's much worse that that. It's dreadful, Adam.' Her eyes filled with tears. 'I've been so wrong. What can I do?'

For a moment, Adam was dumbfounded. This was the first time he could ever remember Catherine admitting that she had been in the wrong. *What can have happened?* he wondered. Aloud, he asked, 'What do you mean? I don't understand?'

For a moment the normal Catherine reasserted herself. 'What's to understand?' she shouted at him. 'I've been wrong, utterly wrong!' Almost immediately, however, tears put out the fire.

'I don't get that.' He handed her a tissue. 'Wrong about what? You haven't told me.'

'Wrong about Magda! I think Philip believes she might be a liar. I told you she must be. You didn't believe it, but I did. I was the one who was supposed to love her. Oh God, how could I have been so stupid and so cruel?'

'You mustn't blame yourself too much.' Wanting to comfort her, he leaned over and patted her hand, but such gestures did not come easily now. 'You were naturally very upset. I wasn't affected so much.'

'*Balls!*' she replied with unexpected ferocity. 'Of all people I was the one who should have believed her and supported her. You can't deny that.'

He couldn't, so he feebly stroked her hand again. 'And do you know,' she asked suddenly, 'I was the only person who never had the slightest suspicion, the only one who truly believed that we were a happy Catholic family. I expect I was useful to them. I helped to maintain the sham and keep Magda happy. Constance, the bloody bitch, was the worst!'

'Why do you say that?'

'She was closest to Mum. She actually told me tonight that she knew that Mum didn't like Magda, in fact that she sometimes seemed to hate her. She noticed that Dad rarely supported Magda, even when Mum was unjust. She had other suspicions, which I think she discussed with Seb, about Mum going away two months before Magda was born and then coming back with a baby. I suppose they carried it off because they were so pious and respectable. But the worst thing of all is that I realised tonight that Constance doesn't care a damn about the truth. Doesn't even want to know it. She only cares that Philip and Magda should be there to make her stupid party a success. I told her that there probably wouldn't be a party and left. I was right, wasn't I?'

Suddenly he realised that she was begging him for support, as she had never done for years. She was lost and frightened. 'Yes,' he replied firmly, 'you were right. Don't worry.' Holding her hand firmly now, he tried to comfort her. 'Remember, Magda doesn't know. And she need never know. Just go on supporting her as you've always done.'

'Thanks, Adam.' She was humbler than he had ever known her to be. 'But what about Philip? I must have made him feel worse.'

'You needn't worry about that. I can tell you a quite a bit about Philip. I actually phoned him tonight.'

'Why did you do that?' She was surprised at such direct action by him.

'I felt sorry for the guy. And I was right. He needed someone to talk to.'

'I never thought of him like that. He always seems so calm and controlled.'

'Maybe, but he wasn't quite like that tonight. In fact, he admitted he was just finishing a bottle of whisky.'

'Not Philip. Surely! He scarcely drinks at all.'

'Well, he had tonight.'

'Well, he must have been pretty drunk, then.' Adam could hear the disapproval in her voice. She was always so ready to judge people.

'Wrong,' he replied firmly. 'He had drink taken but he was not drunk. I'm quite sure it wasn't the first time Philip had drunk a bottle of whisky. You forget he was in the Army for years – Special Services in Northern Ireland, I think. We don't know what horrors he's been through. We are in no position to judge.'

'You don't like judging, do you? But sometimes, I think, you have to take a stand.'

Exasperated, he burst out, 'Can't you forget all that for once? Do you or do you not want to hear what Philip told me?'

'Of course I want to know.' He noticed that she was folding the tissue he had given her into smaller and smaller squares – a sure sign that she was trying to control herself – so he hastened to give her the most important information.

'Magda is definitely not with Conrad, so all our suspicions were wrong.'

'How can you be sure of that?'

'Conrad himself visited Philip. He came back as he said he would to talk to Magda. He confirmed that he and Magda had not met for years, but that Lisa had invited him to her flat to meet Magda.'

'So he did meet her?'

'Only briefly, because when he got there on the Sunday evening Lisa and Magda were in the midst of a terrible quarrel. Lisa was furious and more or less pushed him out of the flat. He hasn't been able to get in touch with Lisa since, and he has no idea where Magda is.'

Catherine stared at him, horrified. 'Do you think it was Lisa who injured Magda?'

'It's possible, but we don't know definitely and we shouldn't rush to conclusions.'

She ignored that. 'What can we do, Adam? I'm afraid for Magda. Poor Philip must be in a terrible state.'

'He's not very happy. I told him we'd do all we could too help him. What else could I say?'

'Nothing. Of course, we must help. I'll go round tomorrow to see him.' She was already more cheerful. Action suited Catherine, but Adam, always cautious, was unsure; although he decided it was wiser to keep his doubts to himself.

Chapter Nine – Lisa's Story

Lisa was apprehensive but nevertheless hopeful. This was the day on which she had planned to meet her daughter for the first time. She was sure the meeting would happen but not at all sure how successful it would be.

On this hot, humid August day she was glad of the shelter of the trees in the wood, even though she was wearing only a thin cotton dress and sandals. She had kept her word and waited for years, but Magda was now eight and she could wait no longer. No promise, she told herself could be valid for ever. She had a right to her chance.

The wood was eerily silent. It seemed to her that Nature, too, was waiting with bated breath to witness this encounter. No breeze, however slight, stirred the leaves; even the birds were hidden and silent. The small patches of sky she could see were a deep unchanging blue, like the blue of her eyes and the blue of the precious stone which she wore suspended on a silver chain round her neck. It was a sapphire, the Fitzgerald inheritance, which might one day be Magda's, if she was indeed a true Fitzgerald.

Suddenly, she heard the sound of footsteps coming along the path towards the clearing. Her heart stood still and then began to beat wildly. It must be Magda... The footsteps stopped for a moment, then the branches were pushed aside and a little girl emerged. They stared intently at each other for a moment.

It was Magda! The first impression was excellent! Magda's long dark hair reached almost to her shoulders in flowing waves. The eyes which stared into hers were as intensely blue as her own. The complexion was as pale and delicate as her own. This was her daughter, the daughter she had longed to see. All these years she had dreamed about Magda, and at last she was going to talk to her.

Even though Magda finally ran away, angry and distressed,

Lisa felt that their meeting had been a satisfactory one. It was natural that the child was upset. It had been a great shock to her to learn that Lisa was her true mother. But in the end, Lisa told herself, the knowledge would make her daughter happier, as she walked slowly back to the main road where a car was waiting for her.

It was wonderful to know that Magda was not at all a Lefevre but a true Fitzgerald: her mother's daughter. Without realising it, the poor child had revealed how lonely she was. She was isolated because of her difference from the rest of the family. She looked different; she felt different, and it was quite clear that they had little love for her, except for Cathy, who looked after her and with whom she had found a refuge.

Cathy's friendship was obviously good for her, especially as Lisa could do little for her daughter at the moment, except arrange to meet her occasionally and gradually win her love and trust. One day, however, Lisa told herself it would be different. At that day she would be able to claim her daughter as her own, and would be able to revenge herself on the man who had ruined her life – Charles Lefevre.

It was clear, she told herself, that he had not kept his promise to her. It had always been obvious that his wife, Rosalind, would resent his 'love child', but he should have been strong enough to overcome that and to make sure that her brothers and sisters accepted her. But then if he had been strong, the whole story would have been different. She was being irrational!

Just as she was leaving the woods, she thought how ironic it was that her first meeting with her child had been in the very same place in which that child had been conceived. Nearly nine years ago... For a painful moment she lingered. How happy she had been that evening in May when she and Charles Lefevre met secretly for the first time in these woods. He had been waiting for her and came quickly to meet her, his fair hair turned to gold by the evening sunlight. *How handsome he is*, she had thought, *tall and bronzed like a Norse god!*

There had been no more time for thought. As he clasped her in his arms, his firm body pressed against her softness, his lips seeking hers more and more passionately. She had not known she could feel like this. She wanted it passionately without knowing exactly what it was she wanted.

She lay on the ground. He was on top of her, caressing her breasts, whispering words of eternal love. She felt his hardness without knowing exactly what it was.

'Lisa, my beautiful Lisa, I never knew what love was until I met you. My darling I love you so much! I can't live without you!'

Joyous and eager, she yielded all without knowing what it was that she yielded. She gave a little cry when he entered her but then ecstasy followed. The earth seemed to stand still and then come to life with an irresistible rhythm. Nothing so wonderful could be wrong. It could never die! It would never end, she had believed. But it had ended. It had been wrong, terribly wrong!

Weeks later, when she had told him, fearful but happy, that she was carrying his child, she had seen it die as she saw the horror in his brown eyes, even before he managed to speak.

When he did speak, it was even more horrible. Her handsome, proud lover had vanished. A scared, guilty man with fumbling excuses stood there in his place. A few minutes later she had run away from him with a mass of words jumbled in her head. Words like, 'Rosalind, my wife, my children, my career will be ruined!' jostled together. Finally, worst of all that cruel, cruel word 'abortion' pierced her heart like a knife. It was then she had fled screaming denial at him. It was then she had begun to hate him. At a terrible cost to herself, she had forced him to save their child. Now, at last, she had seen that child, who had only been allowed life and a proper upbringing because of her insistence.

It was getting late. She must not linger any longer or her lover would be annoyed. The Rolls was waiting for her; the chauffeur opened the back door. Her lover leaned across to kiss her. 'I hope that everything went according to plan?' he asked.

'It did,' she assured him, smiling. 'It was brilliant.'

'And what did you think of your daughter?'

'She is beautiful,' she told him.

'Not more beautiful than her mother,' he replied. 'That would be impossible.'

Without contradicting him, she returned his kiss. In her heart, however, she told herself, *But she is. She is more beautiful than I am, and that means she is more perfect for achieving what I desire.* That, however, must be left to the future.

Now, just over ten years later, she was able to start putting her plan for Magda into action. The meetings between them, after the first, had been short and irregular and always difficult to arrange. In fact, they would have hardly been possible, if Magda had not been so extraordinarily discreet, especially for a child. She had told no one about them – not even her devoted Cathy.

Sometimes, Lisa had wondered uneasily what that indicated about her daughter's character. Had she done her a great harm by revealing the truth? Had Magda, as a result, become incapable of loving?

But this morning she had no such doubts. She was happy to rejoice in her success. Of course it had been easier since Catherine had left home to study Geography at Cambridge, where she had done well. Magda had greatly missed her, and it had been a further blow when Cathy had decided to spend an extra year at Cambridge; and even more distressing when she had accepted a job in that area to be near her boyfriend, Adam, who was also working there.

Hiding her secret joy, Lisa had done her best to comfort and encourage her daughter. Now she was to have her reward. Magda had decided to come to London to study English and Drama, as she, Lisa, had suggested, and she had finally agreed to accept her mother's help in finding a place in which to live. There was apparently nobody else willing to help or advise her.

Jumping out of bed, where she had been having a late break-fast of toast and black coffee, Lisa hurried to the bathroom. She had much to arrange and no time to waste. She had already made a list of addresses which she intended to inspect before Magda arrived, in order to make the girl's choice easier. The next day was to be her day and Magda's, the first they had ever spent together. She was surprised how happy she felt at the thought. As she stepped into the shower, she reminded herself that she must never forget her main objective. But, surely, that needn't prevent her being happy in the company of her daughter?

Their meeting the next day was a surprise to both of them. Lisa had been abroad and Magda had been working for her A levels, so it was some time since they had actually met. To Lisa it seemed that in those few months her daughter had changed from a pretty, young girl into an incredibly beautiful young woman. While to Magda it seemed almost impossible to believe that this elegant and sophisticated woman standing smiling on the platform of Victoria Station could possibly be her mother.

It had been a happy and successful day. Looking back so many years later, it seemed to Lisa that this was the least troubled day that they had ever spent together.

First of all she had taken Magda to lunch in a quietly expensive restaurant, which had obviously pleased her greatly. Then they had inspected the three rooms that Lisa had still kept on her list. They were all fairly central and close to the college, but Lisa cleverly kept the best to the last. It was not only central and close to the college, but also within walking distance of many amenities. The room was larger than average, light and pleasant with a view over nearby gardens. The furniture was sparse but of good quality.

'What do you think?' Lisa asked.

Magda was obviously charmed by it, but when the landlady told her the price, she shook her head sadly. 'I can't possibly afford that,' she told Lisa softly.

'Have another look round, while I talk to Mrs Wilson,' Lisa replied. She did not attempt to haggle about the price but simply asked the landlady if they could have a few minutes before coming to a decision.

As soon as they were alone, she turned to Magda, 'Don't look so glum, darling!' she exclaimed. 'With a few pictures and cushions it will look really good. Surely, you can see that?'

'Of course I can, but can't you understand?' Magda was suddenly cross. 'I can't possibly afford it! My money won't stretch to that.'

'Surely, your father is rich enough to help,' Lisa protested, 'especially now Catherine no longer needs anything from him. He subsidised her, didn't he?'

'Yes, he helped her and Sebastien too, but he won't help me. I'm different. I've always been different. You know that and you know why.' Defiantly, she blinked back her tears. 'Besides,

Rosalind is ill. She has cancer and Dad's paying for a new, expensive treatment.'

'I see.' Lisa stood for a moment, obviously considering, then she replied suddenly and decisively. 'I'll pay your rent. That's the obvious answer.'

'*You*! Why should you?' Magda stared at her.

'You may have forgotten, darling, but I am actually your mother.' She smiled at Magda. 'It's about time I performed some motherly gesture, don't you think? That is, if you've no objection?'

'Objection! Of course not. It's really generous of you to suggest it. But,' she hesitated, 'can you really afford it?'

Lisa laughed. 'Do I look poor, Magda? I assure you I can now afford it.'

'You must be a very successful illustrator!' Magda looked at her mother with admiration. In her elegant black suit with white ruffles at the neck and a diamond brooch in the lapel, Lisa certainly looked very different from the young woman she had first met in her blue cotton dress and sandals.

'I am good at my job, but that's not my only source of income. I have some business ventures with my friend, Conrad, whom I hope you will meet one day soon.' She hesitated for a moment, wondering if she should tell the whole truth. Finally, she decided against it. Now, looking back she wondered, not for the first time, what difference it would have made. How could one tell? Instead, she had said, 'Stop worrying. You're my daughter. I can help you; I want to help you and I will. Isn't that enough?'

'Of course. It's absolutely wonderful!' Impulsively, Magda hugged her mother, her brilliant eyes sparkling like sapphires.

Lisa embraced her warmly. 'You're not worrying about your father, are you?' she asked as she stroked Magda's hair tenderly.

'No, not at all. I don't suppose he'll even think about it. And, if he does, he'll be quite satisfied when I tell him I can manage.' It was a simple statement of fact, without self-pity and without tears.

'How about Catherine? She cares about you, doesn't she?'

'Normally but she's preoccupied no with her new job and her engagement. I scarcely see her. I've found it hard but that's how it is. I've never told her anything,' she added suddenly, 'I've kept my promise.'

'I know you have. You've been very good.' Lisa kissed her. 'Now we'll just fix this and have a happy day together. It's time that we did.'

And they had done just that. In the afternoon they had shopped together buying some things for the room, and finally they had bought Magda a new dress which for the first time revealed her true beauty. *I'm not mistaken about her*, Lisa thought triumphantly. *She will be perfect.* She had played the part of the loving mother but now looking back, she wondered if Magda, too, had played a part – and played it just as perfectly…

Now, twenty-two years later, there seemed to be nothing left. She and Magda had parted violently, as they had done on the first occasion. The difference was that she did not know how to get in touch with her daughter, and there was so little time left. All the excuses she had made during the years were meaningless. But did it matter? Was it fear of death or love which made her want her daughter? She had no clear answer. Probably, she told herself, Magda had become a monster, like her mother. What choice had either of them had?

Chapter Ten

It was several days before Philip heard anything from Magda except for a brief text message. It told him that she was sorry but her sorting out would take longer than she had thought, and that she sent him all her love. Conrad, true to his promise, had told him that Magda had phoned him briefly but he did not know how to get in touch with her because she had withheld her number. Catherine had heard nothing, and Adam advised Philip not to speak to her about it. Privately, Philip thought that Adam was expressing his own inclination to avoid trouble, but he lacked the will himself to confront Catherine.

And now this Friday morning the letter had arrived. It had slid quietly onto the doormat and had lain there all day like an unexploded bomb. Totally unprepared, he had picked it up casually and had been about to toss it on one side until he had noticed the Belfast postmark, and on the back the name and address of the sender. Unbelieving, he read it over and over, but there was no mistake. After seventeen years his past, long buried, was reaching out to him. He remembered that someone had once said that the past never dies. It comes back to haunt us when we least expect it.

It was while he was hesitating about opening the letter that the telephone rang. To his complete surprise and delight it was Magda. 'Magda, darling!' he exclaimed, dropping the letter on to the table. 'Are you all right?'

'Perfectly. I'm just ringing to say that I'll be back this evening in about half an hour.' Her voice was unusually quiet and surprisingly unemotional. 'I hope that won't upset your plans?'

He was amazed that she should say that but decided to ignore it. 'Darling,' he asked, 'what could be more important to me than seeing you again? I'll have a meal ready – but would you like me to pick you up?'

'You don't need to do that. I'll get a taxi, it will be easier. I'll be with you in about thirty minutes.' Without more explanation, she rang off.

He had no time to consider the strange manner of her call, for he must quickly plan and cook a special meal for them. Picking up the letter on the table, he shoved it into the drawer. He couldn't face opening it at this moment. Magda's return was more important. He knew, however, that he would be unable to forget it.

It was just over half an hour later when he heard her key in the front door. He hurried into the hall to greet her. He had imagined himself embracing her as she clung to him, but it was not like that. For a moment they simply stood and looked at each other as if waiting for a camera to click before they moved into the appropriate actions.

After a moment, he encircled her in his arms and she lifted up her face to receive his kiss. As they walked together across the hall, she paused while he removed her coat and kissed her again. 'It's a bitterly cold night,' he said, 'come and sit by the fire for a moment.' While she settled herself comfortably in one of the armchairs he watched her. How beautiful she was, he thought, even in her rather severe grey skirt and jacket, relieved only by the soft blue and purple of her gracefully draped chiffon scarf.

Neither of them spoke at first. The silence was unnatural but hard to break. At last Philip forced himself to speak. 'It's wonderful to have you back, my darling. I've missed you.'

For the first time she smiled slightly. 'It's very good to be back at home,' she said with unexpected feeling.

'Would you like a cup of coffee?' he asked, since she seemed disinclined to say more. 'I'm afraid it'll be nearly another half an hour before the meal's ready. I'm sorry to keep you waiting, but I think you'll enjoy it. It's one of your favourite dishes.'

Now she smiled directly at him. 'I'm sure it'll be worth waiting for. And I would love a coffee in the meantime.'

This is all wrong, he told himself, as he prepared the tray of coffee. Apart from the obligatory embrace and kiss, they were meeting each other like old acquaintances after a short absence. Surely I should be the wronged husband, and she the erring wife asking for forgiveness? But then, he admitted to himself, it would be hard for them to play these roles, since during all their fifteen years together they had skilfully avoided emotional scenes and had usually tried to discuss inevitable differences reasonably, or even left them. *Are we then*, he further wondered, *nothing more that acquaintances who somehow make each other extremely happy in bed?*

This seemed intolerable. Therefore, as they sipped their coffee, he asked abruptly, 'Why have you come back?'

She gave him a startled look. 'Is it so strange that I should come back to my husband and my home? I should have thought that was what you hoped for.'

'Of course it was. I'm sorry I asked the wrong question. I should have asked, why did you go away so suddenly without any explanation?'

'I tried to tell you but it was so very difficult.'

'You mean,' he asked, 'that you couldn't talk to me?'

'I couldn't talk to anyone.'

But I'm not anyone, he wanted to protest, *I'm your husband*. He bit the words back, however, for, if you had to say them, they were meaningless. 'I'm not sure I understand,' he said instead.

For a few moments she did not answer then she began to speak with obvious difficulty. 'I could not remember what had happened that weekend... but I had a strong conviction that something very important and upsetting had been said and done and that it was necessary for me to remember it. All I knew after Conrad's visit was that I had met Lisa and that he had been there at some point but I only knew that because of what he said. The more questions were asked, the more confused I seemed to become... I suppose the whole experience had made me a bit unbalanced.'

'That's not surprising,' he told her gently.

'I kept thinking of Lisa now after what Conrad had said. Worst of all, I thought of her with a strange mixture of fear and loathing. I felt I must get away and sort things out by myself. I seemed to want to be anonymous.'

'And you were successful,' he began, but before he could finish his sentence, the phone rang. 'I imagine that's Catherine,' he said. 'Adam said she would be ringing.'

While Magda was answering the phone, he completed the

cooking of the evening meal. He was preparing to pour out the wine when Magda came into the dining room. 'That smells delicious!' she exclaimed as she lifted up the lid of the main dish. 'Philip, you are so good to me – that's my favourite lamb and apricot dish!' She sat down, obviously eager to eat.

Does she really think that we can carry on as if nothing has happened? he wondered. Aloud, he asked, 'How is Catherine?'

'Fine and very pleased to know that I am safely back. Of course I had a long lecture on how unkind I had been to her – and to you, incidentally. I apologised humbly and tried to explain, but I don't think that she understood.'

'It isn't easy to understand, you know,' he remarked as her passed her plate to her.

'No, I suppose not,' was her only reply. Before he could say any more, she took a mouthful of her food. 'This is absolutely wonderful. You have surpassed yourself.'

'Thank you.' He felt that she was deliberately evading him.

'Incidentally,' she said suddenly. 'Catherine reminded me of something I'd almost completely forgotten.'

'What is that?'

'The great Family Event, Father's birthday party on Saturday, the day after tomorrow.'

'Surely we don't have to go? We need time to ourselves, and you're still recovering.'

'I know,' she agreed. 'But I'm afraid we do have to go for two reasons. The first and most important is that we are guests of honour, especially you, because you have got yourself some kind of advisory post with the Treasury.'

'Rubbish! It's extremely unimportant.'

'You may say that, but they don't think so. The second reason, however, is even more compelling. Cathy has been asked for the first time to help Constance organise the party, since Vivienne is out of favour. Catherine has been terrified that we might not be there. You may not realise, this but Cathy has always felt herself to be inferior to Constance.'

'How ridiculous! Catherine is far more intelligent than Constance, and a more interesting person.'

'Of course she is! I agree, but Cathy herself has never been quite convinced. Now, she seems almost scared of telling Constance and, of course, Dad, that we won't be there. I don't really understand it but I don't like to let her down, so perhaps we'd better go. What do you think?'

Putting down his knife and fork, Philip considered the question. 'Do you mean, Magda,' he asked finally, 'that you really want to go?'

'Yes,' she answered without hesitation, smiling beguilingly at him. 'But I won't insist if you hate the idea.'

'I don't hate the idea any more than I have in the past fourteen years, but I'm puzzled after what you have told me that you should be so keen now.'

She gave herself a second helping before answering. 'There are lots of reasons,' she then replied lightly. 'First of all, perhaps I'd like to please Cathy; secondly I'd like to show that we are still united; and lastly, and most frivolously of all, I want an excuse to buy a beautiful, new dress. Please don't look so disapproving,' she begged him, 'I simply want to make a stand. Do you know that Cathy told me that Constance said that I was truly the ugly duckling who had become a swan? Not only had I the luck to marry you, but also I had actually become quite beautiful and kept you interested. What do you think of that?'

As he looked at her he saw that her eyes were full of tears. Finally, he replied, trying to hide his anger, 'I think that Constance is a fool and Cathy – as so often – a tactless idiot. But don't distress yourself, darling. You shall go to the ball in the most magnificent gown with your adoring Treasury Adviser with you.' He smiled at her.

'And will my adoring TA come shopping with me tomorrow to find the gown?'

'Certainly – and pay for it, I suppose?'

'Of course! What are husbands for? You don't object, surely?' She was smiling again now.

'I'll devote the whole day to your pleasure on one condition.'

'Oh dear, I don't know that I like "condition". It's apt to be a sting in the tail.'

'Not this. My condition simply is that you wear a dress similar to the one you wore when we first met.' She looked disappointed. 'A more extravagant version,' he added.

'I like that better!' she declared. 'The dress I was wearing when we first met was really cheap. I hadn't much money then.'

'It's the colour I like – that deep blue. It was perfect with your eyes.'

'You're being very romantic.'

Why are we talking this nonsense, he thought, *when we have so many serious matters to discuss?* It was obvious, however, that she was determined to avoid any serious conversation. He had very rarely seen her like this. He found himself wondering what was frightening her.

It was not until they were finishing the meal with a coffee and liqueur that he forced her to confront some questions. 'Why didn't you come home earlier today?' he asked.

'I was hoping to speak to Conrad,' she told him. She spoke calmly but avoided his eyes.

'Why? You spoke to him earlier this week, didn't you?'

'How do you know that?' She was startled.

'Because he told me when he came here again. He could not get in touch with you, however, because you had withheld your number.'

'Because I didn't want him to try to find me.'

'But now you want to talk to him again. That's rather contradictory, isn't it?'

'It isn't really. The first time I rang him I simply wanted him to confirm that I had actually met Lisa that weekend. When he had filled in a few details I began to remember more clearly what had happened. And suddenly I remembered something terrible that Lisa had said. She was very angry and so it might not even be true. Conrad is the only person who might be able to confirm the truth or otherwise of what she said.'

'And has he been able to do that?'

'Not yet – he wasn't available.'

'And I can't help? Or is it that you don't trust me?'

She was silent. Finally, she said, 'I must know if it is true first. I don't want to cause anyone unnecessary pain.'

Although he did not understand, it was clear to him that she was determined not to say anymore at the moment, so he turned to another subject. 'You were angry with Lisa,' he said, 'even before you remembered this. Can you tell me why? Or is this another secret between you and Conrad?' He tried but failed to hide his bitterness.

'No. Forget Conrad, Philip. Lisa first made me very angry that evening because she mocked our marriage.' She stopped suddenly. Obviously, she had not intended to say this.

'What do you mean?' he demanded. 'How could she do that? What had it do with her?'

'It's nothing important.' She was very upset.

'Rubbish! It's clearly important. And I have a right to know. I am your husband.'

'Please,' she begged him. Her eyes were full of tears. He refused to be moved.

'It's too late to stop now, Magda.' His voice was gentler but he was definitely determined. 'So much has become known recently that we have to go on. You can't hold back now. Tell me what she had to say.'

After wiping her eyes with a tissue, Magda sat up and spoke with surprising calm. 'Very well. It's not pleasant, but you deserve the truth. I've run away too long. To put it bluntly, Lisa congratulated me on being an extremely successful whore. I had benefited from my training and I'd surpassed even her. She had had wealthy lovers but I had managed to get a wealthy and highly desirable man, not only to marry me but also to remain faithful to me. I had even surpassed my great-grandmother, the well-known Irish mistress of an English earl. She was left penniless in the end. That could never be my fate now.' She stared at him defiantly. 'That is what she said and more.'

Utterly amazed, he stared at her. He had never expected anything like this. 'This is crazy!' he exclaimed. 'Why on earth should your mother say things like that? It's horrible, of course, that she should, but there's no reason for you to be upset. It's all so ridiculous! Quite mad!'

'But it isn't,' she replied. 'That's what I never wanted you to know. It's got to be told now, because Lisa has had such an effect on me.' She hurried on before he could interrupt her. 'She trained me while I was still a student to be an expensive courtesan. I had the beauty and attraction, she said. All I needed was the technique, and she gave me that. Conrad was my first real lover, chosen by her. I was lucky. He wasn't too unpleasant.' She stopped abruptly, staring at him. 'It's true,' she told him.

'But why, in God's name, should she want you to do it, and why should you do it?' He stared back at her. 'Why, Magda?'

'It was quite simple. I owed her money. For a year, to prove herself a loving mother, she had paid for my nice room and lots of extras. I thought she actually loved me but then she told me that she needed the money, and that I would have to contribute to our income. Why shouldn't I use my best asset?' she asked.

'Why didn't you ask your family to help?'

'Because,' she told him, 'I had no family. Lisa had already more or less detached me from them when I was eight. Now she completed the job by telling me quite unemotionally that, instead of being forced to give me up, she had blackmailed my father into adopting me. She was using me to obtain her revenge. I belonged to no one. I didn't know what to do. It was almost like dying.'

'What about Catherine?' Philip asked her.

She looked at him, smiling slightly. 'I know what you really think about Cathy and you're right, I suppose; but I still cling to her because she is the only person who showed me any affection. At that time, however, she was in Cambridge busily pursuing her career and Adam. There was nothing she could do, even if she had wanted to. So I accepted my fate, which for the time being was Conrad. He was pretty generous.' Suddenly her tears flowed silently. 'Oh, Philip!' she sobbed, 'I'm so very sorry. I didn't want you to know ever. You must despise me. I can quite understand.'

What a stupid fool he had been, he realised. Why had he never cared enough to ask any questions? How could he blame Catherine? Without a word, he moved over to Magda and took her in his arms. 'Why ever should I despise you? I've always told you that I love you. That is hard, perhaps, for you to understand, but it always was true and still is true. You've suffered enough. I don't want to make you suffer any more.' After wiping her eyes, he kissed her gently. 'In the end, you left them, didn't you? You rejected Lisa's way of life. That must have taken a lot of courage.'

'It wasn't easy. I took a job teaching in the North but Lisa threatened to expose me, if I didn't come back, so I decided to get lost overseas. I had luckily just inherited some money, so I used that to finance myself. I went first to Calcutta and helped in Mother Teresa's home there, then I got several jobs teaching in Africa. It was interesting but hard. I'm not a saintly character. I wanted to come back and at least to see Cathy again. I went home, and Sebastien took to me to that reception where I met you.'

'That was lucky for me,' he said, kissing her again.

'And for me...' She hesitated, then continued. 'I didn't tell you much about my past. I wanted to wipe it out and start again. It was easier for me that way, because Lisa had trained me to be secretive from my earliest years. Does that make sense?' She sounded worried again.

'I understand,' he replied, 'but it doesn't entirely explain something much more recent which I found very puzzling and upsetting.'

'What do you mean?' Sensing her withdrawal, he was tempted to leave it but he knew it would be wrong.

'When I rang up the hospital with the intention of telling them that you were ill, I discovered before I made an absolute fool of myself that you had apparently left over two months ago just before we went on holiday. It seems to me that I had no real part in your life anymore, if I ever had.'

'That's not true,' she protested.

'That is how it seems. This is something which happened recently, not a long time ago, and I knew nothing about it. Can you explain it? Does Cathy know? Does Conrad perhaps know?' He couldn't quite hide the bitterness he felt.

'No!' she replied fiercely. 'No one knows, not even Cathy. You still don't understand, do you? That is the sort of person Lisa made me into. I was taught not to confide but to conceal.'

'Even from me?'

'Yes, even from you. I felt I couldn't carry on. I felt it was irrational but I couldn't. I wanted to tell you, but this ingrained habit of secrecy seemed to hold me back. I suppose I'm afraid of being rejected. Please try to understand.'

'It's hard, but I will.' He spoke in his normal calm manner and she was reassured. 'But, for your part, you must make an effort to trust me. What changed? I thought you enjoyed your work.'

'I did enjoy it until this year when I had several difficult cases and, finally, one which seemed to break me. I took on a family – Mum, Dad and baby. They had severe drug problems, but they seemed to be very fond of each other and of the baby and determined to try. Suddenly, everything went wrong. The father left without a word, but the mum was ready to try and carry on, and I thought she was doing well. Then one day, she simply smothered the baby and hanged herself. It was horrible, Philip, I simply couldn't understand it! I felt very guilty.'

'I'm so very sorry, darling. You should have told me.'

'I know, but I couldn't bear to speak about it. I think that it reminded me too much of my own life. I didn't want to spoil our holiday, and when I was with you then I felt secure and wanted to forget about it. When I came back there was an enquiry and I was completely exonerated, but I still felt guilty. I knew I couldn't carry on. I wanted to change my life. You were very busy, so I thought I'd tell you when I'd sorted things out a bit. You don't think I was very wrong, do you?' When he did not immediately reply, she continued quickly, 'You might understand more than most people. After all, you changed your life pretty drastically when you left the Army and went into the bank, didn't you? I've sometimes wondered if you didn't have some kind of crisis then but, rather like me, you never talked about your past.'

He had to respond, hard though it was, at that moment. 'You're right, of course. I did make a pretty drastic change, then but it was more or less forced up on me by my brother's unexpected death. For the first time my father wanted me in the bank.'

'Nevertheless, it must have been difficult, and I expect you had to rethink your life, just as I was trying to do after this terrible thing happened. Would you have found it easy to talk about it?'

'No,' he replied quickly, 'it's never easy. I appreciate what you're saying.' He looked at his watch. 'It's getting late, darling. Perhaps we should postpone further talk for another day.'

Unexpectedly, she smiled at him. 'You're right, Philip darling. It's time to make love, not to talk.' She stood up. 'We're always much better at that.'

Without a word, he too stood up and took the hand she offered him.

Chapter Eleven

A quick look into the dining room left Constance with a feeling of satisfaction. Everything was as it should be. The beautifully polished mahogany gleamed in the soft lights. The table was laid with lace mats, the finest china, shining silver and polished glasses. The bottles of wine were lined up; the champagne was in the ice bucket. With her daily woman's help, she had maintained the Lefevre standards even into this vulgar twenty-first century. Other people might make concessions to so-called modern manners, but she and her father would never do so. She was quite sure that her guests would respect this, even the grandchildren, although they would certainly be reluctant and inwardly rebellious.

As she entered the drawing room, she felt even more pleased. It was a long, spacious room with patio doors opening onto the terrace. The dark red velvet curtains were now drawn over these. The trolley with drinks and interesting tapas was in place. The lighting was discreet and carefully arranged to highlight some of the expensive and beautiful china ornaments her mother and father had collected, and the watercolours painted by a young artist friend whose pictures had grown more valuable since her father had acquired them.

Most of the guests had already arrived. White-haired Charles Lefevre, still looking remarkably young and handsome in his dinner jacket, was seated in his favourite armchair. Lucy, looking unusually pretty, was looking after him.

A swift inspection reassured Constance that all the grand-children had dressed for the occasion, even her errant twenty-five-year-old son, Kim, who much to his grandfather's disgust had not yet decided on his career, or on anything else. He too had made the effort.

Catherine was aware immediately Constance entered the room, feeling the usual constriction in her stomach. She had tried her utmost to be helpful, in spite of her worries about Magda. She had even bought a new and expensive outfit especially for the occasion. But once she had seen Vivienne's discreetly elegant black dress and Constance's oyster chiffon, with its delicate traces of gold thread, she had realised that her red and white dress, although it suited her, was far too flamboyant.

She had, however, been able to impart one wonderful piece of news. Magda was back, and she and Philip were definitely coming! The only trouble was that they were not here yet; they were ten minutes late, in fact, and Constance was looking at her watch and frowning. And soon, she was sure, her father would become aware and would make some cutting comment.

At that moment the front doorbell rang. Constance's frown disappeared; she smiled. 'That must be Philip and Magda!' she exclaimed.

'I'll let them in,' Lucy said immediately. It was obvious that she had decided to outshine all the other grandchildren.

Catherine waited in some dread. She was longing to see Magda again but she was afraid. Their conversation on the Friday evening had been friendly, but she had sensed a difference in Magda. Could Philip have possibly told Magda about her suspicions with regard to Conrad? she had wondered. Lucy's return prevented further worry.

Magda, with Philip behind her, stood for a few seconds in the doorway, smiling at everyone. It was a wonderful, perfectly planned entrance. Catherine had never realised before how incredibly beautiful and attractive her 'baby' sister had become. Her dress of gleaming deep blue silk clung closely to her body until it swirled out dramatically below the hips.

It wasn't simply the dress, however, although it did enhance the startling blue of her eyes. It was those blue eyes themselves, the masses of shining dark hair, the pale skin and delicate features, and above all her enchanting smile. She had a rare loveliness and fascination which made Helen of Troy and Cleopatra entirely believable.

After pausing for a brief moment, Magda hurried gracefully across to her father. 'Happy birthday, Father,' she said, bending to kiss him on the cheek.

111

He was pleased. 'You look very beautiful, my dear,' he replied.

She smiled. 'That's in your honour.' Turning towards Philip, who stood a little behind her she added, 'Philip has our gift.'

'Many happy returns,' Philip said as he handed over a small, beautifully wrapped box.

How theatrical and unreal it all seems, Catherine thought, as she watched. She looked round. Everyone else seemed to be absorbed in watching Charles as he tore off the wrapping to reveal an elegant leather case. As he opened it, he was clearly delighted with the gold cufflinks and matching tie clip engraved with his initials.

'They're *beautiful*, Granddad!' Lucy exclaimed. 'You'll look like a millionaire when you wear these.'

'Thank you, my dears!' Charles exclaimed, embracing Magda and shaking Philip's hand. 'It's a wonderful gift.'

Why has Magda done this? Catherine asked herself. *She can't love him, unless she's changed completely…*

'Why don't you wear them now?' Magda suggested. 'Philip can help you off with your jacket, and Lucy can help me replace the old cufflinks with the new.' While Philip held his father-in-law's coat and Lucy helped Magda to change the cufflinks, everyone gathered round.

Catherine, standing aloof, felt a nudge from Adam. 'Aren't you going to join in the fun?' he asked.

'I suppose so,' she replied, allowing him to lead her forward.

She felt sad and detached. It all seemed so unreal, so theatrical. A scene for some reason arranged by Magda, who, she was sure, could not possibly feel what she was pretending to feel. She looked towards Philip, but he was no help. Whatever he felt, his face did not reveal it; but then he rarely revealed his feelings.

Finally, she came close enough to admire the cufflinks, as her father expected her to do. As she moved away, she heard Adam, with his usual lack of tact, whisper to Philip, 'They must have cost a fortune!'

Philip only seemed to be amused. 'It was what Magda wanted,' he replied as they walked away with their drinks. *It is odd,* she thought, *how they have recently become friendly.*

As Catherine stood in the corner by the window, she felt very much alone, until she heard Magda say, 'It's lovely to see you

again, Cathy! Come and sit over here with me for a few minutes.'
As they sat down, Magda asked, 'You're not angry with me, are
you, Cathy?'

'No, of course not! Why should I be?'

'Because I ran away without a word. It was wrong, I know but
I had to sort things out on my own.'

'I think I understand, but you were hard on Philip.'

'I know, but he's been very good about it.'

'And did you manage to sort things out?'

'Yes, I rang up Conrad and he confirmed that I had spent the
weekend with Lisa, and that we had quarrelled. It all began to
come back then. You remember Conrad, don't you?'

Catherine was amazed that Magda should mention Conrad so
casually. 'Of course, I remember him,' she said. 'I even wondered
if you'd gone off with him.'

Magda laughed. 'Never! I know him too well!'

'You never mentioned him before. How long have you actually known him?' Catherine asked.

'I met him when I was a student. He was a friend of Lisa's.'
Magda spoke with a strange coldness. 'The truth is,' she continued, 'that I hadn't seen him for seventeen years until Lisa
apparently invited him to meet me at her flat.'

'Why on earth would she do that?'

'God knows! She had some ideas of making mischief, I suppose.'

The scorn with which she spoke surprised Catherine. 'It
doesn't sound as if you like her much.'

'Why should I?'

'She is your mother. I know she abandoned you, but she
seems to have regretted that.'

'Stop it, Cathy!' Magda said impatiently. 'You don't know
what you're talking about!'

'Only because you have never told me. I thought we were
friends, but you didn't trust me.'

'I couldn't trust you. Lisa made me swear not to tell anyone.'
Magda's eyes flashed blue fire, then suddenly softened as she took
Catherine's hand in hers. 'Please, Cathy dear, you must trust me.
We are friends. I love you. I always have and I always will.' Her
eyes were clouded with sudden tears.

Catherine pressed her hand. 'I'll always be there for you,' she promised.

'Even if I can't tell you everything?'

'Even then.'

There was no time to say any more, as Constance was summoning them to the meal. Philip and Adam came to collect them. Philip and Magda were put on either side of Charles, as guests of honour. The meal was excellent and everything went smoothly. Constance was obviously delighted with her success.

When they had finished the main meal, Constance went out and came back carrying a large and beautifully decorated birthday cake. There were twelve candles on it, seven blue ones for each decade and five white ones for the single years. Sebastien came forward with his cigarette lighter and began to light them all. While this was happening, Catherine brought forward the bottles of champagne. Philip opened the bottles and Adam and he filled the glasses. Sebastien finished lighting the candles while a couple of grandchildren switched off the lights. The room was now in darkness except for the flickering candles, which illuminated the happy faces of the family as they gathered round, making grotesque shadows on the walls.

Catherine took out her new camera, as did Kim. This was the climax of every birthday party and was always recorded. Catherine forgot all her previous anxieties. The family was united. This was a wonderful moment. As she was the best singer, Catherine led them in the singing of 'Happy Birthday'. They all joined in and ended with a tremendous cheer as Charles bent over the cake and with a mighty effort blew out all the candles. The lights were instantly switched on as they all sipped their drinks and toasted Charles.

It was at this moment that Constance decided to do something unexpected. 'As our special guest,' she said, standing up, 'I'm asking Philip to give the toast this year.' This job had normally been given to Sebastien, as the only son. Catherine felt apprehensive, but Sebastien seemed quite unmoved. *But then why shouldn't he be?* Catherine asked herself. *Most of his promotion is due to Philip's influence.*

She looked quickly at Philip, wondering if he had been

expecting this. It was impossible to tell. He spoke quickly and pleasantly without any sign of embarrassment. When everyone sat down again to receive their slices of cake, Catherine relaxed. A dangerous moment had passed.

She might have been right, and all might have been well had it not been for Charles Lefevre himself. To everyone's surprise, he stood up, holding his half-empty glass. 'Just a moment,' he said, 'I want to say a few words.' His face was red; his eyes had an unusual sparkle; even his words were slightly slurred. It was obvious that he had had a little too much to drink. Catherine held her breath.

'I want to thank you all for coming. When you're seventy-five it's good to know that your family still loves and respects you, even your grandchildren, especially in these days when I believe that's no longer fashionable. First of all I want to thank Constance for this memorable meal. She has even surpassed her own high standards. I must also thank Catherine, who has been a willing and able helper. Sebastien too has done so much to help, as he always does, as does Vivienne.' He paused, looking round. Catherine's heart stood still. Surely he must mention Magda?

'And that leaves Philip and Magda. As you all know, Philip has been appointed a Government adviser. We are all proud of him and pleased that he is a member of our family. And that only leaves Magda, our youngest daughter and his devoted wife. As the youngest, she has naturally always had a special place in my heart. I'm very proud of her and I'm sure that her mother would have been too, if—'

'Stop! Don't say any more, Father!' Magda's voice rang out as she stood up and faced her father with flashing eyes. There was a deadly silence.

'What do you mean?' Charles looked bewildered. 'Why shouldn't I tell the family how proud I am of you?'

'Because,' Magda answered in a cold, hard voice, quite unlike her usual voice, 'enough lies have been told over the years. There has been enough hypocrisy. It's time to end it.'

Catherine knew what Magda was referring to, but Charles seemed quite unaware, perhaps because he was convinced that his secret was safe. No one else had any idea. 'Magda, darling,' she begged her, 'not now.'

'Why not now?' Magda demanded. 'What better time can there be? All the family will learn the truth at the same time about me – and about him!' She pointed at her father. 'There will be no chance for anyone to hide anything any more.'

'What truth?' Constance demanded suddenly. It was obvious that she was furious at the ruin of her perfect party. 'What are you talking about, Magda? You're not making sense to any of us.'

'I'm making sense to Father,' Magda replied, 'that at least is quite clear. Why don't you ask him?' Everyone looked at Charles who had suddenly turned pale and now sat down slowly, staring at Magda.

When he did not answer, Constance asked him impatiently, 'Are you going to tell us about it, since Magda is either unable or unwilling?'

'I'm not sure,' he replied slowly. 'I'm not sure.' He stopped and looked directly at Magda.

'How much I know… Is that what you mean? I know it all. I've known ever since I was eight when Lisa met me and told me. She wanted me to know but she also swore me to secrecy. I've kept my promise until now, but now I can't keep it any longer, especially when you talk of Rosalind being proud of me.'

Charles continued to stare at her but seemed unable to answer. 'What the hell are you talking about?' Sebastien asked angrily. 'Either spit it out or shut up.'

'Who is Lisa?' Constance seemed worried now.

Oh dear, Catherine thought suddenly. *Nothing can save us now. But then why should we be saved?*

Magda sat down. 'I'll tell you. Lisa is my birth mother.'

'I don't understand!' Constance exclaimed. 'How can that be? You were born in our family. I remember Mother bringing you home as a tiny baby. We all do.'

'She did bring me home, and I was supposed to be her baby. She didn't tell you I was the bastard Father forced her to accept.'

For a moment there was a shocked silence. 'Is that true?' Constance asked a last.

'It can't be,' Sebastien almost shouted, 'it's just ridiculous! You must say so, Dad.'

'I'm afraid it is true,' Charles Lefevre spoke slowly and reluctantly. He could not meet Magda's eyes. 'It's not right that you should suffer any more, Magda. I had no idea that you knew. Lisa promised.'

'A promise she couldn't keep,' Magda told him quietly. 'She wanted to know if I was happy and somehow she arranged to meet me when I was eight. Although I didn't mean to give anything away, she realised that I wasn't happy, and that made her angry. And perhaps very bitter.'

'Lisa is, I suppose,' Constance asked, 'the woman with whom you committed adultery forty years ago?' When Charles nodded, she added, 'I suppose she trapped you into a stupid affair?'

Magda's brilliant eyes flashed dangerously. Catherine held her breath but before Magda could say anything, Charles spoke. 'I'm afraid I can't pretend I was trapped, Constance, as much as I would like to. If anyone was trapped, it was Lisa. She was an innocent girl of eighteen and I was thirty-five. She adored me and I enjoyed it.'

'Men do fall for temptation,' Sebastien interrupted. 'It wasn't so terrible.'

'Aren't you forgetting the Ten Commandments?' Vivienne asked with obvious irony. 'Of course, I'm not a Catholic but I always imagined that you thought they were important. But, of course, I'd forgotten about confession. It makes things right, I suppose?'

'It doesn't mend a young girl's broken heart,' Magda said quietly.

Vivienne looked sympathetically at her. 'No, I wouldn't suggest that it did.'

'I'm very sorry,' Charles stammered. 'I've always been very sorry. And I did try to make amends by having you brought up as my child.'

Magda laughed. 'Can't you even be honest now? That was never your idea. You know it wasn't. In fact, you broke Lisa's heart by saying that you would pay for an abortion. That was all you could or would do.'

'That was, of course, the obvious solution,' Vivienne said calmly. 'Sorry, Magda, I don't mean that personally.'

'*Abortion!*' Constance exclaimed in horrified tones before

Magda could reply. 'Was that really your idea, Father, that the wretched girl should have an abortion? Adultery was bad, but nothing can excuse the taking of an innocent life. I can only say that I'm pleased she had the courage to resist that.' When her father seemed unable to reply, she continued, 'But I still don't see how Magda was apparently born as a member of our family. That surely wasn't necessary?'

Before Charles could reply, Magda said, 'I'm afraid it was all rather sordid. My mother was heartbroken at the treatment she was offered and so she determined that not only would her baby not be destroyed but that she would also blackmail her lover for refusing to honour his promises. She threatened to expose him if he didn't take me as his child.'

'Obviously a girl of spirit,' Vivienne murmured.

'And you made my mother agree to this!' Constance exclaimed. 'Oh my God! That explains so many things. A lot of people have suffered as a result. And that's mostly your fault, Father.' Everyone stared at Charles but no one said anything.

After a moment, Constance turned towards Magda. 'But why did you want to bring it up tonight when we were having a happy family party? Did you have to be so cruel?'

It was her own son, Kim, who answered her. 'Good God, Mum!' he exclaimed. 'Haven't you learned anything? It wasn't a happy family party. It was our usual "pretend happy" party. I expect Magda would have stuck it out once more if Granddad hadn't decided to make his somewhat inappropriate speech. I'm right, aren't I?' he asked, turning towards Magda.

'Yes,' she said quietly. 'I came chiefly because I promised Catherine, but I've had some very unpleasant news from my mother recently and, in the circumstances, that speech was more than I could bear.'

'You might have spared the grandchildren,' Constance retorted.

Kim laughed again. 'My God, Mum, you really are unbelievable! They're twenty-first-century kids like me. They know the facts of life, and I'm pretty sure that like me they'd rather have the truth.'

'I know I would,' Lucy spoke up suddenly, to Catherine's

surprise and pleasure. 'I'm sorry, Aunt Magda. I'm sure we all are.'

'Thank you,' Magda smiled at her niece. Suddenly she stood up. 'I'm sorry but I'm afraid I must go now.' She sounded tired and sad. 'There are things I still have to do.' She turned towards Philip who having all the time remained quietly beside her, now stood up and put his arm round her.

'I'm ready,' he said.

Charles, who had been sitting with his head in his hands now also stood up. 'Please don't go, Magda, without a word to me,' he begged her. 'I loved your mother, and I've always regretted what I did. I'm very weak, you see.'

Magda took the hand he offered her. 'I know.'

'Can't you try to forgive me?'

Magda hesitated. 'I think I can,' she said finally. 'But that makes little difference. It was Lisa's life that was ruined, and many other people have been affected. We don't know how far the ripples will spread from the bad choices we make. Yours has had a very wide effect. The past is always with us. I can't change that. Goodbye, Father.' Moving towards him, she kissed him gently on the cheek. 'I must go now.'

Philip took her arm and they left the room before another word could be spoken. A few moments later there was the sound of the front door shutting. 'I can't let her go like that!' Cathy cried.

She tried to move, but Adam held her arm tightly. 'You have to let her go,' he told her firmly.

Chapter Twelve

As they entered the flat Magda felt drained and apprehensive. The drive home had been silent. Before they left the family home Philip had carefully wrapped her fur-trimmed velvet cloak around her and, as he had shut the door behind them, he had murmured, 'Not quite the ending I expected.' After that he had not spoken.

At first, trembling and shivering, she had only wanted to seek the comfort of the warm wrap. Philip had carefully fastened her seat belt and, after fastening his own, he had set off.

It was not a good night for driving; dark clouds low in the sky, heavy rain and sudden violent gusts of wind. She would not have expected him to speak much but surely, she thought, he must have some idea of how shattered she felt and could have managed a few, reassuring words. She tried to steal a look at him but it was too dark to see his expression.

Leaning back, she shut her eyes and allowed the soft regular *shush* of the windscreen wipers to lull her into a nightmarish doze, peopled with menacing faces. It seemed in her dream that her father was lying back in his chair clutching his chest, and might have had a heart attack; while Constance, instead of helping him, was glaring at him and shouting, 'Baby murderer, you ought to die!' Vivienne was laughing ironically. 'You might say that Magda behaved like a bastard, but then you can't blame her, can you?'

Sebastien, ugly with anger, hissed, 'Shut up, you bitch! This is serious, but you wouldn't understand.'

Vivienne still laughed. 'You're only afraid you've lost Philip and your next bit of promotion!'

Kim was phoning the doctor... *And Cathy? Where is Cathy? Surely she will understand*, Magda hoped. But Cathy was sobbing in a corner and frantically clutching Adam. 'Oh, why did she do it? I wanted us all to be happy.'

Magda forced herself to open her eyes. Looking out of the window, she saw that they were now in the London suburbs. The streets were unusually deserted and they would soon be home. While she waited in the foyer for Philip to garage the car, she was sure he would speak some kindly words to her when he returned. But he didn't. As if understanding her feeling of weakness, he put a reassuring arm around her but that was all. While he set the locks for the night, she walked ahead of him into the drawing room, sinking down on the settee, still huddled in her cloak.

'You look cold,' he said, walking across the room to switch on the fire. 'I think you need a brandy.' She watched silently as he poured a small brandy for her and a double whisky for himself.

Taking the glass from him, she silently placed it on the small table nearby. 'Drink it,' he ordered, 'you need it. You're suffering from shock.'

Obediently, she sipped the brandy, grateful for its healing warmth. 'Are you suffering from shock?' she asked, as she saw him swallow his whisky swiftly in several gulps.

'Probably,' he replied.

'I suppose I was rather shocking,' she said, noticing that her hand trembled slightly.

'You might say that,' he replied, finishing his drink. As he put the glass down, the phone rang. 'Finish your drink,' he told her, before she could move. 'I'll answer that.' He walked into the hall to take the call there.

She was just finishing her drink when he returned. 'It was Catherine, as I expected,' he told her.

'Is she angry? Doesn't she want to speak to me?'

'She isn't in the least bit angry with you,' he quickly reassured her. 'She could only get away for a few moments but she twice asked me to tell you that, although she's upset, she loves you lots and will soon be in touch.'

'I'm so glad,' Magda whispered.

Philip smiled. 'You have no need to worry about Catherine, but the entire Lefevre household is in a state of chaos, as you might expect.'

'What do you mean?'

'Surely you didn't expect to drop a bomb without causing an explosion and a few casualties?' After pouring himself another drink, he sat down next to her and placed his hand on hers.

'I didn't quite see it in that military way.' Then, feeling the comforting pressure of his hand, she asked boldly, 'Are you also angry with me?'

Leaning back more comfortably, he replied slowly, 'I wouldn't say I was angry but I would have preferred it if you had warned me. As it was, I felt at a bit of a loss. After all, we spent a lot of time and a lot of money on Friday preparing you for the ball and then suddenly you exploded the bomb.'

'I couldn't warn you. I had no intention of doing it until I did it. I suppose I wanted to outdo them all and prove that I really was the beautiful swan.'

'With your devoted partner swimming close by,' he added with a smile. 'Well, you managed it from the beginning. It was a great act.'

'That's the trouble,' she told him, 'that's all it was, a stupid act. And when I realised that, I was ashamed that I had lowered myself to their standards. When I saw how surprised Cathy looked, I felt terrible. Then my father started that stupid speech and I couldn't stand it any more. To endure this after what had just happened with Lisa was too much. Could *you* have stood it?' she demanded. 'Oh, Philip!' She clutched his hand. 'I can't bear it if you don't understand. I thought you would, especially when you understood the shameful life Lisa taught me to live and the weak way I accepted it But perhaps you didn't really understand.'

'Don't say any more,' he told her firmly. 'I did understand, and I do now. Although you seem to find it difficult to believe, I actually love you.'

'And you don't mind about Conrad and the horrid way Lisa encouraged me to behave? I thought you would despise me or be jealous of Conrad. That's why I never told you.'

'Darling, that's all seventeen years ago. Why should I despise a poor, unhappy girl who had no one to turn to? Although, I must tell you I could be jealous of Conrad, even now, if I thought you were attracted by him.'

'You have no need to worry. I'm not tempted in the least. But, Philip, I've often wondered how you could decide you really wanted to marry me after three weeks. I didn't believe you then, but I have to now – yet I still don't understand it.'

He laughed. 'I'm not sure that I do. I only know that half an hour after I met you I was convinced that you were the woman for me. And the years have proved me right. But what about you? Why did you marry me?'

'You seem to be assuming that I didn't love you. Or even that I don't love you now. Is that right?'

'You have never actually said that you do love me,' he replied calmly, 'so I've rather assumed that, although you're fond of me, you don't actually love me. But then this is one of the many subjects we've never discussed.'

'Don't you care?' She was astonished at his calm manner. 'Please be serious,' she begged him suddenly.

'I am serious,' he told her, taking his hand in hers. 'I've always been serious but I've also always felt that you didn't entirely believe me, so I ceased making my protestations of love. I was right, wasn't I?'

'I'm afraid so,' she admitted. 'I didn't understand because Lisa had persuaded me to see things differently.'

'And now I understand more, since I know what you suffered. I understand that you thought I was another Conrad, but better than Conrad because I was deluded enough to want to marry you. Am I right?'

As he turned to look at her, her eyes were clouded with tears. 'Don't,' she begged him, 'it sounds so horrible.'

'It would be, if it were true, but fortunately it isn't. And to be honest I'm indebted to Lisa. She trained you to be the most perfect lover a man could wish for. But that wasn't why I wanted to marry you. I only found that out, after we were married. I insisted on wedding before bedding, as I'm sure you remember.'

She smiled at him. 'I certainly do. It surprised me.'

'My meeting you,' he told her, 'upset my whole life all over again. In the two years since I'd left the Army, I thought I'd got things sorted out. I'd become reconciled to the bank, which was more interesting than I'd expected. I had this flat, and in the six months before I met you, I'd slipped into a relationship – comfortable but not very exciting.'

Sitting up, she stared at him. 'You never told me that!'

'Of course I didn't. I was determined not to lose you so, after I'd known you for a week, I ended it.'

She was still staring at him. 'I don't think I've ever known you properly at all!'

'Perhaps not.' He seemed quite unrepentant.

'Was she very upset?'

'Not really – more disappointed. She was a bank executive in one of the central banks, about my age, hoping, I imagine, to settle down and have a baby or two before it was too late. But she had no desire to stand against true love.'

'Have you always been so determined?' she asked.

'Possibly, but I've never really thought about it.'

'I don't suppose determined people ever do. They just go ahead.'

He made no comment on that, but continued, 'I noticed you were beautiful, of course, but it was your smile and the brightness of your eyes that attracted me. And when we talked during that first meal we had together, I discovered that you, like me, had found it necessary to change your life and, like me, you'd had to break with the past. That takes courage, as I know.'

'I didn't really have any alternative,' she murmured.

'That's not true,' he told her firmly. 'You refused finally to accept Lisa's false values. You had to show far more courage than I did for you actually set off on your own for two years and, in spite of everything, you came back still fresh and innocent.'

'Innocent!' she exclaimed. 'You could hardly call me that, Philip, after what I had done.'

'That is nonsense,' he told her. 'In spite of all that had happened, you weren't the slightest bit corrupted. Unlike the rest of your family, you weren't even interested in my money, were you?'

'No,' she agreed, 'but that was because I learned on my travels that lots of money and possessions have nothing to do with happiness. Of course, people who are forced to be poor may be unhappy, but never those who choose to be poor. They are happy and free.'

Impressed by her sincerity and intensity, he asked, 'How did you learn that?'

'My first lesson was when I spent three months in an orphanage run by the Missionaries of Charity. Three of the nuns had been wealthy and privileged, but they had willingly given up all their comforts to live in this barely furnished house on a spartan diet inspired by their love for Jesus and his poor. It was a happy place and I was happy there. It was a therapy I badly needed.'

'You mean that you needed to experience the power of love?'

'Yes, and to see unwanted children loved.' There was more she could have said, but she stopped and he did not press her. She had suddenly told him so much and he was happy to be trusted.

'How can I not love you?' he asked with unusual tenderness. 'You were just the person I needed.'

'But weren't you disappointed that I never responded more?'

'I always hoped that you would one day, just as you have now. In the meantime you were a person who obviously needed loving, and I was ready to love you.'

Suddenly, she moved close to him. 'I think I really do love you, Philip,' she whispered. Before he could you reply, she kissed him with an unusual passion. In fifteen years he had never felt so close to her. Unexpectedly, he lifted her to her feet and then picked her up in his arms. 'What are you doing?' she asked him.

'I'm carrying my bride to bed. This is our real wedding night, darling.'

Disaster struck late on Sunday afternoon. After a wonderful night together, they had spent a lazy, happy day together – the happiest they had ever had, or so it seemed to Philip. They were lying together on the couch trifling with the Sunday papers when the telephone rang. It went on insistently, demanding a reply. 'Let it ring,' Philip suggested, but Magda was already on her feet.

'It might be Conrad. I've been trying to get him.'

'Damn Conrad!' he remarked, but he was not worried.

It was a few minutes later when she came back to the room, switching on the lights as she did so, for the November dusk was falling over the city. 'Was it Conrad?' he asked idly.

'No, it was his secretary, but she gave me a number where I can reach him tomorrow.'

How beautiful she is, he thought, as she stood before him in a deep blue velvet housecoat. Then he noticed she was holding a letter. *Surely it can't be...?* 'What are you holding?' he asked, sitting up.

'I found this in the hall table drawer when I opened it to find a pad to write on.' What a fool he had been to leave it there, he thought. 'I suppose you were going to readdress it,' she continued, 'but you must have forgotten it. I thought I'd better remind you. It might be important.'

'Yes, I should have attended to it,' he said, holding out his hand.

She was looking at it, puzzled. 'It has the right address,' she said, 'but it's made out to Mr Gerard O'Dowd. Who is he? I've never heard you mention him. Why should you have his letter?'

He was completely at a loss. For a moment he was tempted to lie but he knew it would not only be wrong but futile. What an absolute fool he had been! He should have destroyed it and what it represented for ever.

Surprised by his silence, Magda was looking earnestly at him. 'Well, at least, it's not your secret mistress,' she remarked, smiling as she sat down again next to him. 'So you can tell me who it is.'

'It's actually me,' he told her, 'my alter ego, as you might say.'

'What do you mean, Philip?'

'It's the name I had when I worked undercover for the Army in Northern Ireland. Surely I've mentioned that to you?'

'Perhaps, but I never understood what it meant. Did you actually have a different name?'

'Yes, and another history, fictitious, of course. I could hardly mingle with the IRA calling myself Lieutenant Colonel Peters, could I?'

'Of course not. It must have been very exciting, but terribly dangerous. But that was all over seventeen years ago. Why has the letter turned up now? It's from Belfast, too.' Before he could answer, she continued, 'How strange that you should have a secret life, just as I did. But yours was much more praiseworthy and you couldn't speak about it, I suppose.'

'That's true,' he said. 'Official Secrets and all that nonsense. The truth is I never wanted to speak about it.'

Surprised by the bitterness in his voice, she stared at him; she felt that she was glimpsing a Philip she had never known. She wasn't sure that she wanted to know more. 'Hadn't you better read the letter?' she asked him.

'Yes. I suppose so.' Opening the envelope carefully, he took out the single sheet and read it slowly, not once but twice. 'God!' he exclaimed. 'What a stupid fool I was!'

Crumpling up the letter, he stuffed it into his pocket. Then, after standing up, he quickly walked across the room towards the window. The curtains were still undrawn, and with his hands in his pockets he stared out into the growing dusk watching the brilliantly lit boats gliding down the river. 'A bloody fool!' he repeated.

Magda joined him. 'Philip, darling,' she asked anxiously, 'what is the matter? Tell me, please.' Slipping one of her hands into his pocket, she clasped his clenched fingers. As she waited, she felt him slowly relax a little.

'I came to hate undercover work,' he explained finally. 'I hadn't understood the true nature of the situation. I went out to Northern Ireland with all the prejudices of the average middle-class Brit. *These people are just terrorists*, I told myself. *They need to be taught a lesson.* In fact, I was the one who needed to be taught a lesson. I soon learned what an arrogant bastard I really was.'

He was silent now, still staring out of the window. In spite of the lights being switched on, the growing darkness seemed menacing. Magda shivered. 'Don't stand here,' she begged him. 'Come and sit down and talk to me.'

For a moment she thought he would resist, but suddenly he unclenched his fingers, clasped her hand and allowed her to lead him back to the settee. After a few minutes he began to explain. 'The trouble about working undercover is that you actually meet the enemy – in this case the ordinary Irish people – and gradually you are forced to realise that the version of the story that you have always been given is not only incomplete but to a large degree untrue. At least, that's what I found.'

'Couldn't you give up?' she asked. 'Or is that impossible in the Army?'

'It would have been difficult,' he told her. 'I might have had to have some kind of psychological assessment. But before I could make up my mind, I was given this important assignment – the last, or so I was told.' He became silent. She had never seen him look so unhappy.

'And this letter is connected with that?' she at last ventured to ask.

'Yes, it is,' he replied slowly. She thought he wasn't going to say any more but, after a few moments, he added, 'It's from a young man called Liam O'Neill. When I last saw him he was a lively, attractive kid of six. We got on well together. I became a sort of honorary uncle.'

'How did you come to know him?' she asked as he paused.

'As Gerry O'Dowd I was working on his father's farm, taking the place of Martin O'Neill, Liam's uncle, who had been shot. Gerry O'Dowd's father was supposed to have been shot, so I was welcomed. Officially, I had been ordered to discover the truth – or otherwise – about a new IRA group and its as yet unknown leader who were thought to be planning a big bombing campaign in the near future.'

'That all sounds very dangerous and unpleasant.' She had never imagined Philip doing things like that.

'It was, and I made it more dangerous and unpleasant by allowing myself to become friendly with Liam's father, Seamas. I broke one of the chief rules of undercover work, and I had no excuse because I was not a novice. Perhaps it was because they were apparently such a loving, happy family, and they welcomed me into it. I simply didn't want to believe that a guy like Seamas could be plotting to kill innocent people. It was some time before he let me see the dark, tormented soul determined to revenge the deaths of his father as well as of his brother. He believed he was fighting a just war and I began to see why.' Philip stopped abruptly.

'How terrible! What did you do?'

'The only thing I could do – my duty as an Army officer. I reported all I knew and hated myself.' He was silent. How impossible it was, even now, to explain his feelings. How sure was he of them, even now?

'That must have been truly terrible,' Magda said gently but even as she tried to express her sympathy she realised how inadequate her words must sound. *Is it impossible for people to be truly honest with each other?* she wondered. *Is it foolish even to try?* She was aware that several matters were still unexplained. She challenged one now. 'Why has this Liam written to you now?' she asked.

'He wants to know the truth about his father's death, and it has been suggested to him that I might be the best person to help him.'

'I don't understand. Surely he has known that for years?'

She felt Philip's withdrawal from her. 'Apparently not,' he replied after a pause. He seems to think that he now has evidence to suggest that his father was deliberately murdered and not accidentally shot, as others were, when their group was ambushed by an Army patrol. If that is so, he wants justice – or more accurately revenge.'

'But why then write to you?'

'Who better?' Philip asked coldly. 'Since I shot his father, although he doesn't yet know it.'

Horrified, she stared at him. 'But why? I thought he was your friend!'

'He was, but he was also the enemy, especially when he was about to shoot me. So, you see, I murdered Seamas O'Neill. That, at least, is how his son will see it. But as the official mind sees it, I killed a dangerous terrorist and saved the lives of innocent people.' He sounded cold, almost indifferent, but she saw the pain in his eyes.

'And how do you see it?' she asked gently.

'I told myself it was self-defence, but I was tormented with doubt and guilt and I was glad of an excuse to leave that intolerable life. I decided that the only thing to do was to start afresh, but it didn't work very well until I met you. Do you know, I believe I'd almost forgotten!' He walked across the room and helped himself to a whisky. 'And now the past has caught up with me, as it did with your father yesterday.' He took a gulp of whisky. 'Strange, isn't it? You told him that one can never escape the past. You were right, my darling.'

After hurrying across the room, she took the glass from him. 'You don't need that. Your situation is quite different. You were not to blame.'

'Can you accept a murderer for a husband?' he asked her.

'Stop it,' she told him. 'You're being melodramatic! That's not like you. We have both made mistakes. You have forgiven me, I forgive you, if there's anything for me to forgive.' Before he could reply, she put her arms round him, pulled him close and kissed him tenderly. As he returned her kiss, the sharp ringing of the phone interrupted them.

'I'll go,' she said. 'I won't be long. Don't touch that whisky.'

When she returned, he was once again sitting on the settee. 'Who was it?' he asked.

'Cathy,' she replied. 'She's in one of her states. Her whole life has been destroyed. I don't realise what an upheaval I have caused.'

'Poor little Cathy. I'm truly sorry for her. She always suffers so much.' His irony was obvious.

'You don't like her, do you?' She was surprised. She had never understood that before.

'Not much, but I tolerate her for your sake.'

'I'm sorry, but I felt I had to invite her and Adam to supper.'

'Thank God for Adam,' he replied. 'I can at least talk to him.' He stood up. 'I'll go and sort out something for an especially comforting supper.'

'I really am sorry. There are still lots of things we need to discuss.'

'Don't worry. We can talk later. That might be better. You have already made the most important point clear.'

'What is that?'

'That you love me.'

'Of course I do. When you've decided what you're going to cook, call me and I'll come and do my bit.' With a quick kiss she pushed him off towards the kitchen. *Perhaps it would be better*, she thought, *to leave the discussion on hold for a while.*

Chapter Thirteen

Catherine took so long to make her sufferings clear to them all that there was no chance for Magda and Philip to talk further when she and the somewhat silent Adam finally left. It was late and they were both tired. 'I'm sorry,' Magda apologised, 'it was difficult to stop Cathy. I'm afraid she was very self-absorbed.'

'When isn't she?' Philip asked.

'She has been very kind to me,' Magda protested.

He was surprised that she was obviously upset by his remark. He had imagined that she saw Catherine as he did, as an egotistic attention-seeker whose kindness always had a price; but obviously this was not so. How lonely the young Magda must have been! He bit back the critical words he had intended to say and, instead, remarked with a smile, 'At least she gave us a vivid picture of the mayhem your outburst caused – Father collapsing apparently, Constance furious about abortion and her party, and Sebastien and Vivienne nearly coming to blows! My God, you certainly had an effect!'

'I'm afraid I did. I didn't realise how upset Cathy would be that the whole family idea had been destroyed.'

'I shouldn't linger on that,' Philip remarked casually. 'After all, she scarcely spent two minutes inquiring how you felt – but perhaps you didn't notice that.' He stood up. 'I think it's time we went to bed. I'm pretty tired and I expect you are, too.'

'I am tired,' Magda admitted, 'but I want to talk to you, Philip, to help you sort things out with regard to this Liam.'

'It can wait until tomorrow. Just now I can think of nothing more comforting than holding you in my arms, unless you object.'

'I'd like nothing more. After all, this is our real honeymoon.' But, when they were undressing, she suddenly said, 'I don't think you should worry too much about that letter. I can just put it in an envelope with a note saying that Gerard O'Dowd is not known at this address.'

'Would you do that for me?'

'Willingly. That should put a stop to it, unless someone knows your real name.'

'I don't see how Liam could.'

'Well then, if I do that, we can forget the past and get on with living.' Even as she spoke, she felt that it was unlikely. She still had other problems. But perhaps, she thought, she should forget those now and concentrate on her relationship with her husband.

'What do you think?' she asked him as they got into bed.

'We'll talk about it tomorrow,' he replied as he took her in his arms.

It was still dark when she awoke, barely six o'clock. Something had disturbed her. Turning to look for Philip, she realised that he was no longer with her. Slipping on a dressing gown, she went to look for him. As she came into the hall, she saw the light shining through the study door, which was slightly ajar. Opening the door a little further, she saw him seated at his desk. His computer was switched on and he was studying the screen by the light of his desk lamp.

'What are you doing?' she asked.

'I am making investigations on the Net,' he told her.

'Investigating what?' Switching on the fire, she tried to warm her hands but she felt a sudden chill that no fire could take away.

'I was wondering if I could get a flight to Belfast later today,' he told her calmly.

She was immediately angry and upset. 'I thought you'd agreed to discuss that! Or don't my feelings matter to you at all?' She turned round to look at him. 'I suppose you intended to tell me at breakfast that it was all settled. Or were you simply going to disappear, leaving a note?'

Standing up he moved swiftly towards her. 'Of course not, Magda darling. You can't possibly believe that. I couldn't sleep, so I thought I would find out what was possible.' He tried to put his arms around her but she moved away.

'I thought you'd agreed,' she said furiously, 'to my returning the letter. I thought that you felt like me that, after we had got to know each other so much better, we could now start a proper life together. But, obviously, I was wrong. You had other ideas, which you didn't bother to mention.' She made no attempt to hide her hurt and anger. They were on the verge of a serious quarrel, something that strangely enough had never happened before.

He appeared to keep his usual calm but answered swiftly. 'I don't want to hurt you, Magda. I didn't intend to settle anything until I'd talked to you.'

'That's not exactly the impression you have given me!' she retorted. 'I suppose that what you mean is that you hoped to persuade me to accept your point of view.'

He was silent for a few moments, then he said slowly, 'I suppose that about sums it up. The trouble is that I realise I have to go back, Magda. I can't run away again.'

She had never heard him so determined or so grim. She tried to comfort him. 'You didn't run away. You did what you were supposed to do. It must have happened before.'

'This was different,' he said. 'This was a betrayal of trust.'

Suddenly the explanation hit her. 'It's the boy, isn't it? You feel you betrayed him…'

'Yes, he was completely innocent and he trusted me. That's what made it different.'

'Then why didn't you tell me?' she began angrily, but stopped as a further realisation hit her. 'You really cared about him, didn't you?'

'I suppose so.' Philip looked at his screen as if wanting to avoid her gaze. 'I knew him for less than a year but we hit it off. I became his adopted uncle. He was the sort of boy—' He stopped suddenly.

'—you would have liked for a son?' she finished the sentence for him.

'Yes, that's about it.'

'Oh Philip, I'm so sorry! You never let me know it mattered so much to you.'

'What do you mean?'

'You know what I mean. Don't push me away again. I'm so sorry that I can't have a baby. I did tell you before we were married.'

'And I accepted it. I needed you more than I needed a child.

And there was always the hope, since you told me that the doctor had said that it wasn't absolutely impossible. In any case, I thought it was worse for you.'

'There is no time to talk about that now. If, as it seems, Liam matters so much to you that you really feel you must go to Belfast to help him, then you have a lot of things to arrange and no time to waste.'

Grateful for her understanding, he replied quickly, 'I can make a reservation for late this afternoon which will give me time to go into the bank first and clear a few days. That is, if you have no objection?'

'If you really want to do it, I have no further objections. I think I ought to warn you, however, that I think it might be dangerous. Liam is no longer a little boy; he might be like his father.'

'I understand that. I promise you that I shall be very careful. I'll try to speak to a few people first but I think I must try.'

'Very well. I'll leave you to make your arrangements while I prepare breakfast.'

There was no point in further discussion. That was clear. It was only while she was later clearing away the breakfast that a sudden thought struck her. How did Liam know this address? There were obviously still things that Philip hadn't told her. She did not feel, however, that she had any right or desire even to complain about that.

It was nearly five o'clock when they finally parted at the airport. There had been so much for Philip to arrange during the day that there had been no time to talk, and now it was impossible. In the last five minutes Philip, apparently oblivious of the people around, put his arms round her. 'There are so many things I intended to say,' he told her, 'but I can only say now I love you with all my heart. I know this is the wrong time for me to be leaving when we have just made so much progress. Please forgive me, darling.'

'I do understand,' she replied. 'Just take care, darling, and keep in touch.'

'I promise I will do both. If you should need me, just call me and I'll come back. You are the most important person in my life, remember.'

In the end, she gently detached herself and moved away. She had not expected the parting to be so hard, but then she had never felt so close to Philip before.

Nevertheless, her first thought when she had left him was that she must ring the number Conrad's secretary had given her. If she left it too late, he might have left. She was lucky; he was still there. Without any preamble, she said, 'There is a question I want to ask you about something Lisa told me.'

'I gather that it is important?'

'Very, at least to me.'

'Strangely enough', he said, 'there is something I want to tell you about Lisa. But I doubt if these matters can be dealt with on the phone.'

'Probably not,' she agreed.

'Where are you now?'

'At the airport. I've just seen Philip off on a business trip to Belfast.'

'Then, perhaps you will have dinner with me later?' When she hesitated, he continued, with some amusement in his voice, 'You don't need to be afraid.'

'What do you suggest?' she asked coldly.

'I'll pick you up at your flat in about two hours' time. Do you agree?' He was still amused.

'Certainly,' she said, and rang off quickly.

It was about ten o'clock when Philip returned to his hotel room, after an expensive dinner with a very senior police officer who was an old acquaintance. With the help of good food, choice wines and the finest brandy, he had managed to elicit information about people they had known in the past, including the O'Neill family. Liam O'Neill was known to the police. He spent little time at the family farm, now run by his mother and her brother, and much more time in shady pursuits in the backstreets of Belfast.

'He's one of those unfortunate youths,' Philip's informant told him, 'who cannot or will not accept the peace. So far he's been lucky and has not been charged, but it's only a matter of time. I should say he's never forgiven or forgotten his father's death.'

This had been depressing news, which had only confirmed Philip's worst fears. He was very weary when he returned to his hotel room. It had been a long day, and the return to Belfast had been more traumatic than he had expected. For him it was a city peopled with ghosts, which he had managed to keep in the background for years.

After taking off his jacket, he drew the curtains, switched on more light and poured himself a whisky. He didn't need it but he wanted it. But more than that, he realised with a sharp pain, he not only wanted Magda but he needed her. Suddenly, he decided to phone her. She would be alone and missing him. To his surprise there was no answer. He tried her mobile three times but it was switched off. He rang an irritated Catherine, who told him that, although she had expected to, she had not heard anything from Magda. He rang off before she could ask any questions and poured himself another whisky to quell the feeling of near panic.

On his fourth try Magda answered the phone. 'Where the hell have you been?' he asked her. 'I've been trying to get you for over an hour!'

'I'm very sorry, Philip,' she replied quickly. 'I've been out to dinner. I didn't expect you would ring again tonight, so I switched off my mobile for a time. Has something bad happened?' She was obviously alarmed now.

'I'm very sorry too,' he replied. 'I shouldn't have spoken like that. I was worried about you. Nothing actually bad has happened but the information I've had so far hasn't been very encouraging.' In a few words he told her what he had learned about Liam.

'That's not good,' she said quickly. 'I think you should leave. Come home please, Philip. I miss you.' There was a sudden break in her voice.

It was his turn to be alarmed. 'What is the matter?' he asked. 'You sound upset. Has something happened? Where have you been? I didn't imagine that you'd go out.' There was a brief pause before she answered him.

Finally, she said, 'I had dinner with Conrad. When I phoned him, he told me that he had something important to tell me about Lisa, and that he preferred not to talk over the phone, so he suggested dinner.' She was obviously uncomfortable but she gave no further explanation.

'And you agreed?' For a moment he was assailed by jealousy but he forced himself to bite back the stupid and hateful words. Magda had actually told him that she loved him and he wanted to believe her.

'Yes, because there were things I couldn't say on the phone.' *And there still are*, she admitted to herself.

'What did he have to tell you? Was it really that important?'

Ignoring his obvious disbelief, she answered quickly, 'Yes it was. He told me that he had met Lisa, and it seems that she really is dying of breast cancer. I didn't believe her but Conrad thinks it's true. She has sold her flat and is going to live in a hospice in France run by some nuns.' Her voice broke. 'I'm so upset that I disbelieved her. It's terrible, Philip.'

'Oh, my dear,' he said softly, 'I'm so sorry. I should be with you. This stupid business doesn't matter compared with you. Does she want to see you?'

'No.' Magda was crying now. 'She's left a package, which Conrad gave to me. I haven't opened it yet. I never imagined… Oh God, I was pleased when she said she was ill, but I didn't really mean it.'

'Of course you didn't.' He was quick to console her. 'You were just angry at that moment. Look, if you want me, I'll come home tomorrow, and forget about Liam.'

'No, that's sweet of you but there's really no need.' She was suddenly much calmer. 'It really isn't necessary. Simply speaking to you has comforted me. If you can help that young man, then you should. I'm not a baby.'

'If you're sure.' He was puzzled by her change of mood.

'I'm sure. Just don't take any risks and be as quick as you can. Remember I love you.'

'I promise. I won't take risks and I'll be back in a few days. You know I love you now and always.' He still felt vaguely puzzled by her. 'What will you do in the meantime?'

'I may try to see Lisa. She is my mother, after all. I can't just abandon her. Do you think I'm right?'

'Of course, darling. You won't be happy if you don't try.

Remember I support you in all you do. But, for God's sake, keep in touch.'

'I will,' she promised.

In a few minutes the conversation was over. To his relief, Magda seemed quite normal again but, as he undressed, he had an uneasy feeling that there was something she had not told him.

As she put down the phone Magda was disturbed by her own behaviour. Why had she not told Philip the full truth, even now? Why had she urged him to stay away, reluctant though he was?

Sipping the coffee she had made for herself, she went over the evening she had spent with Conrad. It had been very different from what she had expected. She had prepared carefully for her meeting with him, choosing a dramatic outfit certain to appeal to him. Looking back, she was amazed to admit that she had done that but at the time it had seemed natural.

She had been right, for he had looked approvingly at her flaring tiered skirt in black and gold satin, topped with a gold camisole and a close-fitting short black jacket. Long gold earrings and a gold necklace completed the outfit. She had been half ashamed to admit that Lisa could not have instructed her better, but she had enjoyed it.

It was not until they had ordered their first courses that Conrad asked her what it was she so urgently wanted to ask him.

'When I last met Lisa,' she began, 'she said some very unpleasant things to me. Most of them I ignored, but there was one too cruel to be dismissed.' She paused as the waiter approached with the wine list. As they discussed the possibilities, she realised how foolish she had been. The matter she wanted to talk about could not possibly be discussed here, where there was no possibility of privacy.

Suddenly she became aware that Conrad was looking at her and obviously expecting an answer to something he had said. 'I'm sorry,' she said. 'I'm afraid my thoughts were far away.'

'I only asked,' he replied, 'if you were now ready to ask your question?'

'No,' she replied abruptly. 'I'm afraid I can't.'

He was obviously puzzled and concerned. 'Why not?' he asked. 'Have I upset you?'

'No, it's not you,' she said quickly. 'I've just realised what a fool I am. This is something I can't possibly discuss in public.'

'Nevertheless, it's something you want to discuss with me…'

'Yes, especially with you.'

'I see.' He did not speak any more until the waiter had brought the first course and departed. 'This is difficult,' he then said. 'I would have invited you to my apartment, although I'm not sure you would trust me. That's irrelevant, however, since I've just sold my apartment and am temporarily living in a hotel.'

'Why ever have you done that?'

'Because I am planning to return to Lebanon, where I came from.'

'I never imagined you would leave England. In fact, I never actually knew where you were born.'

'That was how I wanted it to be. That's why I changed my name. My family actually came from Palestine but I was born in a refugee camp near Beirut. I lived with my mother, as my father had been killed by the Israelis.' He stopped as the waiter approached again. As soon as he had gone he continued with a slightly mocking smile. 'I apologise. I didn't intend to bore you with my sob story. I should have tried it on you when you were young and innocent.'

Magda determined to know more, ignored his last remark and simply asked, 'However did you get away? It must have been difficult.'

'It was, but I was helped by my elder brother who had married a wealthy Lebanese girl. My mother too helped me, although it meant that she would be alone, but I promised that I would make a fortune and return when she needed me. She now needs me, as she is in her late seventies and far from well, so I'm keeping my promise.'

Magda felt humble. It was clear to her that she had never bothered before to know Conrad; she had merely used him. 'It must be very difficult for you to make such a change!' she exclaimed. 'I admire you for doing it.'

'It's not been as difficult as I thought it might be. In spite of the invasion this summer, Lebanon is the only place I can think of as home. It's a very troubled place, of course, but it's also amazingly beautiful. My brother is helping me to find a house in the mountains, where my mother can hope for a safe refuge.'

'What about your business?'

He shrugged. 'A man like me can always make money, especially in troubled times. Surely you know that?'

She was suddenly cross with him. 'Why do you always imply horrid things about yourself?'

He smiled. 'Perhaps to prevent you from saying them.'

'I'm in no position to criticise. I imagine you must have a pretty low opinion of me.'

'On the contrary,' he replied with an unexpected seriousness. 'I admire your courage. You remade your life and it can't have been easy.'

'I've simply been lucky,' she told him quickly. 'But don't let's talk about me. I want to hear about Lebanon, which is so beautiful, and about your mother who is so brave.'

Since she was obviously determined now to avoid the question she had originally intended to ask him, he obliged her, and for the rest of the meal he told her his memories of Lebanon and of the courageous way in which his mother had faced difficulties. They seemed almost unbelievable to Magda.

At the end of the meal, as they emerged into the cold Mayfair street, Conrad said firmly to her, 'You can't put it off any longer. I think we have some serious talking to do, unless I have misunderstood you.'

'You haven't,' she told him. 'I desperately need to talk to you, to ask you a question.'

'And I have things which must be said to you. The question is where can we do this?'

She shivered. The late November night was already frosty and promised to be colder. 'I suggest,' she said finally, 'that we take a taxi to my flat, where we can have coffee and talk uninterruptedly.' Startled at her own suggestion, she waited to see how he would react.

'Thank you for your invitation and your trust.' There was no mockery in his voice or manner. 'I am extremely pleased to accept.'

Chapter Fourteen

As soon as she had led Conrad into the sitting room, Magda hurried into the kitchen to prepare coffee for them both. While she did so, she wondered whether she had been foolish to invite him into her home when Philip was absent. She even considered whether it was her old nature reasserting itself. During the dinner she had felt more than once that Conrad was attracted by her and that she was enjoying it. *Don't be ridiculous*, she told herself. *I have to know the truth and this is the only way to discover it.*

The telephone was ringing as she came into the sitting room with the coffee. 'Aren't you going to answer it?' Conrad asked. He had settled himself comfortably on the settee with a book.

'No, it's probably Catherine, and I do not want to speak to her at this moment.'

'Might it not be your husband?'

'No, he rang earlier to tell me of his safe arrival and to give me his address.' After putting down the coffee, she sat down opposite him. 'It's strong and black,' she told him 'and there's cream and sugar, as I think you like that, unless your tastes have changed.'

'They have not,' he replied, helping himself to both. 'I'm flattered that you still remember.' His smile was slightly mocking, as was his tone. After taking a sip of his coffee, he asked directly, 'Isn't it time you put your question, Magda?'

To her surprise, she found herself still unwilling to ask him, so she said quickly, 'You said you had met Lisa and had a message for me. Perhaps you should give me that first.'

'If you wait a moment,' he said, 'I'll get the envelope from my overcoat pocket.'

Without waiting for her reply he stood up and left the room. Coming back a few minutes later he handed her a large and bulky envelope. 'Lisa asked me to give you this,' he told her. 'I believe that it contains a letter and some things she wants you to have.'

'I don't understand.' Magda looked at the envelope without

attempting to open it. She felt almost afraid to touch it. 'I thought she'd gone away.'

'She had, but then she came back to her flat and asked me to go and see her, which I did reluctantly. Her flat is up for sale and she is leaving England in a few days, I believe.'

'Why?' was all she said.

'She told me that she is ill and is going into a private hospital run by some nuns in France. She gave me the impression that she is terminally ill.'

'That is what she tried to tell me,' Magda said coldly, 'but it didn't stop her attacking me. Do you believe her?'

He considered the question. 'I think I do,' he said at last.

Suddenly making a decision, she put the envelope down. 'I'll deal with that later. Now, I'll ask my question.' The telephone rang again but she ignored it. 'When I met Lisa that weekend she said some terrible things to me, but only one that mattered.' She paused.

'What was that?'

Clearly and slowly she told him. 'She said that my baby – our baby – had not died but that she had had it taken away to a foster mother when I was still unconscious. Do you know if that is true?' She waited in agony for his reply.

'It is true.'

'Is that all you can say? If you knew all about it, how could you let it happen? I know we'd disagreed, but I never thought you hated me so much!' She was deathly pale, her voice low and penetrating; her brilliant blue eyes were completely dry. She was obviously exerting an immense self-control. 'Oh, God, how could you be so cruel?'

'I never hated you, Magda. You know that. I wasn't there. Don't you remember? The baby came early. I hurried back as soon as you phoned me but I arrived too late. Lisa told me that the baby had died at birth and she had had the body removed to save you further suffering. Fool that I was, I believed her.' His bitter anger was obvious.

'It was lies, all lies!' Magda cried. Suddenly her control collapsed completely. Huddled in her chair she began to sob, terrible wracking sobs. Her eyes were filled with tears that rolled unheeded down her cheeks. It was as if she had never cried before. *Perhaps*, Conrad thought, *she never had.*

He moved swiftly across the room to comfort her. Sitting on the arm of her chair he enclosed her in his embrace. She did not resist but leaned against his chest. His shirt was wet with her tears. He murmured loving, comforting words in Arabic. She did not know what he was saying but his tone comforted her. As her sobs became more controllable, she murmured an apology but did not move.

After a few moments he lifted her face and gently wiped her eyes and cheeks with his handkerchief. Suddenly, without premeditation he bent and kissed her on the lips. It was not the passionate kiss of a lover but the comforting kiss of a friend. She did not pull away but, after a few moments, she rested her face against his chest again.

'Thank you,' she whispered. 'I never knew you could be so comforting.'

'I'm not wholly bad,' he said. The telephone rang again, but neither of them took any notice. As soon as she was completely in control, he released her and moved back to the settee.

'When did you find out?' she asked.

'It was about eighteen months later. You had gone, and Lisa did not know where you were. She seemed quite unaware of the cruelty of her actions but boasted that you would be grateful to her one day for freeing you from a useless burden. She said that it was my fault too for finally deciding with you against an abortion. I don't know how she managed the legal arrangements, but she never allowed a little illegality to stop her.'

'I was surprised that you supported me against abortion, although I was grateful. Why did you?'

'I couldn't agree finally. It was against the faith I had been brought up in. It is difficult to sever oneself entirely from the beliefs of one's youth.'

'But if I had agreed to an abortion, you would have let it happen?'

He shrugged. 'That is the sort of man I am. You know that.'

'I'm not sure what I know now,' she murmured.

'Actually,' he told her, 'I was very angry with Lisa. I reminded her that this was my child, too. She only laughed and said it was a bit late for me to pretend to be the fatherly type, if there was such a man. Ignoring that, I finally managed to get some useful information from her.'

She sat up and demanded urgently, 'What did you find out?'

'Only that our daughter was registered as Isobel Lefevre, and the name of the children's home to which the foster mother took her.'

'And that was all?' her disappointment was clear.

'Not all. I was later able to discover that Isobel had been fostered by a pleasant sounding couple who intended to adopt her.'

'You didn't think to tell me,' she said, accusing him.

'No. I had recently heard that, much to Lisa's satisfaction, you had married Philip Peters, the banker. Lisa easily persuaded me that it would be stupid to upset everyone. I had no desire to play the part of father and I did not imagine that you would want to produce an illegitimate daughter, unless of course you had told your husband everything.'

'I hadn't,' she admitted.

'That was what Lisa thought, so I dismissed the whole matter and went to the United States for a couple of years.'

'With the information you have already, you could surely get more, couldn't you?' Magda suggested eagerly.

'Possibly,' he said coolly, 'but why should I want to?'

'To please me, to make me happier. Surely you don't object to doing that?'

'In theory I'm very much in favour of your being happier, but I'm not at all convinced that this would be a good way to do it.' He was cool and detached. 'You know that your daughter is alive and has been adopted. Is it not rather selfish of you, my dear, to think of disturbing all that now? It is very sad for you, but it happened eighteen years ago and should now be forgotten.'

'But I can't, not now. You can't imagine how much it hurts, Conrad. I want so much to see my child – or at least to be sure that's she's happy. If that is selfish then I am selfish.'

'I can't pretend to be a judge of selfishness.' He spoke more gently. In his heart he was secretly cursing Lisa for telling Magda what she had. 'But,' he continued, 'there are many aspects to be considered. Even I can see that.'

'Such as?' she challenged him.

'First of all, there is the girl herself. If she is happy with her adopted family why should you want to upset that? What good would you do?'

'I don't want to upset them,' she protested. 'I just want to know. She might not be.'

'And your appearance would change all that?' he asked mockingly.

She didn't answer him but instead walked across the room and sat down beside him on the settee. Resting her hand lightly on his arm, she into his eyes, smiling slightly. 'Please, Conrad,' she appealed to him. 'Surely you will help me?' Now she was a different woman – one he remembered well.

For a moment he did not answer her, then firmly but gently he removed her hand from his arm, moving away from her at the same time. 'My God!' he exclaimed. 'Lisa was a wonderful teacher. You have not forgotten any of your lessons.'

'What the hell do you mean?' she asked angrily.

'Surely that is obvious. You can't deny it. You are trying all your old seductive methods on me – the appealing look, the tender smile, the gentle touch and, above all, the voice. Unfortunately, I'm twenty years older and no longer ready to respond. What has happened to you, Magda? Your husband is a decent man. I've met him, remember? Surely, he deserves better than that!'

She tried to laugh. 'I'm amazed that you of all people should have become so moral.'

'And I'm amazed,' he replied coldly, 'that you should behave in this way. Don't you love your husband at all? I know you never loved me, but I would have imagined that he would inspire some love or at least loyalty.'

Suddenly she had a sudden vision of herself in this same room only two nights before, telling Philip that she loved him. 'You're right,' she told Conrad. 'I've been behaving horribly, just like the whore Lisa said I was. She said she thought that I was incapable of love. Perhaps she was right. Do you think so?'

'I know little about love. Surely, you are aware of that?' He seemed to be still mocking her, when suddenly he added in a changed tone, 'But I do believe that you are capable of appreciating the loyalty of your husband. What is this romantic love? What lasting value has it? Is it anything more than lust dressed up in a pretty costume?' He shrugged his shoulders. 'I think not.'

She was looking at him quite differently now as she slowly answered, 'I agree with you. Philip has not only given me a lot of kindness but a secure home for fifteen years, the first home I ever had. In return for that I've always been faithful to him and given him as much pleasure as I could. I don't know if that means that I love him, but I do value him.'

'I'm pleased to hear you say that and to know that Lisa is wrong, as she often has been.'

'But must that mean that I cannot and must not know any more about my daughter? I learned to cope with the grief of believing that my only child was dead; but to know that she is alive and to know no more torments me. Can you possibly understand?'

He was silent for a few agonising moments and then he said slowly, 'I think I can, Magda. I think perhaps that I should gather what information I can and then we can discuss whether any further action would be desirable on our part.'

'You say on *our* part!' Do you really mean that, Conrad? I understood that you had no further interest in her.'

'I have changed,' he told her calmly. 'I have come to accept that she is my daughter, too, and therefore that I have a responsibility towards her. Do you deny that?' He spoke very formally.

'Of course not, but...'

'...as her mother you are the one chiefly concerned. I understand that. I only want to help you and to do what is right, if I can.'

'And what do you think that is?' Magda was suspicious and wary, feeling that she had never understood Conrad.

'We can't really decide that until we know more. I would suggest, however, that if we find, as I expect we shall, that she is happy with her adopted parents, we do nothing to disturb her. If she ever wants to find you, she can.'

Magda was not happy with this suggestion but she saw its justice. 'I hate the thought of never seeing her but I agree.'

'In that case, I'll set one of my agents on to discover all he can. And I'll ring you as soon as I have any information.'

'You do promise?' she pleaded with him.

'Of course. You can rely on that.' He looked steadily at her for a moment then, standing up suddenly, he announced, 'I must go now.'

She followed him as he moved towards the hall to retrieve his coat. As he fastened his coat, he turned towards her. 'You must not look so worried and so sad, my dear.' Without warning, he drew her towards him and kissed her gently. As he did so, the telephone began to ring again.

'I think I'd better answer that,' she said, rather shaken. 'It must be Philip. Cathy would never ring so late.' As she picked up the phone, Conrad left her with a smile, closing the door quietly behind him.

When she had finished speaking to Philip, she felt even more dissatisfied with herself. Why had she lied to him again? And yet how could she have avoided it. Her emotions were in turmoil, her thought confused. How impossible to tell him over the phone what she had just discovered from Conrad, who seemed so changed. *The past is truly catching up with us*, she thought with a shiver.

It was at this moment that she decided that she should read Lisa's letter before saying any more to Philip. On opening the large packet she discovered a smaller one inside together with a separate letter. The smaller packet contained three jewellery boxes, the largest of which held a moonstone and diamond pendant. Inside the second there were earrings to match the pendant. She recognised both of these as having been in Lisa's possession for years. She must think she is dying to have parted with these, was her first thought. The third box was a ring case, inside which was a magnificent diamond solitaire ring.

The letter was much shorter than Magda had expected. She read:

Dear Magda,

These I'm afraid are the only legacy I can afford to leave you. As Conrad may already have told you, I'm going to a hospice in France, my final destination, or so it seems. My attempt to meet you that weekend ended so badly that it seems wiser that we don't meet again. In my own way I have loved you and tried to do what I thought was best for you. Taking your baby away saved you a lot of misery and I don't really regret it but I do very much regret telling you. I would never have done it had not my envy and my anger at your obvious distaste for me overcome my good sense. I hope you can understand and forgive me. Tell your father, if you wish, that I try to forgive him.

But my real wish is that you will get in touch with my mother, your grandmother. She is a good woman who deserved a better daughter. She is old now and a widow and may very well need help that you can easily give. I hope you will be able to do so. I enclose her name and address separately. She knows that you exist.

I must say goodbye now, Magda. Please don't let any of this disturb your marriage with Philip. Try to be wiser than I have been.

All my love and very best wishes,

Your Mother, Lisa

After she had carefully reread it, Magda put the letter back into its envelope. She felt frozen – unable to cry, almost unable to comprehend. She needed someone desperately. If Philip had been here she might have been able to tell him everything now. Catherine would never understand. Even Conrad might have helped, but he had gone.

Suddenly she made a decision. She would go to visit her grandmother. She would surely understand and, at least, she was someone she had a claim on and someone who might need her. As soon as she had made the decision, she felt happier. She was almost ridiculously sure that her grandmother was the person she needed.

Chapter Fifteen

This was definitely another world, Magda decided, as her train drew into the station of the West Midlands town where her grandmother lived. The approach had been along a line built on a high embankment with a surprising view of green fields and a pleasant housing estate among trees and gardens. Immediately before the station, however, it had become grimmer, with a view only of factories and dark warehouses – more what she had expected of the industrial North and Midlands.

The station, although not particularly large, had three long platforms to accommodate the main line trains from London to the North and Scotland, many of which stopped there. On this grey November morning there were few people around. Joining the half-dozen or so who disembarked from her train, she walked across the steep bridge, which led to Platform One and the exit.

As the others went out through the exit gate, she hesitated. 'Can I get a taxi?' she asked a solitary porter.

'You'll find plenty queuing up outside,' he told her. His accent and his voice seemed rough to her. Refusing his offer to take her small bag, she decided to try the door marked 'Refreshments'. She needed time, she felt, to consider her future actions.

She had done everything so quickly after deciding to visit her grandmother. She had booked a seat on the train, and left a text message for Cathy to say that she would be away for a few days. She knew that this would infuriate Cathy but she was not prepared to discuss anything with her. Finally, she had phoned Philip to tell him that she would be visiting her grandmother, as this was Lisa's wish. It was a relief to tell him some truth but she was not tempted to give him the full story. He told her that he did not expect to be away long but she must not worry about him; she was right, he said to support her grandmother in these circumstances. Suddenly, perhaps with a liar's ear for another, she decided that he was not telling her the whole truth. But she had left it alone.

On the train she had experienced a wonderful sense of freedom. There was no longer any need to pretend or to lie. She could be herself or at least try to make some decisions about herself. Unfortunately all she had actually done had been to sit back comfortably and watch the scenery slide past. Now she must make a plan.

The almost deserted refreshment room was not exactly a place of beauty and badly needed a coat of paint. Many of the empty tables were still uncleared, cluttered with empty cups and glasses, the remains of food and many cigarette ends. It was all rather distasteful but, after buying a cup of coffee at the counter, Magda managed to find an empty table as far away as possible from two mothers with their unmanageable and whingeing children.

She tried to think seriously but instead suddenly realised that it was not very thoughtful of her to visit her grandmother without warning. She was over eighty and might be unwilling to receive visitors in the morning or at any other time if they were unexpected. Lisa had assured her that her mother was aware of Magda's existence, but could she even trust that?

As she sat in the sad little refreshment room, it occurred to her that she had acted on a mad impulse. It might be said, she thought, that she had been in a state of shock ever since Conrad had told her the truth. Still, she was here now, nearly two hours away from London, and she did not intend to return without seeing her relation.

Consulting Lisa's letter, she confirmed that her grandmother's name was Margaret Vaughan (commonly known as Maggy) and that she lived at 12 Wilson Avenue, wherever that was. Thank God there was a telephone number! Leaving her half-finished coffee, she hurried through the other door to the station forecourt. After finding a seat in a quiet corner, she dialled the number on her mobile. After many rings the phone was answered by a woman with a quiet, pleasant voice, who gave her number.

'Can I speak to Mrs Vaughan?' Magda asked nervously.

'I am Mrs Vaughan,' the woman replied. 'Who is that speaking?'

This was the time to be direct, Magda decided. 'I'm afraid it may be a bit of a shock for you. You've never met me and I'm not even sure if you are aware of my existence. I'm your grand-daughter, Magda.'

After a moment's pause, Mrs Vaughan replied with surprising calm. 'Then you must be Lisa's daughter. I have heard of you, of course, and have often hoped to meet you. It's very kind of you to get in touch.' She stopped, obviously needing more information.

Magda rushed in. 'I'm hoping to meet you. I've come especially from London.'

'Where are you now?' Her grandmother asked.

'At the station. I can get a taxi if you're willing to meet me.'

'I shall be delighted to see you.' There was no doubting the warmth in Mrs Vaughan's voice. 'It should take you about fifteen minutes. I'll have a cup of coffee ready.'

Melford was not a very attractive town, Magda decided as the taxi turned out of the station and crawled towards what was obviously the High Street. The traffic was much heavier that she had expected but then she remembered that the town was only about two miles from the M6 motorway. It was a dull, grey day with a biting wind and many of the people jostling in the streets or waiting at the bus stops looked depressed and weary. The shops were small and the houses, which succeeded them, were mostly three-storey Victorian terraced houses with little or no gardens.

The taxi turned right off the main street and then took the first turning on the right, finally stopping before a modest-sized semi-detached house probably built in the 1930s. 'Here you are, love,' the taxi driver told her, '12 Wilson Avenue.'

'Thanks.' Without considering the fare she offered him a five-pound note, which seemed to please him.

She stood for a moment by the iron double gates. On one side of the path leading to the front door an ancient car was parked. On the other side there was a small but tidy garden. It all seemed rather dreary. Had she made a hideous mistake? Magda wondered as she walked up to the front door and rang the bell. Her heart was beating fast as the door opened and she saw her grandmother for the first time. She had a quick vision of a small, plump, white-haired old lady wearing a jade green velour housecoat. The eyes which looked directly into hers were remarkable; however, they were not blue like her own and Lisa's, but a deep, warm brown.

For a frightening moment they simply stared at each other until Magda, feeling the fear of rejection, smiled hopefully. Whereupon her fear was swept away, as Mrs Vaughan smiled the most loving and welcoming smile that could be imagined.

'Oh, my dear!' she exclaimed, as she took Magda in her arms. 'You're so like Lisa. I was almost afraid for a moment, but when you smiled I saw that it wasn't her.' She kissed Magda on the cheek, half laughing and half crying. 'Come straight in, my dear. How good it is to meet you! I never thought!'

She led Magda along the narrow hall, then through a door on the left into what was obviously the main living room. It was larger than Magda had expected and at a first glance it seemed to be almost entirely furnished with bookcases packed with books.

As her grandmother took her coat, Magda exclaimed, 'What a lot of books you have! How lovely! So few people seem to have any these days!'

'I was an English teacher,' her grandmother explained.

'How strange! I taught English and Drama for a time. Well, I suppose it's not really strange. After all, I am your granddaughter. But Lisa...' She hesitated.

'...Lisa was quite different,' Mrs Vaughan finished the sentence quietly. 'But do come and have some coffee. It's waiting.'

Magda sat down in an armchair, shabby but comfortable. Nearby was a coffee table laid with cups and saucers, a coffee pot and a plate of tempting chocolate biscuits. The warmth from the gas fire was very comforting. A black and white cat lay curled up in a basket near. It lazily opened one eye and then firmly turned his back on her. Mrs Vaughan sat down opposite Magda and began to pour out the coffee carefully.

Magda relaxed happily. The coffee was excellent, and she willingly allowed her grandmother to persuade her to choose the most tempting biscuits. She had a feeling she'd never had before. She was being lovingly mothered.

'This is lovely, Grannie!' she exclaimed. Then, startled at herself, she asked, 'May I call you Grannie?'

Mrs Vaughan smiled. 'I should be unhappy if you didn't. It's wonderful to see you here. I can't imagine any better surprise. God is good.' She spoke simply and sincerely.

As she sipped her coffee Magda remembered why she had come. The message she brought was neither happy nor pleasant. It would be wrong to delay giving it, she decided.

'What is the matter, dear?' her grandmother asked. 'You look worried.'

'I'm afraid I shall make you unhappy when I tell you why I've come.'

'Lisa must have sent you,' Mrs Vaughan remarked quietly, 'or you wouldn't have known where to come. You need not worry. I'm eighty-two years old and I've survived many disappointments and difficulties. I'm afraid I don't expect comfort from Lisa, so just say what you have to say.'

Since any preamble seemed a waste of time, Magda plunged straight into her story. 'Lisa and I parted company many years ago,' she told her grandmother, 'and I heard nothing from her until quite recently when she suddenly asked me to meet her, saying that she was ill. The meeting was a disaster.' She paused and then decided not to go into detail. 'Lisa was in a vile mood. We quarrelled, and I left after she had attacked me.' She stopped there.

'Lisa has a violent temper, I know,' Mrs Vaughan murmured, as if trying to comfort her granddaughter.

Reassured Magda continued. 'A couple of days ago I heard from a mutual friend, who told me that Lisa had given him a packet and a letter to pass on to me. She had sent me some jewellery and a letter in which she told me that she was going to a hospice in France, probably to die.' She paused for a moment wondering what effect her words might have, but Maggy Vaughan continued to gaze steadily at her.

'Go on,' she said gently.

'That's really all,' Magda replied. 'She said she thought it would be better if we didn't try to meet again. But she gave me your address and asked me to visit you. She said she loved me, and that you were a good woman who deserved a better daughter.' She stared straight ahead, refusing to allow herself to cry.

'Oh, my dear, come here.' Mrs Vaughan was holding out her arms and, as Magda moved towards her, she found herself embraced warmly and lovingly. It was a mother's embrace – something she had never experienced before. The tears came now, but they were gentle, healing tears as she relaxed into her grandmother's sheltering arms.

After a few minutes she managed to say. 'You must be very sorry too, Grannie. Lisa is your daughter. I'm really sorry that I've brought such terrible news.'

The answer came quickly and quietly. 'I'm sorry, of course, that my daughter is suffering and perhaps dying and, most of all, I'm sad that she's doing it all alone. But that is her choice. She rejected not only me but also her father, her brother and her home – not just once but several times.' She stopped talking and tightened her embrace a little. After a while she said, 'I think we have a lot to tell each other, and perhaps it will help us both to talk.'

'It'll certainly help me,' Magda replied. 'I need to talk. It seems clear to me now that, mostly because of Lisa, I've never been able to talk honestly to anyone.'

'I'm puzzled that you even know of her existence,' Maggy said. 'The only thing she told me was that she had forced your father to take you as his own child and give you the life you were entitled to but that it was on condition that she should never make herself known to you. I thought it was wrong and foolish, but Lisa was not interested in my opinion.'

'It was wrong,' Magda agreed. 'It might have worked, I suppose, if she had kept the conditions, but she didn't.'

'What do you mean?'

Quickly, Magda told her incredulous grandmother how Lisa had met her when she was eight and many times afterwards, forcing her to swear to keep their meetings secret. 'I did it for her sake but it meant that I was forced to live a life of lies and secrecy. Can you imagine that? I even had to lie to the one sister who loved me. I hated Lisa at times and then I felt guilty.'

'Did you see her often?'

'Yes, quite often, but always secretly. Why was she so cruel? She has told me so many lies that I don't even know if she's telling me the truth now. I'm sorry. You're her mother. I suppose that shocks you?'

'I'm afraid not,' Maggy answered gently. 'She taught her father and myself some hard lessons before she left.'

Magda sat up suddenly. 'Her *father*! She didn't even mention him. Have I a grandfather? Of course not.' She answered her own question quickly. 'You're a widow. Lisa did say that. Did he die recently?'

'No, not recently. Quite a few years ago.' She paused and hugged Magda again. 'It seems that you and I have a lot to talk about – that is, if you want to talk to me?'

'I do very much. I desperately need someone to talk to.'

'I think it will be good for both of us, but it's nearly time for lunch now. We must have food and I must have my afternoon rest. I'm in pretty good health, but I'm old and I do need a rest after lunch.'

'Of course!' Magda jumped up. 'I'll prepare the food if you'll give me directions.'

'Good. I'll sit in the kitchen and you can do the work.'

Lunch was a simple meal soon prepared. During the course of it a neighbour, who obviously kept a friendly eye on Mrs Vaughan, popped in and seemed delighted to meet the new granddaughter. In an odd way, Magda felt as if she had always belonged here.

After lunch, Maggy went upstairs for a rest. 'I hope you won't be lonely,' she said.

'Of course not.' Magda laughed. 'In a room full of books? It'll be bliss!' As soon as her grandmother had gone upstairs, Magda curled up by the fire with several books and Catullus, the cat, for company. She had intended to think seriously but found it much pleasanter to doze and read instead. It was easier to accept without question these unforeseen events and each new situation.

At the same time as Magda phoned her grandmother from the station, Philip made a call to a once familiar number in Belfast. After a few rings a woman's voice answered. 'Noreen O'Neill speaking.'

'Good morning, Noreen,' Philip replied in a chilly tone, and with an accent that Magda would not have recognised.

'Who is that?' The woman asked. There was a hint of fear in her voice.

'Do you really not recognise me? Or is it your guilty conscience that makes you hope that you are wrong?'

'I don't understand,' the woman stammered. 'Who are you?'

'You already know that,' Philip answered, 'and you understand but you don't want to. I'll help you. It's the voice of the man whose confidence you have betrayed – Gerard O'Dowd.'

'Oh Gerry, I'm so very sorry. I didn't mean to I—'

'But you did!' he interrupted her. 'Let me remind you of the circumstances. When I left Northern Ireland many years ago we both agreed that it was safest for us to sever all connections. At least, I thought we agreed.'

'Yes, we did.' She spoke more firmly now. 'But you were the one who actually gave me your address, Gerry, in case I needed help.'

'Yes,' Philip agreed, 'I was the sentimental fool who felt sorry for the widow and orphan I might be said to have deserted. In case you were in dire need, I let you have an address by which I could be reached. I felt worried about you.'

'Or was it that you felt a bit guilty too?' she asked him quietly.

There was a silence, so long that she thought he might have ended the call but then he replied calmly, 'You may well be right, Noreen, but you too had reason to feel guilty.'

'I've never forgotten that,' she replied bitterly.

'Nevertheless, you didn't write to me. As time passed, it was clear that you had sorted your life out. I admit I was glad and felt free to remake my own life.'

'I did write but you never replied. I thought you had been killed but I'm pleased to hear that you're happy now, Gerry.'

'Are you really?' His tone was mocking. 'Then why did I a few days ago receive a letter addressed to Gerry O'Dowd and sent by Liam, your son, to whom you have obviously betrayed me.'

'I had to, Gerry. He has become so mad and so violent. I don't know what to do. He's convinced that you, his Uncle Gerry, whom he has always remembered, are the only person who can help him to discover the truth about his father's disappearance. He only wants the truth.'

'No. Don't lie to yourself or to me. He doesn't want truth, he wants revenge. He wants to perpetuate the whole horror.'

'You're wrong. He's only a boy!'

Philip laughed. 'He's no boy. He's twenty-three. I've been told quite a bit about him. He associates with those idiots who don't want peace or closure. He wants more killing.'

'Oh, no. Don't say that, please.'

'I'm afraid it's true, Noreen. He's only just escaped prison a couple of times already. You say he wants the truth. Very well, I'll meet him and give it to him.'

'No! Please don't, Gerry! He's mad and dangerous. I don't know how to deal with him.'

'So, that's why you thought you would hand him over to me. What did you expect?'

'To put him off. I thought you would have left there years ago.'

'Well, I haven't. I live there with my wife.'

'You could have ignored it.'

'Unfortunately, no. My wife found the letter. Besides, I owe him something, don't I? I've come to pay my debt.'

'Gerry,' she begged him, 'go home while you can!'

'I can't go now. I have to get in touch with him, as he has asked me to. I thought I should warn you, Noreen. You have sown the wind, you may reap the whirlwind.'

Before she could answer him the receiver was firmly put down.

During the next two days Magda found herself telling her grandmother most of her story. She found it easy to talk to someone so loving and so undemanding. In this shabby little house, she found a comfort and ease that she had never known before. She had found a safe home, and for the first time she experienced motherly love. It felt as if she had stepped into another world. The old world in London was still there, and one day, she supposed, she would have to return to it. But, for the moment, it no longer seemed to matter.

She did not, however, tell of Lisa's terrible act of betrayal until the end of the second day. That evening she tried twice to ring Philip, only to find that his mobile was switched off. She shrank from ringing the hotel because she did not know what name he was using there.

She was puzzled and upset. Why hadn't he attempted to ring her? Why had he cut himself off? It was so unlike him… It was then that the unasked question returned to her mind. To whom had he once given his London address? Obviously it was someone he cared for and was willing to help. It could not have been the five-year-old son, so perhaps it had been his mother. She tried to control her disordered thoughts but was hit with a sudden sense of betrayal. Even Philip? Could it be possible?

It was then that her phone rang. It was not Philip, however, but Conrad. Although he did not know where she was he had her number. 'Have you any news?' she asked eagerly.

'Nothing definite yet, but I think I shall be able to tell you in a couple of days our daughter's story and her present whereabouts. Where are you now? Can you easily come to London?'

'I'm with my grandmother,' she told him, 'and I'd like to stay as long as possible, but I'm ready to come as soon as you summon me. You've been very faithful in your search.'

'Our daughter matters to me,' he replied, 'but your happiness matters most of all. Goodnight, Magda.' Then he was gone.

It was when she re-entered the sitting room that Magda finally decided to tell Maggy, about Lisa's final betrayal. Without considering her words, she went straight across the room and sat on the floor, leaning against her grandmother's lap. There was silence when she finished then tears that were made less bitter since they were mingled with those of her grandmother, who held her closely.

'Why did she have to take my only child?' she asked. 'It was too cruel. I need to forgive her, but how can I?'

'Perhaps you need to know more and to understand more,' her grandmother said gently. 'I think that I failed her and that I have some blame.'

'I don't believe that,' Magda replied passionately. 'You are too good!'

'Unfortunately,' her grandmother replied sadly, 'all our actions have consequences – sometimes very different from what we intended. They may stretch very far but we cannot escape them.'

'I don't see how you can be blamed for Lisa's cruelty.'

'Not entirely, of course, but if I tell you my story and Lisa's, it will help you to understand everything more easily.'

Chapter Sixteen – Maggy's Story

'I grew up in the years of the Depression,' Maggy began. 'The time when long queues of men could be seen snaking along the streets just off the centre of the industrial city where I lived. They all seemed to wear caps and mufflers and shabby jackets. Their hands always seemed to be plunged deeply into their pockets, in the hope of keeping warm, I supposed. They looked grey and hopeless.

' "Why are all those men standing there?" I asked my dad as we drove past in a bus.

' "They're queuing up to get their miserable dole at the labour exchange," he told me. "Of course, that's where they're supposed to get a job, but there's not much hope of that these days. Poor devils!"

'I became aware that my normally cheerful and confident father was angry – very angry. "Don't they *want* a job?" I asked, surprised. I had never thought before that the job was something you couldn't get, even if you wanted it.

' "Of course, they want one!" My father sounded almost savage in his anger. "But there aren't any. Most of the factories are closed down, since the banks demanded their money back. In one night almost half the men in this town were thrown on to the streets."

'I was very young, but I always liked to understand things and my father, unusually, respected this; so now I had my first lesson in politics – that's why I remember it so vividly. My father explained, in simple terms, that most of the factories depended on loans from the banks. Trade was bad; the banks didn't want to risk anything, so they called for the immediate repayment of the money, and as a result the factories closed and thousands of men were jobless and their families were facing near starvation.

'The thought horrified me as I stared again at the scarcely moving queue of men. I tried to find some degree of comfort.

"But you work in a factory, Dad," I said, "and you aren't out of work."

'He laughed. "Only because I realised some years ago that you've got to be better than average if you want to survive! Don't you worry, Maggy! Just trust your old dad. He knows a thing or two!"

'I did trust him and I wasn't wrong to. Although soon he was only working three days a week for a time, he was a key worker with more than average knowledge and skill, so he was kept on. Resourceful as always, he made up his income by selling small insurance policies to friends, acquaintances and even relatives. He was, at the same time, an important member of his trades union.

'I felt secure, simply because my dad always seemed confident. Our position was better than that of many we knew. We did not live in a rented old terraced house but in a new, three-bedroomed semi-detached one which my dad had managed to secure a mortgage for, and he managed to maintain it even in those bad times. We had hot water and a bathroom, simple luxuries which were denied to most of my friends.

'I accepted this without much thought. I didn't feel superior to my poorer friends; and later, when I secured a scholarship to a well-known girls' independent school, I didn't feel inferior to the middle-class girls I met there. It was just the way things were, and I still had my own friends.' Maggy paused.

'I suppose that surprises you?' She looked across at Magda.

'I suppose it is a bit surprising,' Magda agreed, 'especially since you did say that you had an inquiring mind.'

'That's true. I did have, but my father directed me into wider ways of thought. Although I was only a working-class girl, he decided that, with his help, I would get the best education possible. He was completely convinced that education was the key to a fulfilled and successful life. I can still see his brilliant blue eyes – rather like yours – fixed on me, almost hypnotically.

'Although he had passed the examination which gave him a place at the grammar school, it was impossible for him to take it up. As the youngest of ten with a drunken father, his mother required him to give her all the help he could. He left school at thirteen, therefore, and went to work. He didn't despair, however, but continued to read books from the library – not any books, but many of the classics, which his schoolteacher had already introduced him to; books which he then introduced to me, such as first class historical novels, some Shakespeare, and most of all, Dickens.

'He wasn't content to remain an ordinary factory worker but went to night school to improve his skills and knowledge, until he was snatched away into the hell of the First World War. He suffered terribly for four years, but even in that he was different. He decided not to join the local regiment, but went south to join a London regiment where he met many highly educated and intelligent men. He learned from them, and many respected his courage and native wit. Many remained his friends for life, and these friendships increased his passion for knowledge and his determination that no child of his would be held back by lack of education.'

'What would have happened if you hadn't been intelligent?' Magda asked.

'I don't know. Fortunately, I was. I enjoyed reading and learning. Backed by my father, I was allowed to join the Senior Library and never lacked for good books. However, we owned very few, apart from the complete works of Dickens and the latest offerings of the Left Book Club. These were stored in a cheap bookcase along with the Bible and papers relating to my father's work with the union and the Labour Party. One day one of the glass doors was broken, but it was never properly repaired, just as our carpet had to become completely threadbare before my genteel mother was allowed to buy a new one, often with weekly payments taken from her meagre housekeeping money. She accused my father of being mean, but their priorities were different.

'Suspecting that his health had been seriously impaired during the War, he saved all he could to provide security for them and the best start for me.'

'Didn't they quarrel?' Magda asked. 'Surely it must have been very difficult?'

'Of course they quarrelled at times, but he only let her win when it suited him. In spite of her protests she was naturally submissive, as most working-class women were then. What else was there for her? I often tried to comfort her but, I suppose, I was, really, my father's daughter. I had no thought of women being inferior; no knowledge really that they were supposed to be so, although my mother warned me that I would find out one day.

'For an intelligent girl encouraged to ask questions, I was surprisingly ignorant about the world. I understood that we were fairly poor but I did not know any middle-class people well enough, to envy them. Our food was limited but we always had enough especially at the weekend.

'When I went on a scholarship to the expensive independent school I didn't worry about the girls there, for I was cleverer than most of them and I still had my friends from primary school, although our lives were going to be so different. My long-standing girl friend, Grace, failed the eleven-plus, so she left school at fourteen and went to work in a shop. She was quite happy with her life, and I almost envied her when I was working hard for examinations.

'My great comfort, however, was my oldest and closest friend, Nick. He was really poor, much poorer than Grace, whose father was only unemployed for about two years. Nick's father never worked when I knew him. I met Nick when he was three, and from that time until he died when Nick was nearly eleven he never did a day's work. I was told he was ill but the exact nature of his illness was never made clear.

'It was only years later that I realised that it was probably serious depression. Mental illness, however, was not a luxury the poor could allow themselves, unless they wanted to risk being incarcerated indefinitely in one of our grim mental hospitals, dreaded by all. He suffered more or less silently, while his wife went out cleaning to get money. One day he mercifully died without any fuss.'

'Oh dear.' Magda shuddered. 'That sounds terribly sad.'

'It was sad. But you know, life often is sad, in spite of all our attempts to hide that with tinsel and pretence in the present time.' Maggy was silent for a moment then continued with renewed vigour. 'I remember Nick's house, particularly the kitchen, very clearly. It's strange as you grow old how some scenes come back vividly into your mind.

'Nick lived in a small, cramped terraced house, one of a row whose doors opened straight onto the main street. When you came through the front door you went straight into a dark, airless parlour and its few bits of "best" furniture. Net curtains kept the light out. I never saw a fire lit in the fireplace. Most people walked through the parlour into the kitchen, but I usually approached it through the back after coming down the yard with its outside privy.

'I went straight into the scullery with its bare tiled floor and large earthenware sink with one cold tap only. One step brought me into the kitchen. This was a bigger room, but rather dark, because there was only one small window which had a depressing and narrow view of the yard. A plain wooden table stood by the window with two wooden chairs beside it. In the middle of the main wall there was an old-fashioned range with fire and oven which had to be painfully black leaded every week. Two large, spotted china dogs stood on the mantelpiece above, with a shabby tea caddy in the middle. It too was large, but usually only contained a small portion of tea, which was carefully measured out into the brown earthenware teapot. A kettle simmered on the hob. Before the range there was the only floor covering, a faded rag rug.

'A large cupboard with shelves above and drawers beneath stood against the wall opposite to the range. The only other furniture I remember was a hard and shiny horsehair sofa and a rocking chair, in which Nick's father spent most of his time.'

Maggy stopped suddenly and stared straight in front of her. It was as if she had slipped back into the past. Magda spoke suddenly in an effort to bring her back. 'It's hard for me to imagine that many people once lived so barely.'

Maggy came back to the present with a start. 'I'm sorry. You must be wondering why I'm talking about all these things when all I promised was to tell you how I might have had a bad effect on Lisa. I suppose the truth is that I want you to know about me and where you come from, because Lisa has obviously not honestly told you anything. But it's difficult to find the beginning.

Do you know what I mean?' She looked anxiously at her granddaughter curled up in the armchair opposite her.

'I'm beginning to,' Magda replied, 'but I find the idea rather frightening.'

'It is frightening. Everything we decide changes the future. Sometimes what happens is very different from what we expected or desired. I'm coming to a very important decision I made, but you have to see how I came to make it.'

'Please go on,' Magda urged her. She had the strange feeling that what Maggy said would ultimately be important to her. At the moment she felt as if this cosy sitting room was her only home. She felt completely cut off from her past life.

'I often went round to Nick's house when he had to be at home with his father when his mother was out cleaning. Most times I was there, Nick's father sat in his rocking chair. Day after day he sat there wearing shabby trousers and a shabby waistcoat over a shirt open at the neck. If it was cold he had a muffler wrapped round his neck. His hair was scanty and grey; his face was grey and badly shaved.

'Much of the time he was either dozing or muttering to himself but sometimes he upset us by shouting at us, "Go away, you noisy brats! Can't you give me a bit of peace?" Then, if the weather was fine, we would take refuge on the back doorstep and talk. It was there that Nick asked me if I would marry him when we grew up. After due thought, I agreed. It was all very innocent. We simply held hands and Nick said, "I'm so glad, Maggy."

'One day Nick's old man really frightened us. He suddenly sat up and began to sing loudly in a harsh, cracked voice, "I've got the joy – joy down in my heart, down in my heart." He repeated it several times, then suddenly fell back and seemed to go to sleep. I think it was the first time that I understood that he was not just an unpleasant old man, but a suffering human being. It taught me a lesson. Unlike Nick, who was amazingly kind and understanding, I was always ready to judge people, often unkindly. Nick was more of a Christian.

'Soon after this, Nick's father died, and life went on almost as if he never existed. It was a hard life for Nick and his mother, but they cared for each other. We both passed the eleven-plus. He went to a city grammar school while I was offered a special scholarship at a "posh" independent school. We remained good friends, although we tried to avoid the silly comments of others.

'Although scarcely spoken of, our future seemed clear. After his School Certificate, Nick would go to the technical college and train for a good job in local industry. I was to go to a training college and be a local primary school teacher. That satisfied my father, although of course we were not to have an early marriage.

'And then without any warning, everything was changed – but not by any decision of ours. Providence intervened. One day soon after leaving school, Nick dropped down dead. His heart had failed! I can still clearly remember the unbelievable horror of it!' She looked straight at Magda. 'I was changed. My life was completely changed, and the results have touched you. I want you to know how interwoven our lives were, and then, perhaps, you'll find some explanation for Lisa.' She leaned back suddenly and closed her eyes, saying, 'I'm very tired, my dear.'

'Of course you are,' Magda replied gently. 'I'm going to help you to bed and we'll talk again tomorrow.'

It was only when she was getting to bed herself that she thought about Philip. He had not rung her. Why not? Should she ring him? Turning out the light, she decided against it.

That evening, Conrad studied once more the information had received earlier. Magda had given him her phone number, and his first instinct had been to ring her. Finally, he decided that he must make sure of all the facts before he disturbed her. So far it seemed that the problem of Isobel Lefevre was not going to be easily solved.

There was no point in blaming Lisa now. It seemed clear that, after all these years, they would have to take responsibility for their own actions. He would ring Magda tomorrow when he was sure of all he had to tell her.

Chapter Seventeen

It was later the next morning when Magda prompted Maggy to continue her story. As they were sitting over a cup of coffee, she said, 'It must have been terrible for you when Nick died. I have never experienced anything like that.'

'It was a terrible shock. But the worst thing was that I was not allowed to mourn openly. My parents scarcely spoke of it. I was not allowed to go to the funeral because I couldn't miss a day from school. I tried to find out what had happened, but the answers I got were vague and I was never told the results of the inquest. I was too numb to protest, so I worked extra hard; but Nick was always with me, especially in my dreams. I felt that he expected something from me but I didn't know what.

'Then one day, about two months later, I was told that Nick's mother would like to speak to me. I hadn't seen her since Nick died as she had been ill. Now, however, she wanted to speak to me before she went to live with her sister. It was a grey sultry day, very much in harmony with the threats of war now gathering closer. I could hardly bear to walk down the yard to the back door.

'I found his mother sitting in the rocking chair in the kitchen. She who had always been so cheerful and strong had suddenly become a fragile old woman. Words were unnecessary. As she held out her arms to me, I knelt by the chair and we hugged each other and wept.

'Finally, I sat down on the sofa near her and she told me that Nick had died of enlarged heart and chronic kidney disease. "He must have been ill for months," she said, "and suffered a lot of pain, but he never told me. He wanted to spare me. There wasn't any money for a doctor, you see. Did he say anything to you?"

' "No," I said, my eyes filling with tears. "Never."

' "He loved you a lot. I always hoped you'd marry one day." Suddenly she stood and walked across the room. Opening one of the drawers, she took out a little book and handed it to me. "It's Nick's Bible. I know he'd like you to have it. There's nothing else, I'm afraid."

'I clasped it tightly. "I'll always keep it," I said. Then I asked the question I could no longer hold back. "How can you bear it? You seem so calm."

' "I accept it as God's will. You know, we have to try to accept God's will: 'The Lord gives; the Lord takes away.' Try to accept that, Maggy dear."

'Soon afterwards I left. I never saw her again. But that answer changed my life. I was angry, very angry. I was sure that my God would never have willed Nick's death in that way.

'During the weeks that followed I began to question many things. It seemed to me that when human beings talk about God's will, they are trying to shift their responsibilities onto Him. It was not God's fault that Nick had died as the result of long years of malnutrition. It was the fault of a society that paid widows such a pitiful amount and that operated a means test on the desperately poor.

'But it wasn't just society. There were individuals like my father who really cared but hadn't noticed Nick. Why had my mother never said anything when I told her of the lard and onion sandwiches that Nick and his mother ate? For that matter, why had I never been concerned when I knew that Nick only had a penny every day for his lunch, which he spent on a bag of chips?

'I decided that I was just as selfish as most people. It's so much easier to assume that everything's all right; to look the other way and to cross by on the other side. It's the good, like Nick and his mother, who suffer silently.'

'I know what you mean!' Magda exclaimed suddenly. 'I know that I'm selfish!' She was startled to hear herself say this and to realise how true it was.

'I expect you think that I'm going to say it made me a better person,' Maggy went on, 'but it didn't. It made me an angry one. One day, I thought, I might be able to do something; but in the meantime, I was going to use my intelligence to get away from my present narrow life.

'I hated the ugly city and the narrow-minded people in it. I hated the factories and the smoke, the slums, and the slag heaps which were my only idea of a mountain. I was determined to escape. I yearned for beauty.

'About this time I became friendly with a middle-class girl from school and became acquainted with a different style of living. It wasn't simply that Rachel's home was large and comfortable, but it was full of books and records, many of them of classical music. Rachel and I went to concerts together and to the theatre. There were many visitors to their home and much lively conversation on a variety of topics. To my delight, I was accepted as one of them.

'It was soon after this that my headmistress told my father that I had considerable talent and should definitely aim for a top university such as Oxford or Cambridge. He was delighted. I would have to work hard for scholarships, but he would back me all the way. I don't think that he suspected that this education might separate us. For my part, I worked tremendously hard and finally found myself in the Promised Land of Oxford. It was even more beautiful and exciting than I had imagined. Here was my chance to study, to learn and, above all, to meet interesting and exciting people who might help me in the future!

'It seemed almost impossible that I should be living in a place as beautiful as this, where all I had to do was to study, write essays, listen to lectures given by famous people and meet many of them. Before I was able to formulate my ideas, however, I fell seriously in love – and for life. I think that most girls have their secret romantic dream, but mine seemed to come true almost before I knew I had it.

'It was the same for Richard, too. We were both nineteen. I was beginning my third term and he was on an Army officers' short course. We seemed very different. I was small, quiet and a good listener. He was tall, apparently very confident, and a passionate talker about himself and everything else. We met at a political meeting, had tea afterwards, and he talked and I listened until it was time for me to return to college at about ten thirty. Our long relationship had begun almost before we realised it!

'For the next few weeks we saw each other every day, if only for a few minutes. Those few minutes gave a glory to each day.

We spent a few enchanted weeks in that beautiful city. Sometimes we went to the theatre or to a concert; on other days we drifted down the river in a punt, stopping under the shade of the willows to eat our picnic. In my memory, the sun shines all the time. We forgot the brutal war, the threat of air raids and the fact that Richard would soon have to go away on active service. Time was suspended…'

Maggy stopped talking for a moment. She seemed to have wandered back to those far-off moments.

'How wonderful!' Magda exclaimed. 'I have never felt like that at any time in my life! I didn't believe that anyone really could. Perhaps that was why Lisa told me recently that I had never loved anyone. In fact, she said that she thought I was incapable of loving.'

'What a terrible thing to say!' Maggy was shocked. 'She of all people had no right to say that of her own daughter.'

'I'm afraid she may be right,' Magda replied. 'I've never had much experience of love. My adopted family mostly ignored me, except for Cathy, who made me her pet, which was at least comforting then, when I was eight and I knew I was an interloper.'

'Perhaps she wanted you to love her,' Maggy suggested.

'Perhaps, but if that was so, she did all the wrong things, didn't she? When I was a student, I thought she loved me, but she soon disabused me of that folly. I understood that I was simply useful to her. And now I'm finding it difficult not to hate her.'

'I can understand that, but surely your marriage has made a difference. You have something she never had, and you did say that it was a successful marriage, didn't you?'

'Successful, yes, but not happy in the way you think.'

Maggy was puzzled. 'I don't understand?'

'Well, you and my grandfather loved each other straightaway and continued to love each other in every way. I'm right, aren't I?'

'Yes,' Maggy agreed, 'we were very blessed for many years, but it wasn't a marriage without difficulties. We had some very hard times indeed.'

'But you always loved each other and were very close, weren't you?'

'Of course.'

'I never felt like that about Philip. I married him because he was kind and intelligent, but most of all because he offered me a home and security – two things I'd never had. I told him that I didn't love him romantically.'

'Then how could you possibly be happy? Physical love is very important, particularly to a man.'

Magda smiled cynically. 'You have forgotten that Lisa trained me how to satisfy a man's physical needs expertly. I was to be a high-class prostitute. I knew what to do, and my marriage has been happy. I believe Lisa was mostly angry because I had succeeded where she had failed and had persuaded a wealthy lover to marry me. I don't know how your daughter has become like that, but that is how she seems to be.'

'I am very, very sorry.' Maggy's eyes filled with tears. 'I'm afraid that Lisa would say it's my fault and to some degree she's right. Remember, I told you in the beginning that I might be responsible for some of her actions. We are coming close to that point now.' Shutting her eyes, she leaned back in her armchair as if she was suddenly very weary.

'It was my decision, and it affected her in a way I never thought it would. I decided what I thought was right for all of us, but Lisa thought I put her father before her, and ruined her life, which I certainly didn't intend to do.'

'Of course you didn't! That's something you would never do.'

After lunch and a rest, Maggy was eager to resume. It was almost as if she wanted to make a confession, or at least to tell a story which had long worried her.

'Richard and I were married,' she began, 'just before the end of the war in Europe, but we were parted after a month because he was transferred to a unit which was advancing into Germany.'

Magda was horrified. 'How could you bear it?'

'It was something which many people had to accept in those days. We parted at Victoria Station. He was going to fight, perhaps to be killed while I was to stay in London, now being attacked daily by the terrifying V-2 missiles. We had had four ecstatic weeks together when we'd tried not to think of the future. But now the future was here. We kissed and hugged, said goodbye, and hurried apart without daring to take a backward look. He went straight to his train while I almost ran out of the exit.

'It was not the end for us, at least. Nearly two years later he was released from the Army and we were able to settle down a few months later in our own home in a pleasant London suburb leading the middle-class life Richard was accustomed to. Fairly soon we had two children: Lisa and three years later our son, Stephen.

'Richard, however, was not a good provider; he had not been prepared for that. He had left his minor public school at eighteen and gone straight into the Army. A few months later he had been put on an Officers' Training Course in Oxford where we met. He had seemed to be a lively, confident, friendly person, but I soon discovered that he was extremely sensitive and suffered from dark bouts of depression. He had been sent to a boarding school at an early age and his home life had been pretty loveless. He needed to love and be loved, and he responded to me passionately. Furthermore I was his first and only real friend, and for me he took the place left empty by Nick. I soon discovered that now he was haunted by several horrific experiences which he'd had on active service.

'With his father's help he managed to get a job in an advertising agency. At his best he was a good salesman, but he was always secretly fighting depression. If this got very bad, he would throw up his job, often to his employer's consternation and to my distress.

'For years we struggled on, apparently prosperous. It was getting harder, however, every time he changed his job, and the moods of depression were becoming deeper and more frequent. Finally, when Lisa was eleven and Stephen nine, disaster struck. Richard was discovered to have cheated on his expenses and was summarily dismissed without a reference. The future looked very grim for all of us, but most of all I was afraid that it would be too much for Richard, so I decided that I would take charge. That was not something that women did fifty years ago.

'I was a graduate with teacher training and some experience. If I could get a job, we wouldn't be rich, but we would have a secure and sufficient income and the strain could be lifted from Richard.

We discussed it for hours and, in the end, he agreed, because, although it was humiliating for him, he agreed with me that the most important thing was that we should stay together and keep our family secure.

'I was very fortunate. After a few months I obtained a job in the best grammar school for girls in this area. My father, who thought I had come to my senses at last, helped to pay off our debts, and we sold our detached house in Kent and bought this smaller house here.'

'You were brave!' Magda exclaimed. 'I don't imagine that married women with children were welcome in full-time jobs at that time?'

'They weren't, but fortunately the headmistress took a liking to me, as I did to her. I was determined not to let her down.'

'Obviously it was a success...'

'To a large degree, yes. Richard accepted the change well, especially when I encouraged him to take up some voluntary work. He still suffered from depression, but the burden was now less for both of us. Stephen soon made friends and eventually went to the local boys' grammar school, where he did brilliantly. I enjoyed my work and was steadily promoted.'

'What about Lisa?'

'She hated it! She missed her friends and thought that the grammar school was a poor substitute for the expensive, private convent school she had previously attended. She said I had ruined her life and, at least, I should have talked to her first. She was sure there could have been another way – if I hadn't put Richard first, as I always did.

'That was very selfish of her. After all, you had only done what you thought was best for the whole family.'

'That is what I had intended. I'd tried to make the right decision, but in one sense she was right. I had put Richard first, as I always did.'

'That can't be wrong,' Magda persisted. 'Surely even Lisa wasn't too selfish to realise that it's important to have your parents happy?'

Maggy, obviously deeply upset, didn't reply. Overwhelmed by an unusual feeling of tenderness, Magda tried to comfort her.

Although she was furious at the thought of Lisa's cruelty, she felt it would be wiser not to mention this.

Instead she said gently, 'Don't be upset, Grannie. You have me now, and I think you made the right decision, the only decision.'

'Thank you for that.' Maggy pressed her hand. 'God must have sent you to me to comfort me. Lisa wouldn't agree with you. She never forgave me. That is why when she was eighteen she decided to stay with my wealthy friend as an au pair, while we went on our first overseas holiday. You know what happened as a result of that?'

'Me!' Magda surprised them both by saying.

Suddenly, her grandmother smiled. 'How wonderful! You couldn't have made a better answer. God has really sent me consolation at last!'

'Me too!' Magda exclaimed. For a few minutes they sat smiling at each other and holding hands.

'Tell me,' Magda finally asked. 'You didn't really refuse to have her home when you knew she was pregnant?'

'Of course not!' Maggy was indignant. 'We both begged her to come home but she refused. Did she tell you differently?'

'I'm afraid so, which seems to prove that she intended to do what she did. She made her own decision. I expect she persuaded herself that it was right, but I don't see how. You shouldn't blame yourself. You tried to do what was right, but it turned out differently because Lisa was always selfish. She made a bad decision because she thought it would help her to get what she wanted. I hope she is beginning to repent, but she can't blame you or God or anyone else. She has to take her own responsibility.' She stopped suddenly. 'I suppose that's what we all have to do. I'm afraid I've never really thought about it properly. I should have done.'

'You're right,' her grandmother agreed. 'Too often we try to blame others or God for our failure, instead of looking at ourselves. Of course there are evil temptations to be considered.'

'That reminds me of school,' Magda answered almost cheerfully. 'The nuns used to try to talk to us about the problem of evil, but it was a bit deep for me, I'm afraid.'

'Perhaps the real problem for us is more practical. Perhaps we should consider why apparently sensible human beings choose to do what is wrong and obviously stupid.'

'That probably belongs to the problem of free will,' Magda replied triumphantly. 'I remember that too, but I think I'll strengthen us with more tea before we discuss it.'

It was while she was making the tea that the phone rang. It was Conrad. He sounded different. His accent was more noticeable; he was less confident. She realised that he was upset. 'I need to talk to you,' he said. 'The situation is very different from what we imagined. Can you come back?'

'No,' Magda said immediately. 'I'm staying with my grand-mother. She needs me. You will have to come here. I'll give you the address and directions.'

When he agreed to this almost without hesitation, she was convinced that her life was about to change radically.

Magda was right. Her life was changed. Conrad had brought news of her daughter, but totally different news from that which they had expected. She had not been happily adopted as Conrad had believed. Instead he had a sad story to tell.

Isobel had been quite quickly fostered with a view to adoption, but the sudden illness and death of her foster mother had caused her to be returned. A second fostering had lasted for several years but had ended when Isobel's headmistress had discovered her true situation. She had apparently been abused physically and mentally by her foster mother for several years. She had tried to tell people, but no one had been prepared to listen to her before.

'People tend not to believe a child,' Maggy commented quietly. 'It makes life easier.'

Isobel had been so badly affected that she had to spend some months in a mental hospital, but amazingly she had managed to obtain several good examination results. At sixteen she had been put into s sheltered flat while she worked for A levels and did a part-time job. At eighteen she was still there and very much alone.

Magda listened to Conrad with growing horror. 'We must go to her at once!' she exclaimed as soon as he had finished his account. When he did not immediately answer, she turned her brilliant blue eyes accusingly on him. 'Surely you agree? You are her father, after all.'

'Of course we need to help her but we must not be rash!'

'How can you talk like that? Our child has suffered for years.' She turned on him passionately 'Now we know we can't possibly let it go on any longer. But there is no need for you to worry. Now you've got the necessary information, I can do the rest by myself. You never wanted her anyway, I know.'

'That is true. There was no reason why I should have wanted her. You know that was not part of our agreement.'

'Are you saying that I cheated you?'

'Yes.' He didn't hesitate. 'But that is no reason why I shouldn't help you now. We must be sure, however, that we help in the best way.'

'I don't understand you. There is only one way to go to her and rescue her.' Magda jumped to her feet. 'I don't want to waste any more time.'

Conrad turned to Maggy with a hopeless shrug. 'Mrs Vaughan, perhaps you can explain?' he suggested.

After a moment's hesitation, Maggy said quietly but firmly, 'Sit down, Magda. Conrad is right. You must give this matter more consideration.'

'I thought you would understand!' Magda exclaimed. Nevertheless, she sat down.

'I do understand,' Maggy told her. 'Years ago you made a decision, a rather reckless one, to have a baby. You suffered greatly because of that decision, and so did that baby, as you now know. At this moment you have to make an equally important decision. It is easy to make a disastrous mistake.'

Magda was crying. 'I don't understand. All these years I've grieved for her, and now I know she is alive, I just want to see her, to love her. What is wrong with that?'

'It isn't wrong,' Maggy told her, 'but it may not be the best thing to do.'

'I don't understand. Why isn't it? Why are you agreeing with Conrad? He doesn't care. He never did!'

'I have always loved you,' Conrad interjected calmly. 'And I still do but I have been forced to be more rational, more cynical, I suppose you would say. When our child was conceived, I was in a precarious position – any small mistake could have forced me back into the world of the stateless and penniless refugee. Fortunately for you, you do not know the horror of that life.' He shrugged. 'I was selfish; I didn't want to face it.'

Magda suddenly put out her hand and touched his. 'No, if you were selfish, I was more so – and stupid, too. I didn't think clearly of the consequences.'

'That is why you must think of them now,' Maggy urged her. 'You could ruin several lives. What are you going to tell her?'

'That I'm her mother,' Magda began, 'and that I want to be a mother to her—'

'But I do not wish to be her father,' Conrad once again interrupted her. 'I've made all my arrangements to return to Lebanon. My family, especially my mother, are expecting me. I must fulfil my promise to her. I'm sorry, Magda. I can give money but nothing else. And you,' he reminded her, 'have a loyal and loving husband. Does he know anything of this? I think not.'

'No! Why should he?' She was defiant. 'I made a decision to start a new life when I married Philip. Perhaps that was silly, too. But you know, don't you, Grannie, how hard it is to make a good decision. You did, however, try. I must admit that I don't think I tried very hard.'

'That means that you must try all the harder now,' Maggy told her. 'You have to tell your husband. You know that.'

'I can't tell him now. He's gone to Belfast on private business. I can't possibly tell him this story on the telephone, even if I could get hold of him.'

'Then you must wait,' Conrad told her. 'It is possible, my dear. After so many years a few days will make little difference.'

'I'm afraid that Conrad is right,' Maggy said before Magda could reply.

'Neither of you understands,' Magda replied with frightening intensity. 'There is no point in waiting for Philip. I have waited over eighteen years, and now I can't wait any longer to hold her in my arms and to give her my love. If Philip says he can't accept her, then I shall have to leave him. I want to be a mother, a good mother. I want to feel real again.'

Conrad and Maggy looked at each other. Maggy spoke very

gently. 'Have you thought that she may not want to see you? She may not want her hard won peace disturbed?'

Magda was sobbing. 'I know you may be right,' she managed to say at last. 'She may blame me. But I have to try. I have to see her.'

To her surprise, Conrad said firmly, 'In that case, I will come with you. I will make the arrangements for us to meet her on condition that it is clear that I do not wish to take on a father's role. I will help in any other way but my first allegiance must be to my family. Do you understand?'

'I do. Thank you, Conrad.' She smiled at him.

Although she was filled with misgivings, Maggy could not think of anything helpful to say. She could see that Magda was determined to follow what might be a disastrous course. But she knew that no one could see the future or know the full consequences. She, who had so wounded her own daughter, was in no position to make a judgment.

And so it was finally decided that Conrad would make the arrangements for them to meet Isobel the following day, if possible.

Before they left, Maggy gave them final words of advice. 'Since you are determined to go, I think you must decide, both of you, to speak the full truth, however hard it may seem. Isobel certainly deserves that. Truth is essential now.'

Without hesitation, Magda agreed, and hugged her grandmother gratefully. Looking over Magda's shoulder, Maggy waited for Conrad.

'You are right,' he replied slowly. 'I'm not a good man but I can speak the truth when it is necessary. You can trust me, now.'

'I do,' Maggy told him.

Chapter Eighteen

Philip looked slowly round the living room of Noreen O'Neill's farmhouse. It was, of course, the same long, low-ceilinged room with windows at both ends that he remembered from seventeen years ago. The heavy curtains were now drawn but there would undoubtedly be the same magnificent view of the countryside.

The appearance of the room itself had changed considerably. The ugly open fire had been replaced by a modern gas fire. The presence of radiators indicated central heating which had not existed before.

Seventeen years before the room had been cold, cheerless and sparsely furnished. Now, one half was furnished as a dining room with an oak table, dresser and chairs – cottage-style oak, but well polished and cared for. This table was now laid for their meal with lace mats, glass and silver. It was all very different from the rough but substantial meals rapidly eaten at the scrubbed kitchen table years before.

The other half of the room was well furnished with a large settee and three armchairs with brightly coloured covers and many cushions. There was a bookcase and a large modern cabinet which, judging by the rack of DVDs next to it, probably contained the television.

The ornaments were mostly nondescript and there was only one picture – a somewhat dismal rendering of a grim, rocky coast. The furnishing was neither particularly tasteful nor expensive, but the room was pleasant and comfortable and indicated that Noreen had prospered since her husband's death.

As Philip's sat down in one of the armchairs, which was as comfortable as it looked, he wondered not for the first time whether he had been wise to come. Soon after their first unpleasant exchange on the phone, Noreen had rung him again, apologising for her behaviour and begging him to come and have an evening meal with her as proof that he had forgiven her. It would also give her a chance, she added, to tell him more about Liam before they met. Philip told himself that it was the latter argument which had persuaded, him but he knew that he had also been curious to meet her again.

On his arrival she had greeted him as she might greet any old friend. After taking his coat, she had ushered him into this room and then hurried away to prepare a couple of whiskeys for them.

As he sat down he took his mobile phone out of his pocket, considering whether he should ring Magda. There was no time, however, for the long talk which was really necessary. What was there for him to tell her? He had not even met Liam. Nevertheless, feeling ashamed to leave her without news which might be worrying to her, he swiftly texted a short message. 'All is well. Will ring soon. All my love, Philip.' As he was returning the phone to his pocket, Noreen came into the room carrying a tray with drinks.

He saw her eyes glance at the phone but she asked nothing; simply offering him a drink. As he was able to observe her more closely, it became obvious that she had aged considerably but gracefully. She had put on weight and her dark hair had obviously been touched up to hide the grey. By wearing an attractive sage green loose jacket over matching trousers and top, she had skilfully minimised the extra weight. True, she had a slight double chin and a few wrinkles, but her complexion was still very good. Her smile was as attractive as ever and her hazel eyes still sparkled at him.

After handing him his glass, she sat down opposite him and took a sip from her own. 'It's good,' she said, 'Bushmills maet. Try it.' Following her advice he found that it was indeed very good.

While he was trying to think what to say, she broke the silence with an abrupt and startling question. 'Gerry,' she asked, 'who the hell are you?'

Philip was not prepared for this, at least not so soon. 'What do you mean?' he challenged her. 'What the hell are you getting at? I know it's seventeen years since we met, but I haven't changed so much, surely?'

She looked at him with a slightly mocking smile. 'You've

changed surprisingly little. You're in very good shape for fifty-two and you're just as good-looking. But you know that isn't what I mean.'

'Do I?'

Ignoring him, she continued. 'Seventeen years ago I knew you as Gerard O'Dowd. You'd lived most of your life in England but your mother was Irish and had brought you up with the idea of revenging the death of her father in Northern Ireland. Because of that you were introduced to Seamas and very quickly became his friend, Liam's adopted uncle, and briefly my lover. Everything seemed to be going well – until suddenly disaster struck. Seamas's group was ambushed by the Army. He and several others were killed or wounded. Two or three others – including you – managed to escape and had to disappear.' She paused.

'That's what happened,' he agreed calmly. 'Because I cared about you, however, I risked my life to tell you. You agreed that we had to part and that I must somehow get back to England. That's the full story, isn't it?'

'Yes,' she said, almost whispering. 'That's true, but I still have no idea who you really are.' Her voice was stronger now and her eyes met his steadily. 'We knew you as Gerard O' Dowd. But who are you really?'

'Does it matter now?'

'Perhaps not. But one naturally likes to know the name of one's friend, don't you think? You see, when you gave me your mobile number, you accidentally mentioned the name of your hotel.'

'So?' he asked, hiding the anger he felt.

'I thought I'd ring the hotel, but no Mr O'Dowd was staying there.'

'Didn't it occur to you,' he asked coldly, 'that I would be very foolish, even now, to come back here as Gerard O'Dowd?'

'You once said that you loved me,' she answered sadly, 'but now you're not even prepared to trust me.'

'It's Liam,' he answered swiftly, 'that I'm not prepared to trust. Telling you might mean that I'm telling him.'

'I suppose that you believe that I deserve that?'

'Well, don't you? I gave you my address seventeen years ago, so that you could reach me if you desperately needed help. I did not expect to be appealed to, especially by Liam. My life has changed completely in those years, and furthermore—' He stopped suddenly seeing tears gathering in her eyes from which the sparkle had vanished. He could not finish the sentence, but the words 'I no longer cared about you' – although unspoken – seemed to ring out in the silent room. After a moment, he added, 'Surely, you must have realised that, if anyone was to write, it should only be you?'

She did not answer immediately but instead looked down at her glass as if the answer was to be found there. As he watched her, he noticed that she no longer wore her wedding ring but a cheap little dress ring he had once given her.

Finally, she lifted her glass, finished off her drink and then spoke directly to him. 'Of course I knew that, and was also pretty sure that you wouldn't want to hear from me after all those years – that it would be embarrassing for you.'

'You were right,' he told her, 'so why did you?'

'I didn't,' she answered at last. 'It was Liam, remember. He knew that I had your address and he forced me to give it to him.'

'Why would he do that?' He was unsure whether or not to believe her.

'Because as the years have passed he has become more and more obsessed with his father's murder and his desire to avenge it. Unfortunately, there are still quite a few in that state of mind.'

'I believe you. I have been told…' He broke off, not wanting to reveal his sources. 'He's in danger of getting into serious trouble,' he continued.

'And I don't know what to do, Gerry,' she interrupted him. 'I really don't. I suppose I had a silly hope that you might be able to help him, although I wasn't sure that the note would reach you.'

He looked closely at her, trying to decide how much truth there was in her appeal. Was it really her son who wanted him, or was it something she herself wanted? Was she, in fact, desperately trying to arouse long dead desires?

She met his look without wavering. 'It's true,' she asserted. 'I know that you're wondering whether I want to tempt you back. I might have done once. I admit I've never forgotten you, but it's obviously a bit late for that now, I'm afraid.' She smiled sadly.

He believed her; nevertheless he protested. 'But I really can't see why Liam puts his hopes on Gerard O'Dowd. After all, it's years ago and he was only five.'

'He still remembers that you were very kind to him. He loved you and he's often talked about you. You were his hero.'

'A hero who ran away! Doesn't that occur to him?'

'He knows you had to leave, as others did.'

Philip considered this calmly. 'I wonder. He may have acquired other ideas by now. Hasn't that occurred to you? Nothing stays the same, you know.'

She smiled. 'I've lived long enough to know that.'

'And what about you?' he asked. 'What did you think about my leaving? Surely, it didn't seem exactly heroic.'

'I was rather tired of heroes,' she replied with a touch of impatience. 'Surely, you must have understood that? Most women wanted peace. Women usually do.'

'And so you actually thought what?'

'That I wanted peace, if only for me. I accepted that you were in a dangerous situation and that you thought it best for all of us if you disappeared back to England and your family for a time.'

'But you thought I might come back, didn't you? That's the truth, isn't it, Noreen?'

'For a time – yes. Particularly after you gave me your address.'

'I was wrong to do that,' he told almost angrily. 'It was impossible for me to come back.' He stopped abruptly. How much could he safely tell her?

She seemed to know his thoughts. 'You can trust me,' she replied. 'I still love you.'

Before he could answer her, she stood up. 'But not now. The meal is cooked and it will be ruined if I leave it any longer. Perhaps we should have a truce while we eat.'

'Agreed.' They smiled at each other. Some of the old magic seemed to steal back.

The meal was a tasty beef casserole, one which he had always liked. They talked little as they ate, mentioning nothing at all of a personal nature. When they had finished, he stacked the dishes in the dishwasher, while she made the coffee. The kitchen, he noticed, had also been modernised. 'It seems that the farm has prospered in the last seventeen years,' he commented.

'My brother, Tom, is a far better farmer that Seamas ever was,' she told him. 'He keeps his mind on the job. He has an adjoining farm and we've run the two together. It's worked well.'

'What about Liam?' he asked as they took the coffee back to the living room.

Her face clouded. The sparkle left her eyes. 'He isn't interested. In fact, he doesn't seem to be interested in anything useful. He tried uni but gave it up after a year. Now I don't really know what he does most of the time. He's supposed to live here, but dosses down with friends in Belfast when he feels like it.' After putting the coffee cups and pot down on a small table, she sank heavily into an armchair. 'I don't know what to do with him. He scares me, Gerry, that's the truth.'

Before he could reply, she continued unexpectedly with an ironic smile, 'But there's no sense in my appealing to Gerry, is there? Gerry doesn't exist. I still have no idea who you are. My Gerry is a kind of phantom who seemed to love me and my son. And now I don't even know what to call you. Why should you care?' She waited, almost scared, for an explanation.

He surprised her and himself by saying quietly, 'Gerry still exists. My Christian names are Philip Gerrard. My father was obviously English and my real surname is Peters.' He stopped abruptly, amazed that he had told her so much. That had not been his intention. *Why did I really come?* he asked himself.

She smiled that gentle, loving smile he still remembered. 'Then you will help Liam, won't you?' she asked him.

'I'll do what I can, but I'm not sure that I can do very much.' *What a bloody liar I still am*, he thought. *I know if I tell him the truth, it'll be destructive, and yet what else can he possibly want from me? Why the hell did I come? I should have let Magda send the letter back. Why didn't I?*

'I knew you would.' Leaning forward, Noreen put her hand on his. It was a kind of caress, and the gesture which accompanied it was a caress, too.

Swiftly, he moved his hand away. 'I'm married, Noreen,' he

said. 'I told you I'd remade my life. There was nothing else I could do. I've been happily married for fifteen years.'

'Then you came because of Liam. You still care about him.'

Philip tried to think of the right answer but nothing occurred to him. Finally, he said slowly, 'I suppose that was the reason since I can't think of a better one.' Then he added, almost without thought, 'I thought of you, too. I've never completely forgotten you, although I hoped you would eventually forget me. It would be best for you.'

'Unfortunately, Gerry dear,' she replied gently, 'one can't always forget to order. I've never stopped loving you, but I would never want to hurt your wife. I'm sure she loves you.'

'She is a good, faithful wife,' he told her.

'Then let us forget everything and put Liam first. Will you try to help him?' Before he could answer they heard the sound of a car drawing up in the yard at the back. 'That must be him!' Noreen exclaimed. 'I didn't expect him tonight.'

Even as she spoke the back door was opened and then quickly and loudly slammed shut. They heard heavy footsteps cross the kitchen. The living room door was violently thrown open.

Liam stood in the doorway. He was wearing jeans with an expensive leather jacket over a black T-shirt with a vivid coloured logo. His hair, black like his father's, was worn fairly long. His face with its high cheekbones and generously curved mouth was like his mother's, but his dark eyes expressing bitter anger and resentment, reminded Philip very much of his father in his darkest moods.

Before either of them could speak, Liam laughed mockingly. 'I was right!' he said. 'I thought I would find you here. You were supposed to be coming to help me. What a joke!' He laughed again. 'Me mam's more attractive, isn't she? Just like she always was. I never realised it at the time, but making a fuss of me was just a way of getting close to her. I bet you've never thought about me since.'

Furious, Noreen jumped to her feet. 'How dare you? You're drunk, as usual, and utterly stupid.'

Standing up, Philip put a hand on her arm to restrain her. 'You're wrong, Liam,' he said calmly. 'I've never forgotten you.

Incidentally, you haven't changed much, except that you're bigger.'

'And what does that mean?' Liam was still suspicious but he seemed less agitated.

'You're furious with me, just as you used to be when I wouldn't let you do something you ought not to do – like drive the tractor. Or don't you remember?'

'Who are you?' Liam asked.

'I'm your Uncle Gerry, and I've come because you asked me to. I came straightaway leaving my job, my wife and my home. Surely that's proof that I remember you and care about you?' He held out his arms in welcome and to his relief Liam rushed towards him and hugged him.

'Uncle Gerry!' he exclaimed. 'Jesus, am I glad to see you. Please help me if you can. You've always seemed like the only real dad I ever had!'

Philip knew that this new friendly attitude could easily be destroyed but he hoped to find a way to deal with this bitter, unhappy boy. As soon as Noreen had produced a meal for her hungry son, and more coffee for herself and Philip, they decided, at Philip's suggestion, to sit round the fire and chat so that they might get to know one another better. He was not ready to be left alone with Liam. Liam even suggested that Philip might spend the night with them. He was already looking more like the lovable little boy Philip had once known. They settled down like a happily reunited family as the tentacles of the past drew them together. Unnoticed, however, the dark shadows too drew even closer.

Chapter Nineteen

The green door of Number 6 slowly opened wide in response to their knock. With almost overwhelming and conflicting emotions, Magda looked at a mirror image of her younger self. Similar large, expressive eyes looked into hers.

For a moment her heart almost seemed to stop beating, as she feared hostility or, worst of all, rejection. Suddenly, however, Isobel smiled at her and put out her hands. 'You must be my mother!' she exclaimed. 'I can't believe you're really here.'

Magda instantly took Isobel's hands in hers. She could scarcely speak but she managed to say, 'You are my daughter! It's like a miracle!'

As they embraced, Isobel looked at Conrad over her mother's shoulder. 'And you are my father, Conrad, aren't you?' she asked.

'That is right,' he acknowledged with a little bow.

At her invitation they followed Isobel along the narrow hall to a large room which was obviously both living room and bedroom. It was sparsely furnished but was extremely neat and tidy, as was Isobel, in her full and long grey skirt with a loose purple top. She wore no make-up and her black hair was brushed severely back and fastened with a purple ribbon.

Sitting now in Philip's car, being driven by his chauffeur to the airport several days later to meet him, Magda recalled clearly every moment of that afternoon. This was an important part of the story which she must tell Philip, who was, as yet, not even aware of Isobel's existence.

It was obvious, as she recalled it, that Isobel had carefully prepared for their visit. A small table by the window was laid for three with china plates and cups and saucers. There was also a plate of scones and a chocolate cake. 'I only have to make the tea,' Isobel told them as she disappeared through a door which apparently led to the kitchen. 'I won't be long.'

It was Conrad's suggestion that they should postpone serious discussion until after the tea. Even then, it was he who started the conversation. Unlike Magda and Isobel, he was calm and controlled. He did, however, Magda noticed give a truthful account of his position. 'Any man,' he said finally, 'would be proud to have such a lovely and courageous daughter, as I certainly am. But I'm not in a position to offer you a home. I am returning to Lebanon in two weeks' time. I promised my mother, who helped me to get out, that I would return when she needed me. She now needs me. I'm not a particularly good man, but that is a promise I must keep.'

'Of course you must,' Isobel replied in a quiet, cool voice. She appeared to be exercising great control over her emotions. 'I am pleased that I have met you but I'm not begging for a home. I have one here. I have learned to be independent.'

Magda, unable to find the right words, looked imploringly at Conrad. He responded quickly. 'But not from your mother, I hope. You have suffered, I know, but so has she. You must hear her story before you decide anything.'

'I'm longing to hear it,' Isobel replied softly, turning towards her mother.

Conrad stood up. 'I will leave you both for a time,' he said with a formal bow. 'I can only be an intruder.' He kissed Isobel on her forehead; took Magda's hand and kissed it; picked up his overcoat and went out through the door, only pausing to say, 'Be very careful, both of you, and try to be honest. I'll be back in an hour.'

Looking out of the car's window on the cold November afternoon, Magda remembered how she and Isobel had looked silently at each other for a few moments. Strangely, it was Isobel who spoke first. 'I think you know my story, or most of it, so perhaps you should start first, as I know scarcely anything about you.'

'You're not sorry that I've come, are you?' Magda asked.

'No, of course not!' Isobel was smiling happily. 'I think it's every orphan child's dream that one day it will find its mother. I can't believe it's actually happened. It's so wonderful! It's a dream come true!'

Magda remembered again how afraid she had been made by

Isobel's joy. Already she was scared that she would be a disappointment. Finally, she had managed to say, 'I think I'd better try to start at the beginning, when I was eight. That's the only way you can possibly understand such a weird story.' It had been even more difficult than she had imagined it would be but somehow she had managed it, while Isobel listened intently and did not interrupt her.

She had to stop when she came to the point of her daughter's birth and apparent death because she could no longer hold back her tears.

'Oh, no!' Isobel exclaimed. 'How could your own mother have been so cruel!' Jumping to her feet, she hugged Magda closely.

'I don't know,' was all Magda could manage to say.

'I think,' Isobel said firmly, 'that she knew in her heart of hearts that she had done a bad thing when she blackmailed your father, but she couldn't bear to admit it and say that she was sorry, so she became all twisted.'

Surprised, Magda looked at her. 'You seem to be wise for your years; you may be right.'

'I've had to become wise,' Isobel replied. 'Anyway, it's easier to see something when you're not involved in it.'

From that moment, everything became easier. They hugged and kissed each other and talked. Remembering her grandmother's advice, Magda had tried to be truly honest, which meant admitting some of the truth about her relationship with Conrad as far as she could bear to.

It was a shock to realise that Conrad would soon be back. 'You must return with me,' Magda said, 'we can't be parted again now that we have found each other. I can't bear to let you go.'

'I don't want to go!' Isobel exclaimed. Then she added. 'But you have a husband. Does he know about me? Or did you even keep the secret from him?'

'He doesn't know,' Magda was forced to admit. 'I decided that the best thing I could do was to forget my past and start life afresh.'

'Was that a good idea?' Isobel asked.

'Perhaps not, but it seemed sensible at the time. I wanted to put Lisa and Conrad right out of my life, even though I was no longer close to my family.'

'You must have felt very isolated, as I often have,' Isobel commented.

'I did, but then I met Philip. He seemed to offer kindness, security and friendship. I knew I could manage the rest so I agreed to marry him.'

'You mean that you weren't in love with him?' Isobel's surprise was obvious.

'Yes but I told him and he accepted that.'

'But he was in love with you?' When Magda hesitated, Isobel continued, 'Any man would be, of course; you're very beautiful.'

'So are you,' Magda answered quickly.

'No, I'm not,' Isobel was quite decided. 'I look like you, but I'm not beautiful.'

Finding herself unable to protest against such clear-sighted honesty, Magda replied, 'I suppose that's why I was tempted to marry Philip. I was weak. I don't think you would have done it.'

'I don't know – perhaps not. But you are happy, aren't you?'

'Yes, I think so.'

'Then why didn't you tell him about me?' Isobel asked earnestly.

'I'm not sure. It didn't seem necessary. But it certainly would have made things easier now.' Magda found herself anxious to get away from these questions. For the first time she realised how odd and disappointing her secrecy must seem.

'Well, you can, at least tell him now.'

'I'm afraid I can't easily do that straight away. He's on a visit to Northern Ireland to help some friends in trouble. I can hardly tell him this story over the phone.'

'Then, we shall have to wait,' Isobel said sadly.

'Of course not. You are coming home with me!' Magda was determined.

'Philip might not want me; he might not like me. You can't force me on him.' Isobel was very hesitant. 'I might not like him.' In spite of her apparent calm, she was upset. She had expected her new-found mother to speak passionately of her love and longing.

At this critical moment, they heard Conrad's knock on the

front door. A decision must be made. Without hesitating, Magda stood up. 'You must come now,' she declared. 'If you prefer it, we can call it a visit, and keep your flat until you're sure. We can get to know each other better. What do you say?'

Isobel could not resist her. 'I would love that. I do so want to know you.' And so it had been settled.

Leaning back in the car four days later, Magda admitted to herself that once again she had had her own way. Her grandmother had not entirely approved and had warned of difficulties, but Magda had hugged her while ignoring what she was saying. *Am I really like Lisa?* she asked herself. It was a disturbing thought, but she didn't let herself dwell on it. She tried instead to think what she would say to Philip in half an hour. She felt strangely remote from him.

They had had little communication while he had been away, except for brief texts. For three days there had been nothing until the message had come asking her to meet him at the airport that afternoon. She had decided that she would tell him the story as they were driven home. There would be plenty of time, she thought. As she approached the airport, however, she suddenly realised that this was neither the right time nor the right place to give him such unexpected news.

The plane was on time but it was a tedious wait until she saw him, tall and erect striding, in her direction. Seeing each other simultaneously they hurried to meet. As they kissed, she was surprised by her happiness at his return. John, the bank chauffeur, came and took Philip's bag, and they were quickly settled in the back seat ready to be driven home.

It was only then she had a chance to see how pale and tired Philip looked. 'What is the matter?' she asked. 'You look dreadful! What have you been doing?'

'I think I've been a bloody fool,' he told her. 'You were right.' She had never heard him speak so grimly.

'What do you mean? Right about what?'

'I should have let you send that letter back to Liam. Instead I went off, thinking I could put right all the bad things that had been done. As if I was some sort of knight in shining armour.'

She wanted to kiss and comfort him but she was confident that such actions would be useless at this moment. He needed to talk. 'You'd better tell me more,' she urged him. 'Do you realise that I haven't heard anything from you in the last three days? Your mobile was apparently switched off. Why did you cut yourself off from me?'

For a moment he was silent and then he said quietly, 'I was in hospital.'

'In hospital?' She stared at him, horrified. 'You're not really ill, are you? You haven't had a heart attack, or something?'

He managed a smile. 'Nothing like that, darling. I was shot in the arm and taken to hospital for treatment.'

'Shot! I don't understand. Who on earth would do that?'

'A member of a breakaway Republican group. A young man with a bitter desire for revenge.'

'You mean Liam, don't you?' Suddenly she understood.

'Yes,' he agreed. 'It was my young admirer, Liam. So much for reconciliation.' His tone was very bitter.

'What went wrong? He didn't sound hostile in the letter.'

'He wasn't quite as he seemed. I made some enquiries when I arrived and quickly discovered that Liam had a reputation. He was suspected of being a member of a breakaway group. That wasn't very promising.'

'Perhaps you should have come home then,' she suggested tentatively.

'I expect you're right.' He sounded even more depressed. 'I should have done but I had foolishly accepted an invitation from Noreen, his mother, to have a meal with her so that we could talk about Liam.' He paused. He had never mentioned Noreen to Magda and he wondered how much it was wise for him to say now. He didn't want to destroy their recently found happiness. But surely, if he had learned anything it was that there could be no security based on evasion. On the other hand his recent encounter with Liam seemed to prove that there was little security in truth.

'I suppose,' Magda said calmly, 'that you were lovers and that's how you came to give her your address which she passed on to Liam. You felt guilty. I supposed there had to be some such explanation.'

To his relief she sounded completely unemotional. 'That's about right,' he admitted gratefully. 'It was stupid, of course.'

'But quite natural,' Magda replied. 'There's no point in worrying about it now. Just tell me what happened.'

'Liam came home as we were finishing our meal. He was drunk and rather hostile, but quite soon he seemed to be friendlier and to accept that I must have come out of affection for him.'

'How ever did he come to shoot you?' Magda asked.

'That came about a quarter of an hour later. Suddenly, his mood changed. It was the sort of thing that often happened with his father. He jumped and shouted, "You haven't fucking well explained anything, Uncle Gerry. I've always known my father was shot. But who shot him, and why? That's what gets me!" He was shouting very loudly. "I reckon it was one of his so-called fucking friends. And you must know more about it. I want the truth. I'm sick of lies!" '

'What did you say?'

'I told him the truth,' Philip replied. 'I told him that an Army officer had shot his father.'

'That was risky, wasn't it?' She knew that she ought to stop this conversation and give him her news. It was impossible, however, for it was clear that her usually controlled husband needed desperately to talk. Perhaps he had been silent about some events for too long and she had never understood.

'He was demanding the truth, and that is the truth,' Philip replied. 'I didn't want him trying to find some scapegoat, so I told him that an undercover British Army officer had betrayed them; that he had shot Seamas and then disappeared. I hoped that would satisfy him, and for the moment it seemed as if it would.'

He was silent. After a minute she asked, 'But that wasn't the end, was it?'

'No, you're right. He wanted to know more.' Philip's voice was grim and cold; he looked old and tired. 'Liam jumped up again suddenly and shouted, "You're still fucking lying, you bastard! If you know that, you must know more. Which is it? Stand up, Uncle Gerry, look me in the eye and tell me the truth if you dare." I stood up and looked at him. He was mad with rage and drink. "Give me the bastard's name and I'll find him and kill him!" He took a revolver out of his pocket to prove that he meant what he said. Noreen tried to intervene but I waved her back. "Are you sure you want the whole truth?" I asked him. "It's not always what you expect, you know." I was pretty angry myself.

'He laughed, "Spit it out if you really do know it. Or admit you just ran away and left him. Stop acting the fool. I'm deadly serious."

' "So am I," I replied. Noreen tried to stop me but I ignored her. "The man was an Army colonel, Philip Gerard Peters," I told him.

'He stared at me, "But Mother said just now that that was your name!" He was almost stuttering.

' "That's right," I said, "it was me. I was working undercover. I discovered what Seamas was planning and I reported him to my superior officer."

' "But you were his friend! What a bloody bastard you are!"

' "Friendship doesn't come into it," I told him. "I did my duty and saved the lives of innocent people. I shot Seamas because he was about to kill me. You have the truth. What are you going to do about it?" ' He tried to find some comfort from Magda but she could only stare at him.

Finally, she asked, 'What did Liam say?'

'He was quite definite. He raised his revolver, pointed it straight at me and said, "I'm going to kill you, of course." Noreen cried out, but we both ignored her. I wasn't afraid. You don't forget the kind of training I have had. I should have acted immediately but I gave him a chance. That's how I got this wound in my arm. I reacted instantly to that. In a few seconds his revolver was skidding across the carpet and I had him pinned to the floor. He hadn't a chance. I could easily have killed him and the terrible truth is, Magda, that for a moment I really wanted to. I thought I'd put all that violence out of my life but I hadn't. Perhaps one never can. Fortunately, Noreen picked up the gun and threatened both of us. She had seen violence before. Ignoring my protests, she rang both police and ambulance.

'Liam was arrested and I was taken to hospital, bleeding rather badly. I don't want him to go to prison, but Noreen seems to think that it is the only way he'll learn. I doubt that but it'll keep him off the streets for a time.'

Putting his elbows on his knees, Philip buried his face in his hands. 'At least I told the truth, but it doesn't make me feel any better.' Lowering his hands, he turned to look at her. 'Do you despise me?'

She encircled him with her arms and then kissed him gently. 'I think you were very brave and I love you.' She knew that he needed to talk more, that he needed help, but as she looked through the car window, she realised that they were only about fifteen minutes away from their flat. She had failed in loving again.

'Philip,' she said urgently, 'I know that we need to talk more about this, but there is something I must tell you before we get home.'

'Surely there can be nothing more important now!' he protested, as he kissed her. 'I need your support.'

'I know you do but there is something I have to tell you. We have a visitor who has been with me for three days. Her name is Isobel Lefevre and she is my daughter.'

Before he could stop her, she swiftly told him about Isobel's birth and supposed death, and then tried to sum up her daughter's unhappy history. It was a terrible way to do it, she was aware, and he was utterly bewildered and only managed to say, 'How did you discover her?'

Although this meant bringing in Conrad, it had to be done. She told a strangely silent Philip how Lisa had told her, and Conrad had finally confirmed the story, and how he had discovered that Isobel had not been happily adopted as he had thought years before. 'When I realised how wretched her situation was, I had to rescue her,' she concluded.

The silence that followed seemed interminably long before Philip slowly raised his head and asked quietly, 'You haven't stated it, but am I to conclude that he is her father? That he was your lover?'

'Love was not involved,' she replied unhappily, 'it was a financial arrangement, but he was kind to me.'

'It is because of her botched birth that we can't have children? Don't you think you should have told me?'

'I simply couldn't,' she replied miserably. 'I wanted to forget all of it and start life afresh. Surely you can understand that?'

'Of course.' He kissed her tenderly. 'But how much of a complication is Conrad?'

'None,' she told him with relief. 'He's already decided to return to the Lebanon. He will give any help I want but he has no fatherly ambitions.' The car had already slowed down in order to turn into the side road which led to their apartments.

'Good.' Philip seemed completely calm. 'That leaves me with a chance.'

'What do you mean?' She had not expected such a response.

'It means that since you love your daughter, I should like to try to be a father to her.'

She was puzzled. 'I thought you would be angry and upset?'

'That would be foolish under the circumstances.' The car had stopped. John was opening the door. 'There is one condition, however. We both – Isobel and I – must be free to make an honest decision. No more evasions, no coercion. Understood?'

'I agree,' she told him, as John opened the door. She was surprised and relieved that Philip had accepted the arrival of Isobel so easily. Nevertheless, she had an unhappy feeling that she had failed him.

As he re-entered his home, Philip felt empty and cold. The words which he had spoken to Magda, words which sounded so calm and magnanimous, were meaningless. The truth was that he longed for the love and reassurance which he had tried to offer her for years. In his need, she had failed him.

He had made an effort to tell her so much but, after the briefest consideration, she had answered by recounting her own story. He felt exhausted in mind and body. The only resource left was to take refuge in the bodily comfort which she had always been ready to give him. It was not the love he craved and which she had seemed to offer before he left for Belfast. That was gone. If he still loved Magda, and he admitted he did, he must try once more to accept the old situation.

Chapter Twenty

Something was wrong. Four days later standing on the balcony overlooking the busy river below, Magda admitted this to herself. Something important was still lacking. Lured by an unexpected gleam of sunshine on this cold, late November day, she had gone outside after wrapping herself in a warm jacket. Her excuse had been that she needed to tend and water her plants.

That job had soon been accomplished but, instead of going in again, she had stood leaning on the rail, looking but not seeing. Glancing now at her watch, she was surprised to see how long she had been there. There was no one to worry about her. Isobel was still curled up on the couch with a book she was studying. Philip had long since departed for a series of meetings. After two days he had gone back to work. There was so much waiting for him after his absence.

She tried to get some coherence into her thoughts. Why was she so disturbed? Superficially, everything seemed to have gone amazingly well. After their arrival back from the airport, Philip had scarcely said anything more about Isobel or Liam. But he had needed the comfort he had always needed. She had made coffee while he had a shower. After that he had quickly persuaded her into bed.

Their lovemaking had been passionate and successful as it had always been. She had told herself that it was more fulfilling for her because she was learning to love him. Now, she looked steadily at that thought and wondered whether it was indeed the truth.

On that first evening when he finally appeared for supper, he had greeted a nervous Isobel with courtesy and kindness. He had appeared to accept her without saying anything that might disturb her. Isobel, who had stayed discreetly in her room until called, had been relieved and certainly not upset by this. Magda had noticed already, after their first hour together, that her daughter shrank from any great display of emotion. She spoke quietly, dressed well but unobtrusively, and seemed to desire, more than anything else, to have a definite order in her life. It seemed to her mother that Isobel had invented this as a protection against her own feeling of instability but she never spoke about it.

She had responded readily to Philip's simple questions about the life she had been living in her flat. He, on his part, had talked quite easily about his visit to Northern Ireland, even admitting that it had not been as successful as he had hoped since he had been shot by an embittered young Republican. It had all been true, but it had remained incomplete. Neither of them had made the slightest attempt to come closer to each other. Magda wondered if she had been foolish to expect that.

She had wanted to talk to both of them but somehow they had eluded her. Or was that her imagination? Some of it, perhaps but not all. Neither of them was someone who easily confided, but she felt that it was nevertheless reasonable to have expected more from them.

She had been disconcerted when, on the previous evening, Philip had told her and Isobel at supper that he had learned from a colleague of his of an excellent private sixth form college not far from their home. It seemed to him, he said, that this might be just what Isobel needed. She would get excellent tuition and much more individual attention. He had waited for them to give their opinions. He did turn first to Magda, but she felt that it should have been discussed privately with her first; nevertheless, she agreed that it seemed to be a good idea.

Isobel when asked said that it sounded ideal but that she was afraid that it would be very expensive. Replying immediately, Philip said, 'You must not worry about that. There is no problem with that. Your mother wants you to have the best, and so do I.'

There had been no more to say and it had been quickly decided that she should arrange an interview for the following week. She had satisfactorily done that before she had come out onto the balcony. Isobel had been delighted but apprehensive and Philip had been pleased. Then, why, Magda asked herself, was she unhappy and somewhat irritated when her husband had accepted her daughter so unreservedly?

It occurred to her unexpectedly that she needed someone to talk to, someone who would advise her. Her first thought had been her grandmother, but such matters could not easily be discussed over the phone. She had already spoken to Cathy and told her most of the story about Isobel. Cathy had accepted the news more calmly than she had expected, but then, as Cathy had said, so many unusual things had happened recently. It soon became quickly clear that Cathy wanted to discuss with Magda something of great importance to herself. As a result it had been agreed that Cathy and Adam should come to supper this Saturday evening. Lucy was also coming so that she could meet her new cousin.

Philip and Isobel had agreed without much comment. Philip had merely said that he preferred not to cook this time, while Isobel had simply remarked that it would be nice to meet her cousin, although she was not lonely.

As she walked back into the main room, Magda decided that she would be more sensible to concentrate on planning a menu and then on shopping for it than worrying about apparently insoluble problems. That was, in fact, the way she had lived most of her life so far.

Uncharacteristically, Philip had spent most of that Saturday working, not even at home but in his office. Isobel, although willing to help her mother, was even quieter than usual and obviously worried at the thought of the evening, although Magda tried to reassure her. Fortunately there was little time for thought or discussion as they shopped and prepared the evening meal. Philip appeared just after 6 p.m. and, for a moment, Magda hoped that there might be a brief time in which to talk; but after a quick greeting, he disappeared into the bathroom.

When he came into the bedroom and found Magda putting the final touch to her make-up, Philip was well aware that he had much to say to her – much, in fact, that he ought to say to her. Instead he said, 'You look very beautiful tonight, darling.' She was wearing a dramatically simple black skirt and close-fitting top with glowing, gold sequinned short jacket. Long gold earrings and a matching necklace completed the outfit. 'Not just beautiful, but very seductive,' he added as he kissed her.

Immediately, he was aware that he had taken the wrong direction again.

Magda was not pleased. 'You had better hurry,' was all she said, but her disappointment was obvious. Philip was surprised. Surely, their situation was as she had always wanted it to be?

There was no time to discuss this, however, for Cathy, Adam and Lucy were very punctual, and Magda had to leave him. When he joined them a little later, Catherine was still enthusiastically greeting Isobel and introducing her to Lucy. Magda was standing by the drinks looking undecided, while Adam, standing next to her, had an unusually withdrawn air.

'You're just in time to serve the drinks,' Magda told her husband, obviously relieved to see him.

They seemed to slip easily into the usual routine: whisky for the men, sherry for the women and soft drinks for the girls, at Catherine's insistence. 'They can have a glass of wine with their meal,' she decided, 'that's enough for them!' Lucy was obviously annoyed but, on getting no support from an indifferent Isobel, she reluctantly accepted the situation.

Magda's unexpected and home-cooked Chinese menu was approved warmly, and the meal passed pleasantly enough, although Adam was unusually silent, even for him; and Isobel clearly found small talk difficult. Catherine, however, was in fine form and ready to dominate the conversation as she often liked to do.

At the end of the meal she dismissed the girls to Isobel's bedroom and the men to the kitchen to sort out and make the coffee so that she and Magda could have time for a real chat.

Adam moved towards the kitchen without a word of protest. Philip looked interrogatively towards Magda to see if she had any explanation, but, when she only shook her head slightly, looking puzzled, he quietly followed Adam.

'Your Isobel is absolutely lovely,' he heard Catherine say as he closed the door, but he had a strong feeling that Isobel was not her primary interest. In his opinion, that was usually reserved for her own affairs.

He would have been amused if he had stayed for, after about two minutes on Isobel, Catherine moved swiftly to what interested her. 'I've been longing to tell you,' she told her sister. 'I've had a wonderful offer of a job! I've actually been headhunted.'

Magda frowned slightly. 'What does that mean exactly? I don't understand.'

'I've been invited to apply for the job of principal of a really first class college. It's just the sort of job I've always dreamed of, and it means about £15,000 more in salary. The buildings are mostly new; the staff's mostly very well qualified, but there's also room for expansion and for new ideas. I've met the present principal and he thinks I'm right for the job. In fact, they seem keen generally to have me. What do you think of that?'

'It sounds brilliant. You are going to apply, I presume?'

'Possibly, but I'm not quite sure. That's why I want to talk to you.' For the moment, Catherine sounded a little less self-assured. As she waited, Magda studied her sister. She looked completely the successful career woman. Her blonde-brown hair had been recently cut short and re-touched with gold. She was wearing a bright jade jacket over elegant and expensive grey trousers and matching top. The jacket cleverly concealed her extra inches. Jade earrings completed her outfit. It was suddenly clear to Magda that her elder sister spent more time and money on her appearance than she had before realised. It was obvious that money and prestige mattered more to Catherine than she had thought.

'Why wouldn't you apply? You say it's just what you've always wanted. Is that true?'

'Yes, definitely. But there's one drawback, it isn't in London. In fact, it's about sixty five miles to the west.'

'Good heavens! Surely you don't want to travel all those miles every day, especially when you're starting a new and very responsible job? But, perhaps Adam would be willing to move...'

Catherine laughed. 'Don't be silly! You know Adam loves his cosy little job. He's not in the least ambitious and he hates change.'

'And, of course, you don't want to move the children in the middle of their exam years. It's a pity, but it seems to have come at the wrong time. I'm so sorry.'

Catherine, however, was not so easily defeated. 'It can be

done,' she answered sharply. 'I can get a little flat near the job and come home at weekends.'

'But surely that would be breaking up your family at a time when they particularly need you? I thought you loved them.' Magda sounded both shocked and surprised.

'Of course I love them. I only went back to work so that they could have a decent education. Adam was never willing to exert himself enough. Soon, they'll need money for university, and I'm the one who's expected to provide it. Well, I'm sick of it. I've devoted myself to them and they just make use of me. They take all they can get and don't care a damn. Adam is the same.'

'Are you saying that you feel unloved?' Magda asked. It wasn't the first time Catherine had hinted at this but she had never before sounded so determined.

'Yes, I bloody well am!' Catherine said fervently. 'All I've ever wanted in life is to have someone who really loves me. You know that.' She was almost crying.

Magda answered her quietly. She was almost afraid of Cathy in these moods. 'It is important, of course, but it's not the only thing that matters, surely?'

'It's easy for you to say that,' Catherine retorted bitterly, 'because you've had it for years! It's obvious that Philip adores you. He always has.'

'It seems to me,' Magda replied without giving it sufficient thought, 'that, although it's flattering to be loved, it's more important to love.' As she spoke, she seemed to hear a little voice in her head saying, *You're absolutely right, Magda. That is what is lacking in your life. You have never loved anyone, have you?* Turning to Catherine, she continued aloud, 'After all, that's what we were taught, isn't it? We were told to love one another.'

'For God's sake,' Catherine almost shouted at her, 'don't bring religion into it! We have had enough hypocrisy in our family, haven't we? Although I never realised how much until you had your demonstration on Father's birthday.'

'I apologise for that.'

'I don't really see why you should. He deserved it. You know, I used to think he loved me, but that was probably another illusion.'

'I don't think so,' Magda said quickly. 'He was always very proud of you. I believe Adam loves you, too. And you know I do.'

'I think you might, but there's an awful lot you never told me until recently.'

'Lisa got between me and everyone. She cut me off from people, I hated it.'

'It seems to me,' Catherine unexpectedly replied. 'that, as I suspected, you've never really loved Philip. It hasn't been possible.' Before Magda could answer her, she continued, 'I suppose you feel differently now you've found Isobel. She's really someone you can love, if that's what you want. Is it?'

'Of course! Don't you?'

'No! I told you that I want to be loved passionately. Since I can't have that, I'm going to put myself first for a change. I'm going to go all out for my career.'

'You always were ambitious – admit it.' Magda smiled at her sister.

'You know I wasn't!' Catherine was indignant. 'I always wanted to have a husband and children and stay at home.'

'Then why didn't you?'

'Because there were more important things to consider. We needed more money. Adam wouldn't bother, so I had to earn it. You've never had any of these problems, Magda. Philip is wealthy and successful and he loves you. You only worked to please yourself.'

'And because I didn't have any children,' Magda reminded her sister. She was also beginning to feel indignant.

'And now that problem's solved. But don't be too sure, Magda. As they grow up, these days, kids seem to have a clever way of being both independent and dependent. It's understood that they go their own way entirely, but you pay for it. Isobel is a charming girl, but I expect she'll soon learn the rules. Lucy will be ready to help her, I'm sure.'

'I don't think I'm ready to face that yet,' Magda told her softly.

'I'm sorry, dearest,' Catherine said quickly. 'I shouldn't have talked like that. Enjoy yourself while you can. Forget my non-sense and tell me if you really think I'm wrong to apply for this job. I don't think I can carry on as I am.'

'Then you'd better apply and see what happens. But do be sure it's what you really want.'

As soon as they were safely in the kitchen, Adam insisted that Philip should sit down, while he did what was necessary. 'I can stack dishes and make coffee,' he insisted, 'and, although you don't say anything, that arm of yours must still be painful.'

'It is, actually,' Philip admitted, smiling. 'But you must remember I was a soldier for several years. I've been wounded before. I know where everything is. I'll be quicker.'

'We don't need to worry about being quick,' Adam told him. 'Catherine needs quite a bit of time to tell her news to her little sister and to persuade her to approve.' He made no attempt to hide his irony.

'What news?' Philip was curious now.

As he began to fill the dishwasher, Adam quietly told him of Catherine's latest plan for her future.

'But surely you don't want her to do that? I can't imagine anything worse!'

Adam shrugged his shoulders. 'Of course not! But that doesn't count for much. Surely, Magda must have mentioned how often Catherine's changed her job?'

'Probably, but I'm afraid I've never really taken much notice.'

'Why should you?' Adam filled the coffee grinder but before he pressed the switch, he remarked, 'Catherine is the sort of person who's never satisfied with what she's got. The grass is always greener, as they say.'

Philip waited while the coffee was being ground then, as Adam transferred it to the percolator, he said, 'But what about you and the children?'

Without looking at Philip, Adam replied quietly, 'I've tried arguing with her in the past but I've never had any effect, even though I've been proved right several times. I hate arguments, particularly useless ones, so I'm not opposing her this time. It probably only makes her more determined anyway.'

'I expect you're right,' Philip agreed. 'But this is a fairly drastic move, isn't it? Can you afford to let it happen unopposed?'

'You're not suggesting that I forbid her, are you? That wouldn't be very popular!'

'God forbid!' Philip smiled at him.

'But seriously,' Adam unexpectedly persisted, 'what would you do or say if Magda wanted to do something like that?' He continued his preparations while waiting for an answer.

Philip tried to consider the question before replying, quickly realising that he had no idea. He and Magda never seemed to have serious arguments; their life together had run pretty smoothly. It was not, however, he admitted to himself, because they had such a close relationship, but more because they had kept their secrets and had avoided upsetting each other. He was surprised that he had never thought about it before. Now things were different. Or were they? Aware that Adam was waiting for an answer, he said quickly, 'I'm afraid I haven't a clue. Nothing like that has ever happened.'

'Obviously, you have the perfect marriage,' Adam replied bitterly. 'We certainly don't.' Before Philip could reply to this embarrassing comment, he added, 'Magda is perhaps the only person who could stop her.'

'Magda doesn't do things like that,' Philip replied quickly, then wondered why on earth he had said it. Adam had never talked in this way before and he found it uncomfortable.

As if sensing this, Adam said briskly, 'Show me the china and I'll prepare the tray.'

'I'll do that.' Philip was relieved. 'You keep your eye on the coffee. It's nearly ready.'

A few minutes later when they re-entered the living room, Catherine exclaimed triumphantly to Adam, 'Magda thinks it a good idea for me to apply for the job! At least I have one supporter.'

'But only if you're really sure that's what you want,' Magda interposed quickly.

It was obvious that Catherine was irritated by Magda's intervention but she merely said, 'I am sure, so I do have your support.' Magda only smiled.

'I won't oppose you,' Adam said quietly, 'if it's what you need to make you happy.'

'It's a challenge,' Catherine replied. 'I'm sure I can do the job, and do it well.' She looked directly at Philip. 'You must know what I mean. You must be ambitious. You're very successful.'

'I'm afraid I didn't have to struggle for it. It was unfairly given to me.' He tried to make his lack of interest clear by his tone.

'But you must have been ambitious when you were in the Army. You rose to quite a high rank, didn't you? That couldn't have been an accident.' Her voice and tone were both challenging.

Astounded, Magda looked at her sister, realising that she had never considered Philip's life in the Army. She wondered what he would say.

'You're right,' he relied coolly. 'Clever of you to think of it. I was ambitious then.'

'So you don't despise ambition, then?' Magda recognised Cathy at her most persistent.

'Of course not! I couldn't, could I?' Philip was unperturbed.

'What would you say, then, if Magda wanted to do what I want to do?'

'Don't be silly, Cathy,' Magda interrupted quickly. 'You know I'm not ambitious. You've always said so.'

Ignoring her, Catherine looked past her at Philip. For some reason she was determined to challenge him. Philip only laughed. 'I think it's unlikely as Magda says. But, if she was determined, I don't think I would forbid her.' He smiled at his wife and then turned towards Catherine. 'I wouldn't be *happy* about it, however, as no doubt you guess.' He too was challenging.

'Why not? Since you say you love her and want to make her happy?'

'It wouldn't make *me* happy,' he replied easily, 'and, therefore, it wouldn't make Magda happy. To give you one important reason, I would miss the happy sex life we enjoy far too much, and I'm sure Magda would, too.'

Magda couldn't help smiling, for it was clear that he had ended the discussion. Catherine flushed red. She hated talk of sex, as Magda knew. 'Well, that puts me in my proper place,' Magda said, to make a joke and to placate her sister.

'If that's where you want to be, good luck to you. I thought you might have higher aspirations.' It was a dangerous moment.

Adam saved the situation by offering Magda a cup of coffee. 'Taste this carefully,' he advised her. 'I made it. I thought your heroic husband should rest his wounded arm after a busy day.'

Catherine took the hint. 'Oh dear!' she exclaimed. 'I'm afraid I haven't asked you how you are. Is it still painful?'

Philip smiled. 'More irritating than painful.'

From then on, much to Magda's relief, and Adam's too, she suspected, the talk became general until it was time go. Isobel and Lucy joined them and it was clear that they were not happy with one another. Lucy was definitely in one of her resentful moods and Isobel was even paler and quieter than usual. Furthermore, Lucy made it very clear that she was ready to depart. Cathy and Magda looked at each other but dared not say anything.

When they had gone, Philip subsided with obvious weariness on to the sofa. Isobel took out the coffee tray while Magda sat down next to her husband. Several matters were worrying her, but she decided that she must tackle Isobel first.

'What is wrong?' she asked her daughter as she came back into the room. 'Didn't you get on with Lucy?'

Isobel hesitated and then said almost defiantly, 'I don't really like her. She's very immature.'

'Look at her mother and you'll understand why,' Philip advised her tiredly, much to their surprise.

'I don't want to be horrid,' Isobel continued. 'It's simply that she thinks she knows everything and she knows nothing. I know you don't like Aunt Catherine, Philip, but she is Lucy's mother, and Lucy shouldn't lie to her and make fun of her, should she?'

'Whatever do you mean?' Magda asked.

'I'm sorry. I'd better go to bed. I shouldn't have said anything.'

'Nonsense!' Philip sat up suddenly and spoke firmly. 'You can't leave it like that. You have to tell your mother the truth. Please.'

As Isobel still hesitated, Magda insisted, 'You must tell me what you mean. Catherine is my sister and I love her.'

Isobel suddenly burst out, 'The truth is that Lucy has a boy-friend and her mother doesn't know. She pretends she's going out with a girl friend but she's with him. I don't think he's at all nice. I told her that she was taking a big risk.'

'Do you mean she is sleeping with him?'

'She hasn't exactly done that – yet – but I think she will soon. She believes that he loves her. I tried to tell her that boys often say that but it doesn't mean much. She asked what I knew about it. In the end, I told her how I know.'

'What did you tell her?' Magda asked. She felt suddenly afraid and clutched Philip's hand. When Isobel hesitated, she said angrily, 'You must tell me. You can't stop now!'

'I hoped I'd never have to tell you,' Isobel replied softly. 'Just before I was sixteen I was raped.'

'Raped!' Magda stared at her daughter. She would have rushed to her, but Philip restrained her while he said calmly, 'Sit down, Isobel, and tell your mother the whole story. If you prefer it, I'll remove myself.'

'No, I'd rather you remained,' Isobel told him. 'You're the first good man I've ever known.'

Her pitiful little tale was soon told, in spite of the obvious anguish it cost her to tell it. Just before she had been put into her flat, she told them, she had been allowed to work on Friday and Saturday evenings in a café. Her job was to help with the clearing of the tables and the washing-up. It was boring but she was glad to be with normal people and earn a little money. 'You see,' she explained, 'I was lonely. I'd spent about three months in a special mental hospital for adolescents. They treated us cruelly sometimes, but if you protested it only made it worse.' She didn't look at them as she whispered her story but stared steadily down at her tightly clasped hands. 'When I came out after I'd taken my GCSEs, I went to a different home, where the care assistant clearly thought I was crazy. That's why I was so glad to get away, and very pleased when this man spoke to me in the café. He knew nothing about me so he didn't think I was mad. We became friends. I trusted him.'

Philip and Magda looked at each other. It was clear what was coming. Magda longed to say something but Philip shook his head. The little whisper carried on. Isobel's hands were more tightly clasped then ever. 'Then, one Saturday,' she told them, 'he caught up with me as I was walking home. It was a lonely road, but I'd never been worried and I certainly wasn't worried with him. After saying he wanted to talk to me, he led me into a little side turning and he raped me there…'

The little voice faded away completely at this point, but Philip still held Magda's hand and restrained her. After a moment's silence Isobel raised her head. She was deathly pale as he gazed at them with her pain-filled dark eyes. 'I was so ignorant,' she told them. 'I didn't realise at first what he wanted to do. I knew the facts, of course, but they'd never seemed possible. I couldn't believe it would just happen, but it did. That was what I was trying to tell Lucy.'

Two large tear formed in her eyes and rolled slowly down her cheeks. 'Do you understand?'

'We understand,' Philip told her gently.

'Oh, my dearest child!' Magda exclaimed, 'What did you do?'

'I couldn't fight back. I didn't know how to. He told me to accept it, then it wouldn't hurt too much. He left me without a word afterwards. Somehow I stumbled back to the home and told them.' Suddenly the whisper became a wail of despair. '*I don't think anyone believed me. They said I must have made it up! Oh, God, how could I?*' She began to shake.

Magda took both of her hands in hers. 'Tell me,' she asked urgently, 'did they take you to a doctor?'

Isobel could hardly speak, but she managed to stammer, 'Yes. I – I think he believed me. At least he gave me the morning after pill.' She couldn't say any more. Shuddering and sobbing, she allowed Magda to hold her in her arms and stroke her hair.

When she was becoming calmer, Philip who had been silent, stood up announcing that he would make a soothing cup of cocoa for them all. His sudden assumption of the fatherly role not only surprised his wife but delighted Isobel. 'He is so very kind,' she murmured, as Magda after wrapping her in a shawl, made her comfortable on the sofa.

In a few moments Isobel began to cry again. 'I should have told you,' she said, holding Magda's hand. 'I was very wrong not to be honest with you when you have both been so open and loving. But I was happy, you see, and afraid that you might despise me and I would be unhappy again. I'm so sorry. You do still love me, don't you?'

'I'm your mother,' Magda replied. 'I love you, Isobel. You need never feel lonely nor afraid now.' *Oh God*, she prayed, *help me to be true to what I say. You know I know nothing about love.*

'Do you think Philip will despise me?' Isobel asked her timidly.

'Of course not,' Magda told her, 'but let him speak for himself.'

About twenty minutes later, when they were sipping their cocoa, Philip did speak for himself. 'I understand more than you imagine, Isobel,' he said quietly.

'That's because you're very kind,' she smiled at him.

'It's more because I had a very unhappy experience that changed my life. I thought I would never get over it but I did.'

'How did you do it?'

'Like you, I was given a chance to start life afresh. I took it, determined to put the past behind me.'

'I thought I could do that, but...' her voice trailed away.

'It is hard,' he admitted, 'but it can be done, especially if you have someone to help you. I had Magda.' He smiled tenderly at his wife. Although she smiled back, she found herself unable to reply in words. Instead, she found herself wondering whether she had ever really helped him, and admitting that she had never actually thought about it before.

'I've got Magda, too,' Isobel said, holding her mother's hand. 'And I've also got you, haven't I? Please don't send me away, Philip,' she begged him. 'I'm so happy here. It's like a miracle.'

'You have no need to worry,' he told her. 'You are Magda's daughter, and that makes you mine.' He stood up. 'I suggest you go to bed now. We'll talk in the morning.' Bending down, he kissed her lightly.

'Don't be too long, darling,' he said to Magda as he reached the door. 'I'll be waiting for you.'

'Perhaps now we will be able to talk properly,' Magda hoped as she slipped into bed where Philip awaited her. But it was the usual comfort of her body that he desired. Tonight, however, she was able to respond with unusual warmth and eagerness. She felt closer to him than ever before. *Perhaps this really is love*, she thought, as she yielded readily to him.

Why did she remember the words that had embarrassed Cathy? 'I would miss the sex we enjoy.' Was that the complete truth? Did love only ever mean that?

Chapter Twenty-one

'It's your sister.' Philip smiled slightly as he handed the phone to Magda. 'I'm afraid she doesn't sound exactly amiable.' Magda had a slight feeling of dread. Cathy in one of her 'moods' was not easy to deal with.

Before she could say anything, Cathy was speaking. 'I suppose you're not very pleased at being bothered so late on a Sunday evening. I'm sorry but I've tried twice to speak to you earlier and your mobile was switched off. I felt I must make one more attempt. Have you been out?'

'Yes. We went to see our house in Chichester and the boat. Philip wanted to get away from London. He's been very busy lately.'

'I suppose Isobel went with you?'

'Of course!' Magda was puzzled. 'We could hardly leave her here. What do want to say? Is it important?'

'I think it's very important. I've just had a flaming row with Lucy and she finally told me all the horrible things that Isobel told her last night. She was very upset. I suppose you haven't heard anything about it?'

'Isobel did tell us eventually,' Magda replied quietly. 'We realised that something was wrong. But why were you so angry with Lucy?'

'She was so difficult last night and today I couldn't put up with her any more. She was so rude. Finally, she told me and I thought I ought to make sure that you knew.'

'Isobel is my daughter,' Magda protested.

'Of course, but you hardly know her, do you, dear? I think we ought to have a talk. I am a bit more experienced than you. I love you dearly and I don't want you to be hurt any more.'

Magda felt herself struggling against the old, protective Cathy. 'I don't really understand you. She shouldn't have spoken to Lucy, perhaps but surely it's best forgotten? Isobel was obviously more sinned against than sinning.'

'Do you believe her story, then? I'm not sure that I do, and Lucy seems to be doubtful. By the way, she's not in the room, is she?'

'Not at the moment. She's helping Philip make us a snack.'

'She is very ready to help Philip. I've noticed that.'

'If I understand you properly, you're being very spiteful!' Magda was angry.

'I'm sorry if I've upset you, dearest, but it struck me once or twice yesterday evening. It's natural, perhaps, in her situation; but you don't really know her, do you?'

Suddenly overwhelmed by that sad truth, Magda agreed unhappily, 'You're right, I don't know her.'

'I'm sorry, love. I know it's not your fault. I only want to help you as I've always wanted to. Other people don't realise it, but I know you are far more vulnerable than you seem.'

'Please, Cathy, tell me what you're trying to say.'

'I just want to remind you that Isobel is Lisa's granddaughter and may be more like her than you, especially after the difficult life she has had. I think—'

'I'm sorry,' Magda interrupted her. 'I can't talk about this now.'

'Do you mean that Isobel has just come into the room? That's why I want us to meet so that we can talk freely. Can you meet me for lunch on Tuesday in that little place near college where we've met before? I have an extra hour for lunch that day, so we can have a good chat. We have a lot to talk about, haven't we?' When Magda still hesitated, Catherine continued, almost pleading, 'I also want to tell you a bit more about my plans. I value your advice, you know. But I do also think that you should hear all that Lucy told me. It might be useful to compare their stories, don't you agree?'

'All right, Cathy, I agree. I'll see you on Tuesday at midday.' Magda ended the conversation abruptly as Isobel offered her a tray of food before seating herself on the sofa next to Philip, Magda's usual seat. She put the phone down quickly, remaining seated in her armchair by the fire and feeling as if she had been deliberately isolated.

Could Cathy have actually observed something which she had

missed? she wondered. Even as she thought this, before she could even tell herself she was being silly, Philip casually changed the situation. He stood up, still holding his plate of sandwiches, and said easily, 'I think I'd prefer a whisky to a coffee. Would you like one, darling?' he asked Magda, as he put his plate down next to hers on the table near her chair. Magda agreed, smiling brilliantly at him. She longed to tell him what Cathy had hinted and wondered if he would agree.

When they were finally alone, however, she merely told him that Cathy was upset by Isobel's conversation with Lucy and wanted to discuss it more with her.

'She's right for once. I think you should discuss it,' he commented to her surprise. 'Neither of us knows Isobel very well. It's a sad story she's told us, but I felt there was an element of manipulation in it. The trouble is, of course, that Catherine is also a manipulator.'

'What do you mean? She has always cared for me.'

'Perhaps.' He wondered how much he dared to say. 'But, if you look back, I think you'll see that she's often been missing when you've needed her most.' He stopped suddenly. Magda waited for him to say more but he had apparently finished. 'Don't let it worry you, just be a bit wary.'

She hoped he would say more but, as he kissed her, she understood that he had no desire to do so at that moment.

Monday lunchtime brought an even more disturbing phone call. Magda had just returned with Isobel from a satisfactory interview when the phone rang in Philip's study.

'Could I speak to Mr Peters, please?' It was musical male voice with a slight accent. She was sure that she hadn't heard it before.

'I'm afraid not,' she replied. 'He's not here, at present. This is his home number.'

'Who is that speaking?' the young man asked somewhat to her surprise.

'I'm Magda Peters,' she told him, 'his wife.'

'Then, for the love of God, can you get a message to him? I must speak to him.' In his agitation his accent was more marked and suddenly it occurred to her that it was an Irish accent. 'Are you Liam?' she asked him.

'Jesus! How did you know that? I didn't mean to tell you.'

'Why not? Is it a secret?'

'No, I just felt you wouldn't want to speak to me. If Uncle Gerry has told you what happened.'

'I could hardly avoid knowing, could I? Especially when he came home with a bandaged arm after days in hospital.'

'Oh my God! You know then that I shot him! It was a terrible, terrible thing to do. I can't believe it!' The words came pouring out of him. As a counsellor for many years, she recognised his need to talk and to tell. Her instinct was to encourage him, to listen to him without moral judgment.

'Yes, he told me, but I imagine you thought you had a reason for what you did.'

'I loved him, you see.' The torrent of words could not be stopped. 'I only knew him for a few months and it was years ago but I loved him, really loved him. He was so good to me. I always thought that, if anyone could help me to find out who killed my dad, it would be Uncle Gerry. But he had disappeared, and everything seemed to get worse as I got older. Then, I discovered that my mam had his address, and so I made her give it to me. She was right. I shouldn't have done it. I should just have left it alone.' There was a sob in his voice now, in spite of his efforts to restrain it. 'She said I should forget the past and get on with my life. What do you think?'

A sudden conviction hit Magda. 'It's true, you know. I have heard it said that you can't change the past, but you can ruin the present. The trouble is that we don't realise it.' She paused struck by the thought. *How true!* she admitted to herself. *I should have understood that long ago!*' Remembering the waiting Liam she said aloud, 'I can't blame you for not realising that.'

'But you must blame me for trying to shoot Uncle Gerry! He is your husband!'

'I certainly don't want him to be shot! But why did you do it? You said you loved him.'

'I did. Jesus, I still do, but I hate him, too. Do you know who killed my dad? It was Uncle Gerry himself! The fucking bastard! He was a British spy. He pretended to be my dad's friend but he killed him. Some fucking friend! I don't suppose he told you that bit.' He was crying openly now.

'You're wrong,' Magda said quietly. 'Philip told me everything.'

'And did he tell you,' he challenged her, 'that he bloody nearly killed me? I thought he was going to break my neck!'

'Yes, he told me that.' Magda remained calm. 'He also told me that for a moment he wanted to kill you. His Army training reasserted itself.'

'Oh my God,' was all Liam could say at first. 'I suppose I deserved it,' he then continued. 'But he killed my dad, remember. What do you think? What is right?'

'There's no easy answer.' Magda spoke slowly, hoping that the words she said would be the right ones. She knew from experience how easy it was to go wrong. 'You have to remember the situation. It was a war really, wasn't it? Your Uncle Gerry was a soldier, who had been ordered to do a dangerous job, to save lives as he believed.'

'But he seemed to be Dad's friend. Don't you understand?' Liam protested. 'How can you kill your friend?'

'There's a lot to discuss.' Magda replied, 'and I can't possibly do it now. I like to give you one thought to consider. Your father was a soldier too, wasn't he?'

'Yes, of course. He was a Commander in the Irish Republican Army.'

'Then, don't you think that, if he had been ordered to do it, he would have killed your Uncle Gerry, although they were friends?' The silence that followed this question made her feel pretty sure that she had said the right words. 'What do you think?'

'Jesus!' He exclaimed finally in a despairing voice. 'I guess you may be right. I just don't understand anything. I don't suppose I ever did. But I wanted to try to put things right. To tell Uncle Gerry how sorry I am for what I did.'

'You don't want to shoot him again?' Magda asked him gently.

'No, especially not after the way he's treated me since.'

Magda was puzzled. 'I don't understand. I thought you had been arrested.'

'I was. That was Mam's idea. She thought it might give me a shock. But Uncle Gerry put an end to that.'

'How? I didn't know.'

'It seems that he got his solicitor to persuade the police by telling them that he didn't intend to press charges because it was all a mistake, a silly game that went wrong. I was sent home with a warning. I was still angry at first, but then it suddenly hit me what an amazing guy Gerry is! You've made it much clearer, too. Thank you. I just hoped I could see him.'

'I didn't say it was totally impossible. I can't put you in touch with him now. He rang me this morning to tell me that he had been summoned to the Treasury for a meeting, so I can't expect to speak freely to him until he comes home. You can ring him this evening, but it might be better if I spoke to him first.' As she said this, she realised that she was both hurt and angry with Philip for keeping her in the dark. *We are no closer than we were*, she thought bitterly.

'That would be brilliant, if you're willing to do it. But I would like to see him tonight, if possible.'

'I thought you were in Belfast!' she exclaimed.

'No, I flew in to London today. I found a room in a cheap hotel someone recommended. Please help me… I do so want to see him. I feel he's the only guy who can put me right. After what he's just done, I'm sure he still cares for me. You'll help me, won't you?' His voice was soft, lilting and very persuasive. 'Uncle Gerry told Mam that you were very beautiful but I think you're also very good. Your voice is beautiful and very kind. Please help me.'

Blatant though it was, Magda found herself still affected by the flattery and willing to help. 'It would be better if I prepared him first.' There was something definitely appealing about Liam. It also seemed right to her that Philip should face the situation he had created. 'Do you understand me?' she asked Liam.

'I do! God bless you! May all the saints be praised!' To her amazement he had gone, leaving her to wonder what arrangements, if any, they had made.

Fortunately, during supper that evening Isobel kept the conversation going by telling Philip about her interview and the books she had been recommended to read. Weary as he was, he seemed glad to relax with this simple conversation while enjoying the good food and well-chosen wine which his wife had provided.

He didn't appear to notice that Magda was unusually silent. At last, after a strong hint from Magda, Isobel retired to her room, leaving them free to talk.

After helping himself to a brandy, Philip seated himself on the sofa, obviously expecting Magda to join him. She, however, sat down on a nearby armchair. As she began to talk to him, she realised that she still felt hurt and angry, although she tried not to show it.

'I received a strange and unexpected phone call at lunchtime,' she began. 'It was actually meant for you, but as you weren't available I did my best to deal with it.' She paused for a moment.

'Who was calling?' he asked as he sipped his brandy.

'I didn't realise at first, but eventually I discovered that it was Liam; he desperately wanted to speak to you.'

'I hope you told him that it was unnecessary.'

'It was difficult for me to deal with him,' she replied coldly, 'because you had forgotten to tell me that you had apparently secured his release through your solicitor. Why didn't you tell me?'

'I wanted to forget the whole business and put it, and Liam, in the past – where they belong.' His voice was cold almost angry.

It was so unlike him that she stared at him. 'Aren't you being rather unkind? Liam doesn't feel like that. He needs help; he's very confused. He loves you and thinks you were splendid to get him off the hook, but at the same time he's still angry and hurt. He really needs to see you.'

'It wouldn't do any good.' Philip was apparently unmoved. 'I know you want to help, darling, but you don't understand mixed-up kids like Liam.'

His apparent condescension angered her more. 'I do understand,' she retorted. 'I'm used to people like Liam. You've forgotten, I've been a counsellor for years. I'm not just a pretty doll!'

'I'm sorry,' he apologised. 'I didn't mean to offend you.'

'It doesn't matter about me,' she told him. 'Liam has come to London to see you and to talk to you. He needs to.'

'London? I'm sorry,' Philip replied firmly. 'I neither want to see him nor talk to him. It would do harm, not good. I'll get my solicitor to see him.'

'I can't do anything about it. He's already come to London, but I don't know how to get in touch with him. I'm sorry. We'll have to wait for him to phone again.'

Suddenly, to their surprise, the front doorbell rang, long and loudly. They heard Isobel hurrying into the hall. 'You must stop her!' Philip exclaimed. 'It is pointless for me to see him.'

It was too late, however. Isobel had already opened the door and was trying to discover the identity of their visitor.

Standing up abruptly, Philip moved into the front hall, followed by an anxious Magda.

'Good evening, Liam,' Philip greeted his visitor calmly but coldly. 'I believe you want to speak to me. If so, we had better go to my study.' Without waiting for an answer, he turned, motioning to Liam to follow him.

'Shall I get you some coffee?' Isobel asked timidly.

'No thanks. It won't be necessary. We shall only be a few minutes.'

'Oh dear!' Isobel exclaimed, 'I think Philip is angry. Was I wrong to let him in?'

'It's not your fault,' Magda reassured her. 'If it's anyone's fault, it's mine. I never imagined that he would turn up just like that.' She sat down again in her armchair by the fire. She felt oddly cold and almost afraid.

'I think I'll go to bed,' Isobel said. 'Or would you rather I stayed?'

Magda looked at her. *This is my daughter*, she thought, *and there is no understanding between us.* But then why should there be? That was what Cathy had been suggesting. 'No, thank you, dear,' she said at last to the waiting Isobel. 'It's better if you go to bed. They may be some time, and Philip may be angry.'

Ignoring Isobel's silent appeal for an explanation, she turned back to the fire. It was a relief when the door closed behind her daughter.

She admitted to herself that because of her hurt and anger she might have made things worse for Liam. She prepared for a long wait. To her surprise, however, it was only a few minutes later when she heard them in the hall. They seemed to part quickly but amicably.

Philip returned immediately to the sitting room and took his favourite place on the sofa, obviously expecting her to join him. 'You were right,' he told her. 'After all the other things I had done, I had to see him. Of course it might have been better if I'd taken your first advice and simply returned the letter. Thank you, darling, for helping me when you spoke to him.'

'I don't understand. How did I help?'

'Apparently by telling him two things which he thought over very carefully.'

'I can't imagine what they were…'

'I'll remind you. One was that however much misery you caused, you couldn't change the past but you might ruin the present! Good advice that – for me too, incidentally! Secondly, you reminded him that his father and I were both soldiers and that, if his father had been in my position, he would probably have shot me! He seemed to find that a telling point.'

'And what do you think?' She was begging silently for his confidence.

He seemed to consider the matter before he said lightly, 'Nothing much, I'm afraid, except relief. They are very good points, and I'm very grateful that you've helped to end this silly crisis and stopped me from acting like a complete idiot! I've had a busy and irritating day, and all I want now is to relax with you at last.'

He held out his arms to her. 'Come over here,' he begged her, 'and let me give you the hug you deserve.' As he held her close, he whispered, 'I would like to go to bed. Do you agree? Or would you like a drink first?'

'I don't need a drink. Let's go to bed.' She returned his kisses as she had done so many times. Perhaps when they made love she would feel something. Later, however, when he had fallen asleep holding her in his arms, she had to admit that all she felt was disappointment added to her original anger and hurt. The love she had recently felt stirring seemed to have died prematurely.

At first, having lunch with Cathy was comforting. It was like opening one's diary and slipping back into a less complicated time. In the past they had often eaten in this quiet, unpretentious restaurant, chatting happily. The menu changed little. There was a limited choice but it was all fresh and home-made. This time they chose wild mushroom soup, followed by steak and kidney pie, knowing it would be tasty and well cooked – much better for them, or so Cathy asserted.

Catherine was wearing a smart brown trouser suit with a gold coloured jumper and a double string of pearls. Her rounded curves and her friendly smile prevented her from looking too much the aggressive career woman. Before slipping into the seat opposite her, Magda took off her dark blue jacket with its artificial fur collar to reveal a simple, close-fitting sapphire blue jersey dress, relieved only by the large sapphire and diamond pendant and a matching ring. The dress emphasised her slim figure, the intense blue of her eyes and the darkness of her hair.

'You just can't help it, can you?' Catherine asked with mock irritation.

'What?' Magda raised her eyebrows.

'Looking beautiful! Still, I know I can't compete, so I simply have to bask in your reflected glory.'

'Rubbish!' Magda smiled at her. 'I'm just your little sister.'

'This is lovely, isn't it?' Catherine said suddenly. 'Just like old times, when things didn't seem to be so complicated, or at least I didn't know they were.'

'Perhaps it's better sometimes not to know the truth,' Magda suggested.

'You can't believe that is right. That's not what we were taught in our youth. But then we were taught by hypocrites, especially if you consider our dishonourable parents!'

'Don't spoil everything,' Magda warned her. 'Choose a half bottle of wine, instead.'

'Sensible suggestion!' Cathy smiled happily at her sister.

It was only when they had been eating for a few minutes that Catherine said, 'I've decided to apply for that post. It's now or never.'

'Why do you say that? You're being a bit melodramatic, aren't you?'

'Because I'm already forty-four, and chances like that don't come often. If I turn it down, I shall soon find myself fifty-plus, wondering why my life is so boring and how I'm going to spend the next ten years or so. No, I'm not being melodramatic; I'm simply being realistic. I have to take this chance and stretch myself.'

'What about Adam and your family?'

Cathy seemed unconcerned. 'Adam will soon reconcile himself to it. We might even enjoy being together at the weekends. And the kids will actually benefit. Nobody except me thinks about it but in less than two years Lucy will be off to university and she'll need financing. Two years later Mark will follow her. We have to subsidise them completely now, you know. I suppose Isobel will go to university?'

'I hope so. She seems to be pretty bright.'

'Still, as long as Philip is agreeable, you won't have to worry about money.'

'I have money of my own,' Magda said quickly. 'I saved most of my salary.'

'Lucky you! Still, it doesn't end with college these days. Good jobs are so difficult to get, and houses and flats so expensive that you either have to have them staying at home for ever or put down a deposit on a place of their own. I have no doubt which I'd prefer!' She looked sympathetically at her sister. 'I'm not being fair. You've had no chance to consider any of this. I ought to leave you to enjoy Isobel now that you've found her. I suppose the truth is I'm a bit jealous. I don't want to share you with anyone.'

'I've been married for fifteen years,' Magda reminded her.

'That's different. Philip has always recognised my rights. It was me he called for when he found you in hospital recently.'

'He knew we would both want it,' Magda said.

'That's what I mean. I don't entirely understand Philip, but he always behaves beautifully. He loves you but he never gets between us. Isobel can't be like that. She'll cling to you and you'll want her to. I'm just a jealous bitch, I'm sorry.'

'I don't think so,' Magda replied slowly. 'I'm not even sure you've got things right.' She broke off suddenly. 'What did you really want to say to me about her? Do you think she has lied to Philip and to me? Please, tell me the truth, Cathy.'

Cathy was upset. She felt as is she was making her way

through a dangerous path with a bottomless bog on either side. 'I didn't mean to upset you, but...'

'But what? There must have been something.'

Catherine felt herself blushing, as she always did when she was embarrassed. Magda looked her usual calm self but her sister suspected that was not so. *She has hidden so much during the years*, she told herself, *that's it's become easy*. Aloud she plunged in, 'Remember I'm only going by what Lucy said. She really thinks that Isobel wasn't raped, that she'd encouraged the guy and then realised too late that she'd gone too far.'

'That's very close to rape,' Magda commented.

'Yes, I suppose so, but Lucy feels that she isn't quite as innocent as she wants everyone to think. In any case, I don't believe she should talk to Lucy so openly about these matters. After all, she's only just seventeen.'

Magda laughed suddenly, 'Cathy, did Lucy perhaps not tell you about her secret meetings with her boyfriend and her lies to you? Isobel seemed to think that she was giving Lucy a necessary warning.'

The sisters stared at each other. 'Perhaps we're both being conned a bit?' Cathy suggested finally.

'I think perhaps we are!' Magda agreed after a moment, and they laughed.

'Well, at least it's brought us together,' Cathy said cheerfully, 'and I don't regret that.'

'Neither do I,' Magda agreed. 'Shall we celebrate with a really delicious chocolate pudding?'

'Really fattening, you mean!'

'Forget it for once, and enjoy yourself with me.'

'You were always good at tempting me,' Cathy complained.

'And you were always good at giving in!'

They had nearly finished their pudding before they returned to serious discussion. After she had ordered coffee, Magda said thoughtfully, 'I think you have too high an opinion of me, Cathy.'

'Whatever do you mean?'

'Well, perhaps I should begin by telling you that I'm not sure I'm this devoted mother you seem to think I am.'

'What are you, then?' Cathy twisted her engagement ring as

she often did when puzzled, looking at it as if she were seeing it for the first time.

'I don't know. When I first heard Isobel hadn't died, I couldn't think of anything else. I had to know. Conrad was the only person who could possibly help me, so I even approached him.'

Noting the word 'even' Catherine realised for the first time that Magda perhaps did not like Conrad and that he was, therefore, no rival to Philip as she had imagined that he might be.

Magda continued, speaking more quickly that usual. 'I forced him to find out what had actually happened to Isobel and if she was settled. The story he finally told me upset me a great deal. I had to see her and to rescue her. Can you understand that, Cathy? It was almost an obsession.'

'Of course, darling,' Cathy said quickly. 'It was a terrible thing to hear about your child. The meeting with Lisa and then that. It must have thrown you off balance, but—'

'I know what you're going to say,' Magda interrupted her, 'I should have waited until I was calmer.' She paused.

'Not really that. But I do think you should have waited a couple of days or so until you could have discussed it with Philip.'

Magda didn't answer for a moment. Then she said sadly, 'I don't quite understand it myself. I think I was a bit crazy.' Breathing deeply, she seemed to be trying to control her agitation. 'I believe that if I had been forced to choose between Isobel and Philip, I would have chosen her without hesitation. It seemed reasonable at the time, but it wasn't.'

'Perhaps meeting Lisa again had somewhat unhinged you,' Cathy suggested.

'Perhaps.' Magda was obviously struggling to keep control. 'She said some terrible things, Cathy. She seemed to want to destroy the little haven I had made for myself. Why?' She was trembling.

Leaning forward, Cathy put her hand lovingly on her sister's arm. 'Don't be so upset, dearest. Forget it now. I'll help you if I can. I've been very selfish.'

'No, I'm the selfish one. I even made Philip accept Isobel into his home when he came back from Belfast after being shot. I was selfish and uncaring. He has always been so kind. I don't deserve it.'

'Philip loves you,' Cathy said firmly, 'you're very lucky, so wipe you eyes.' She handed Magda a handkerchief. 'Have a hot cup of coffee. Remember, I'm with you now, as I always used to be.' She tried to convey her love to her sister.

'Thank you,' Magda managed a smile as she wiped her eyes.

'I suggest as a start coffee with soothing cream,' Cathy began. But before she could say more, Magda's mobile rang. 'Answer it,' Cathy advised, 'it might be important.'

It was Philip but an unusually angry Philip. 'Where the hell are you?' he demanded, 'I've been trying to get you at home.'

'I'm lunching with Cathy,' she told him amazed at his tone. 'I did tell you…'

'Not this morning,' he replied sharply, 'you scarcely spoke to me this morning!'

'I'm sorry, but why are you so angry?'

'Because of something Isobel has just told me.'

Magda was worried. 'What do you mean?'

'When she answered the phone she told me you were out and then launched into an outrageous story about Liam, without an explanation. She told me that Liam had called to see you.' His voice was icy now. 'That he had apparently brought you a bunch of red roses. Isobel thought this a romantic gesture, and she was apparently sorry for him, so she invited him to have lunch with her.'

'I knew nothing about this. It's ridiculous, and I'm sorry she was so silly. Please, believe me, Philip.'

'I do, of course.' His voice was gentler now. 'I told Isobel, however, that I did not want him in my home again, and that she had no right to invite him without my permission. I was harsh, perhaps, but it was the truth.'

Magda was silent. There seemed to be nothing for her to say. She felt as if she was on the edge of a steep and dangerous cliff and might easily take a fatal step. There was so much that she did not understand.

'I must talk to you,' Philip said suddenly, 'but in private.' It was clear to her that he was deeply upset, and much of it was her fault. 'Will you come here to the office?' He seemed to be almost pleading with her. 'I'll arrange for us to have an undisturbed tea. What do you say, darling?'

'Of course I will', she replied immediately. 'You're absolutely right. We need to talk. I'll be with you in about an hour.'

'Thank you for understanding. I'll be waiting.' The line went dead.

Chapter Twenty-two

As she was escorted into Philip's office, Magda still felt unusually perturbed. Once again, as on previous occasions, she was impressed by the austerity of it. Apart from the large antique desk, three or four chairs and several bookcases, the large room was pretty bare. *No one*, she thought, *who has seen this office would believe that it was I who forced him to live in comparative simplicity. It's obviously as much his choice as mine.*

Standing up, he came immediately to meet her. Tall, slim and erect, his dark hair only slightly touched with grey, he looked younger than his fifty-two years; still handsome, although at the moment somewhat forbidding.

Overwhelmed by the thought that she did not want him to be angry with her, she hurried towards him. Before he could greet her, she put her arms round him, burying her face in his jacket. Why had she never realised so clearly before, she asked herself, how much she had come to depend on him? He was her security, the only lasting security she had ever known.

Somewhat surprised by her unexpected approach, he embraced her warmly. 'Please don't be angry with me,' she begged him.

'Of course not,' he reassured her. 'There is no good reason why I should be, is there?' Lifting up her face, he kissed her gently.

After that, he released her and helped her off with her jacket. 'I'm afraid,' he told her, 'that I was angry with Isobel, and perhaps rather unkind to her.'

'You certainly sounded exceptionally angry,' she told him as she sat down by the desk. 'I felt quite scared.'

'I apologise, darling,' he replied. 'I'm afraid I was childishly angry because I couldn't immediately get hold of you. It's been difficult lately for me to have time alone with you. It may be selfish but I've missed it. Perhaps you haven't thought about it?'

She glanced up at him. His face was set in its usual firm lines but, as she looked into his grey eyes under their level brows, she seemed to catch a moment's appeal in them. His eyes pleaded with her as his words never would. She was filled with compunction. 'I'm very sorry that I've acted so stupidly and so selfishly— No, don't stop me,' she begged him as he seemed about to interrupt her. 'It's time I faced it and admitted it. I think I've been a bit mad.'

'Perhaps it was the blow on the head,' he suggested. 'We all took it too lightly, I think.'

'That may have had an effect. But it was the meeting with Lisa which was the real cause, I think. At first I couldn't remember much, then bits came back until I had to meet Conrad, although I had intended never to see him again.'

Although her comment about Conrad puzzled Philip, he made no comment, but simply only waited for her to continue.

'When I discovered Isobel's true situation from him, I couldn't bear it. I felt I had to do something immediately.' She paused.

'That's understandable.' Philip tried to console her. He could see how distressed she was, even now.

'No,' she said fiercely, 'I should have waited until I could talk to you! My grandmother insisted on that. Even Conrad agreed with her. But I wouldn't listen. If I had been asked to choose between you and her, I would have chosen her, I believe. I felt so guilty.'

'It would never have been necessary. Surely you know me better than that?' He wondered why she said 'guilty' but decided that this was not the right time to ask.

'Of course I do, really. The further difficulty, of course, was that when you came back from Belfast, it wasn't possible for me to talk to you as I should have done. But that only makes it clearer how stupid I had been not to wait. I was cruel to you. I'm sorry.'

He took her hands in his. 'You're forgiven. I would never want to deprive you of your daughter, especially when you have suffered so much. I don't want your daughter to feel unwelcome but I will not have Liam brought into my home.' His tone of voice was cold at first but, as he continued he spoke more gently. 'I don't want, however, to increase your unhappiness. I can scarcely imagine what a dreadful wound you suffered and I certainly don't want to make it worse. I was angry today but I don't want the girl to feel unwelcome. Nor do I want to increase your difficulties.'

She nodded to show that she understood but remained silent for a time looking down at their hands. When she finally looked up at him he was surprised to see that her eyes were full of tears.

'What is the matter?' he asked. When she failed again to answer him, he continued, 'In addition to reasons I may have, it is surely clear that Isobel is very vulnerable and it would be wiser not to expose her to him. Surely you agree?'

'But Philip,' she suggested almost nervously, 'he's surely not so bad. He's only young and his life has been very difficult.'

'That's true. But he's like his father. He has, as we know, a dark, violent side to him. Isobel should be protected from him, especially as he has considerable charm.'

'Oh, Philip,' she whispered, 'I don't know what to say. I don't think that I really know what I feel. I'm not even sure that I love her. Sometimes I still think that I don't know her at all and, what is worse, I don't want to make the effort. She reminds me somehow of Lisa. Tell me the truth, Philip. Do you think that Lisa was right when she said that I was incapable of loving?'

'That's nonsense,' he replied firmly 'It might be true if she said it of herself. You're new to being a mother, that's all. Remember, darling, you are not alone. We share this job, and all we have to do now is to decide to give Isobel a home and an education for a year or two. She'll soon be ready to live her own life, especially if she knows we care about her.'

'That's what Cathy said,' she told him.

He smiled. 'For once I agree with Cathy. You must persuade Isobel, however, that we need some time to ourselves, and she must not interfere in my personal affairs.'

'I'm sure I can do that, especially since you have spoken to her.'

'Good. I'll order tea and we can have a happy half hour together.' He was smiling cheerfully now.

She was grateful to him but realised sadly that he did not understand her. *I'm emotionally crippled*, she thought, *and need healing, but Philip does not seem to understand that. Perhaps he can't and it will never happen.*

Later, Magda had to admit that she was in fact baffled by Isobel's response, or more truthfully her lack of response. Isobel admitted to being upset by Philip's anger but said calmly that she now understood that she had been wrong and that she was very sorry. But it was her final words that worried Magda. 'I realise,' she said, looking straight at her mother, 'that I ought not to forget, although Philip is very kind, that I'm only a visitor here. I suppose that it would have been different with my own father.'

Magda felt unreasonably angry. 'Whatever do you mean?' she demanded. 'Who are you thinking of?'

'Conrad, of course. He is my father, isn't he? It was he after all who found me.'

Magda struggled to find the right words – words that would be truthful but not too hurtful. 'He and I both,' she said finally. 'I instigated the search. He believed that you were perfectly happy and that the past was best forgotten.'

The dark eyes looked horrified now. 'Are you saying that Conrad knew I was alive, but did nothing about it? It's horrible! If he knew, you must have known.'

'No,' Magda insisted firmly. 'Lisa told him about two years after I had left. He discovered that you were happily settled in your first home so he thought it best to leave everything as it was.'

'And what were you doing?' Isobel's eyes were full of tears.

'I was about to marry Philip, having spent two years travelling. Conrad and I were separated.'

'You haven't told me any of this,' Isobel accused her. 'We talked a lot that first day but scarcely at all since.'

'You didn't ask.'

'Was that necessary?' There was a definite hostility in Isobel's voice.

'Perhaps not. I was wrong, I think.' Magda looked sadly at her daughter. 'There was so much to arrange and there have been several difficulties, as you know. I hadn't had time to prepare Philip. Of course, I didn't know he would have such trouble in Belfast. I'm afraid that I'm a bit of a failure at personal relations.

I'm sorry. Please forgive me.' She smiled at her daughter but Isobel did not respond.

After pausing, Magda continued, 'It's an unusual and difficult situation for all of us and it's bound to take time for us to adjust. Philip's relationship with Liam goes back to his time in the Army. I know little about it but I'm sure he didn't mean to hurt you. He asked me to explain—'

'I've no quarrel with Philip,' Isobel interrupted her. 'I was stupid to butt in when he's been so kind. I expect I've been annoying him by being around such a lot, but he's always been pleasant and polite. I think I should spend more time in my own room in the evening. What do you think?'

Somewhat amazed at her perception, Magda agreed. 'It will be easier when I start college,' Isobel added. Her tears had disappeared. She seemed completely calm. In an odd way, Magda was again reminded of Lisa. It was not a comforting thought.

For a few moments Isobel was silent until she surprised Magda by saying, 'I would like to know more about you and Conrad. After all you are my parents. It's natural for me to want to know more about you both, isn't it? Why did you part? It must have been very painful. I suppose that it why you don't say anything about it.' When her mother did not immediately answer, she continued, 'Do you think I could talk to him? We had such a short time.'

'He is returning to Lebanon very soon,' Magda reminded her.

'But surely he has time to see you and me. Can't you ask him?'

Magda tried to find the best answer. 'He made his attitude clear to you, didn't he? He admires you but he does not wish to make any claims on you. He is completely ready to put you in my care. I thought you understood and agreed.' She tried not to sound irritated but it was difficult. She had the feeling that Isobel was dramatising the situation in spite of her apparent calm. That was what had reminded her of Lisa. 'Are you regretting coming here with Philip and me?'

'Of course not,' Isobel said quickly. 'You have been so lovely to me and Philip is wonderfully generous. I just thought I might talk once more, before he disappears.'

'I'll try to speak to him,' Magda promised, anxious to get away from the subject. 'But I have no idea what he'll say.' She looked quickly at her watch. 'I'm afraid I must think about the evening meal now.'

Isobel's reluctance to accept this was clear, but by hurrying off to the kitchen Magda was able to ignore her.

Alone in her room soon after supper, Isobel, lying on her bed, went over this conversation. She had made her peace with Philip easily but she was aware that Magda remained aloof.

It seemed to her that, at last, she had the answer to something that had been puzzling her. She had soon become aware that although Philip was still deeply in love with her mother, Magda did not appear to have the same strong feeling for him. *Perhaps,* she thought, *I'm mistaken, I know so little about happy family life.* This was not the family she had so often dreamed about. It was, however, she comforted herself, better than no family.

Now, it seemed to her she had the answer. It was clear to her now that Magda and Conrad had been passionately in love but that Lisa, her grandmother, had been determined to end this. It seemed clear to Isobel that Lisa had wanted a much more successful marriage for her beautiful daughter. She had been so determined that she had even taken their child away. She was a cruel and resolute woman. Isobel's eyes filled with tears at the thought of Magda's suffering. She must have been heartbroken, so much so that she had finally broken away completely from her domineering mother. Conrad – still a poor, struggling and despised immigrant – could do nothing to help her.

It was a sad and romantic story that Isobel told herself. She had often comforted herself with stories but this was different because it was true. Magda had finally found security by marrying Philip. Who could blame her?

But when she heard that I had not died, her thoughts continued, *she did not turn to Philip but to Conrad. It was Magda and Conrad who had looked for her and found her. She was sure he had really cared.*

Then why had he renounced her? she asked herself. The answer, of course, was obvious. Magda was married to Philip. She pondered over what seemed to her to be a tragic story. Magda clearly felt she must be loyal to Philip. Conrad, respecting that decision, had decided to leave England for good. He and Magda would never meet again.

I would never have spoken to my mother, as I did, she told herself, *if I had known the truth. She was so brave. I must somehow let her know that I understand what she has suffered. I must see Conrad once more before he goes. He is my father who loves me and I have a right to know him.* It was wonderful, she decided, to be the child of true lovers. She resolved that she would talk to Magda openly the next day.

The decision to tackle Magda had to be postponed, however, because of an unexpected telephone call soon after breakfast the next morning. It was, surprisingly, from Magda's father. About ten minutes later, Magda came into Isobel's room and told her that she had arranged to meet her father for lunch.

'I thought you weren't friendly,' Isobel was surprised.

'We're not, especially since his last birthday. But he was upset and very insistent, so I agreed. I'm sorry to leave you again. Will you be all right?'

'Of course.' Isobel could not think of being unkind to a mother who had suffered so much. 'Don't worry about me.' She kissed Magda and then lay down to plan the talk she would have later with her.

When Magda returned, however, she went straight to her own room after greeting Isobel briefly. It was about half an hour before she emerged. She had taken off her suit, put on her favourite blue gown and brushed out her hair. Although she tried to appear so, she was obviously not at all relaxed.

'How did it go?' Isobel ventured to ask. For a moment Magda did not answer but looked at her daughter as if the question had further irritated her. 'You don't have to tell me, if you don't want to.'

'There's no reason why I shouldn't. He's your grandfather, after all.' She stopped suddenly and for a moment pressed her lips together as if to keep back the words.

But it was useless. They burst out. Isobel had never seen her so agitated. 'He's upset and irritated me so much that I need to talk. You're probably the best person for me to talk to.'

Pleased, Isobel stood up and moved to kneel beside her mother's chair, taking hold of her restless hands. 'Do tell me.'

'He wants to meet her,' Magda announced furiously.

Isobel was puzzled. 'Who do you mean?'

'*Lisa*, of course! My mother and your grandmother.' Magda was angry and distressed. 'They haven't seen each other since before I was born and now he wants to meet her again. He's a bigger fool than I thought he was! Oh God, how can he be so ridiculous?' She looked in Isobel's eyes as if seeking the answer there.

'Why does he want that now?' Isobel asked her.

'Probably because Catherine has told my elder sister, Constance. I know really that I should never confide in Cathy. She gets me to trust her, then she lets me down because she can't help wanting to be the person who is always in the know.'

'I won't let you down, ever.' Isobel was flattered to think that she could be more helpful than Cathy. 'But what did Constance do?'

'She told father that Lisa had written to me saying that she was suffering from a terminal illness, and that's why I had gone to see her.'

'Was that true?'

'I don't know. I never know when Lisa is speaking the truth. She didn't act as if she was dying. She said a lot of foul things, attacked me so viciously that I fell on my head and got concussion.'

'Oh, no! Whatever did you do?'

'I managed somehow to get to the nearby hospital, where Philip eventually found me.' Magda stopped suddenly. 'But that's not important at the moment.'

'If your father knows what happened then, why does he want to meet Lisa?'

'He says he wants to make his peace with her. He is seventy-five and doesn't think he has a lot of time, even if she isn't really dying. He says he wants her to know the truth before it's too late.'

'But that's not a bad thing, is it?' Isobel was puzzled. 'Surely it's right for people to try to speak the truth to each other, isn't it? Surely you would prefer that?'

Magda answered slowly after a pause. 'It may not always be the best thing. It may only cause more hurt.'

'I suppose it depends,' Isobel ventured to say, 'on whether it is really the truth.'

Magda replied quickly, 'In this case, I very much doubt that it is.'

'What does your father want to say to Lisa? Did he tell you?'

'Oh, yes, he told me. The trouble is that it seemed like another fantasy.'

'What do you mean? I don't understand.'

'Well, on his seventy-fifth birthday I destroyed his image of the respected, successful doctor and family man by telling everyone the truth about him and Lisa. This didn't quite fit in with his own idea of himself.'

Isobel stared at her. 'Why did you do that? Wasn't it rather cruel?'

'Perhaps,' Magda agreed calmly, 'but I had to do it. I couldn't stand the lies and hypocrisy any longer. I'm afraid you don't really know what I'm like. But then, you can't be blamed for that. Neither of us can.'

She sounded so sad that Isobel immediately repented of her critical thoughts. 'I think I can understand,' she said gently. 'What is he saying now?'

'He says that Lisa is the great love of his life,' Magda said bitterly. 'He wants her to know because he says it will comfort her that she is the only woman he has ever loved and that he still loves her.'

'If that's true, why did he abandon her?'

'Because he was weak and cowardly, and because he didn't want to hurt his wife and family. He never really loved Rosalind but she was a faithful wife to him.' Magda laughed. 'Don't look so surprised, Isobel. Many people are good at inventing flattering excuses for their actions.'

'But he did hurt his wife.'

'Yes, of course he did, and me and finally everyone. That's why I was so upset and angry.'

'I don't blame you.' Isobel pressed her mother's hands again. 'What did you do?'

'In the end, I gave him Lisa's address.'

'Why ever did you do that? Especially if you don't think he's speaking the truth!'

Magda did not answer at first; then she said wearily, 'I can't really judge, can I? I believe that even Lisa has the right to hear what he has to say. They must decide for themselves. People should have that right, don't you think?'

'Is that what you really think? It is very generous!' Impulsively, Isobel kissed her mother's hands.

'I don't know whether or not it's generous. Perhaps the truth is that I don't care enough any more.'

Apparently ignoring that, Isobel said unexpectedly, 'Then you'll understand why I want you to arrange for me to meet my father again.'

'Your father? Do you mean Conrad?'

'Of course. He is my father, isn't he? When I asked you to get in touch with him, I meant it. I know it will be painful for you, but—'

Magda interrupted her coldly. 'I doubt if he'll agree. But, in any case, he's irrelevant.'

Jumping to her feet, Isobel stared at her mother, exclaiming, 'Why do you say that? It's *horrible!*'

'I say it because I think it's true.' Magda seemed untouched by Isobel's emotion. 'He told you when he met you that he admired you but that he had no wish to play the part of your father.' Inwardly, Magda was afraid. How much truth should she tell to this girl, whom she now realised was far less stable than she had seemed.

'I don't believe he really meant it,' Isobel protested. 'He needed more time. But you can't really speak for him, can you? I realise that it must hurt you, but I need to speak to him.'

'In that case, you shall,' Magda had made a decision.

'How?'

'I'll ring him. If he's willing, I'll pass him over to you.' She wondered if she was crazy to do this, but she felt sure that Conrad would know how to handle the situation.

She didn't believe that he would think it would be to his advantage to tell the whole truth. That would involve him too much. She dialled Conrad's number.

He answered immediately, recognising her voice. 'Magda, darling, I was intending to ring you before I left.'

'When are you leaving?'

'In three days. I shall be happy to go. You are the only person who could have kept me here and you wisely don't want to. You know you are much more secure with Philip. But perhaps you have changed your mind?'

Before he could say any more, she said a definite no to him. She could almost see his shrug and his smile. 'In that case, what do you want?' he asked her.

'Our daughter wants to speak to you.'

'Why? You intrigue me.'

'She wants to speak to her father. She is insisting on her right.'

There was a long pause before Conrad answered. 'Do I understand that you want me to tell an appropriate story but not the sordid truth? In fact, my dear, you want me to lie for you? She's a sentimental young person, I imagine.'

'You've guessed right, but if you think you can't—'

He interrupted her. 'For you, I can. Is she there? Let me speak to her.'

Handing the phone to Isobel, Magda told her that Conrad would like to speak to her. 'He's leaving in three days. I'll leave you to it.' After handing over the phone, she walked out of the room.

It was some time before Isobel came seeking Magda again. She had obviously been crying but she was able to greet her mother with a smile.

'Thank you for letting me talk to him. He was kind and understanding. He said that our situation couldn't be changed. He had to return to Lebanon and you could not possibly desert Philip. He said that as I grew older I would understand that life sometimes has to be sad. I agreed with him. I also respected him very much when he told me that he could not possibly discuss your relationship, even with me, but he wanted me to know that you were the only woman who had ever mattered to him and that you still did. He said I was now very lucky and I agreed with him.'

She kissed her mother warmly. As she returned the kiss, Magda wished she could accept the illusion so skilfully created by Conrad.

Chapter Twenty-three

The next two weeks were more or less uneventful, and then the storm broke and continued with growing violence. There had been no obvious intimations except that Magda had sometimes felt, as one feels on a humid summer evening, that the quiet is unbearable and unnatural and cannot last.

Philip was working long hours because of the growing tension in the City, but he seemed unchanged at home, now that Isobel obligingly retired to her own room most evenings. Having been given books to read by her new college, she had an easily acceptable excuse.

It was Isobel, however, who worried Magda from time to time. Her frequent disappearances on the pretext of getting to know London were puzzling, although she always had plausible reasons. Magda blamed her own suspicious nature but, nevertheless, Isobel still seemed too docile and too quiet. Most puzzling of all, however, was her daughter's tender solicitude for herself. Why did Isobel often treat her as if she were a heroine in a tragedy? she wondered. That did not, however, seem to be a question she could easily ask.

There was also the time bomb of Lisa. Magda doubted many times whether she had been sensible to give her father Lisa's address. Perhaps he had loved her, but Magda was sure that he could have no idea how much his young lover had changed, how ruthless she seemed to have become.

She would have liked to have been able to consult with her sister, but Cathy was very busy with the approaching end of term and with the application for her new post. She would not have time for vague thoughts about Lisa. It was during these weeks that Magda was given an opportunity to return to her old counselling job. It could be full-time or part-time, she was told, whatever she wished. It was pleasing to know that she was much valued but, to her surprise, she found herself postponing the decision. She felt herself too weary to consider it. Recently, it had taken all her energy just to get through the day. She was surprised to discover how stressed and emotional she often felt. Obviously the events of the last few weeks had depleted her strength more than she had realised. She felt that she ought to talk with Isobel, but seemed unable to find the energy to do it.

When the storm finally came, she did not at first recognise it. It came quietly with no lightning flashes and rolls of thunder but simply a change of wind, as it were, which at first seemed refreshing. In fact, she was pleased when it came. One thing that worried her was that, since the episode with Isobel, Philip seemed to be more remote. He was happy to be with her but, for the first time in their married life, he no longer desired the frequent physical intimacy he had always wanted before. Most nights he kissed her and went to sleep. At first she had been relieved because she had felt so tired, but more recently she had become worried.

She was, therefore, pleased when he asked her to travel with him to a meeting and banquet in Edinburgh, where he was to be the chief speaker. 'We can fly up on Saturday,' he suggested, 'stay in the best hotel and fly back late on Sunday, or even Monday morning. What do you think?'

'Are wives welcome?' she asked.

'Of course, especially mine. Do say yes, darling. We need a little break, just the two of us, don't you think?'

It was clear that he was still finding Isobel's presence difficult. She had just been about to ask what she should do about her daughter, but when he made clear his wish to be with her alone, she bit back the words. She must solve this problem alone. 'It will be lovely!' she told him.

He had only given her a week's notice so she did not have much time in which to make arrangements. Surprisingly, it was all quite quickly settled as soon as she mentioned the matter to Cathy. 'I really don't want to leave Isobel on her own,' she explained, 'but Philip has made his wishes quite clear.'

'I can quite understand that. It's been a big upset for him. He needs fussing over. You'll have to learn how to do it.' Cathy seemed prepared to be helpful.

'Do you think you could have her?'

'No, I'm afraid not.' Cathy was quite decisive. 'She would be miserable with us, but I rather think that Lucy would be delighted to have a weekend in your grand flat and away from Mark.'

'Lucy!' Magda was amazed. 'I thought they were sworn enemies!'

'You're out of date,' Cathy told her cheerfully. 'Apparently Isobel rang Lucy to apologise and they've become Internet and phone friends. I'll put it to her, if you like?'

Magda was pleased to have her problem so easily solved, but not entirely happy. There was something here that worried her. She tried to explain this to her sister but Cathy only laughed, saying, 'When you've had a bit more experience, like me, you won't try to understand today's young, you'll simply be pleased when they fit in with your plans without argument!'

Philip was obviously pleased that she had solved the problem so Magda suppressed her doubts, which in any case were not very clear.

Everything seemed to go brilliantly in Edinburgh. Philip's speech was well received and Magda was undoubtedly the shining star of the evening. She had decided to wear a close-fitting silver sheath of a dress, which frothed out below her knees, and had put a midnight blue filmy jacket over it. Her only jewellery was a pair of long, sparkling diamond earrings. Philip clearly appreciated the admiration his unusually beautiful wife received. Magda was relieved.

Her real happiness, however, came when they were at last alone. As he took her in his arms she found herself shivering with delight at his touch. Something which a few weeks before had come briefly to life and had then faded away was now suddenly and wonderfully completely alive. She had never felt anything as strong as this before. She was prepared to surrender herself completely. 'Oh, Philip darling,' she exclaimed, 'I love you, I really do!' She had never before said that to any man, not even to her husband.

He asked no questions, but readily accepted the happiness and love which was at last offered to him. The main storm might still have been averted if Philip had not insisted that they take an earlier return flight because of the strong possibility of a blizzard later. As a result, they arrived home several hours earlier than they had been expected. Magda tried twice to ring Isobel but her calls had not been answered. The girls were obviously out.

As they entered the hall of their flat they heard sounds of very loud music. 'I'm afraid Lucy's tastes have prevailed,' Magda remarked, remembering Isobel's expressed preference for classical music.

Philip smiled. 'Young people usually go with the crowd. Remember?' He drew her close to him. 'One kiss before we enter the fray.' It was a long kiss, which neither of them wanted to end.

'I never knew I could be so happy,' Magda told him as they walked towards the sitting room.

Their elegant room was hardly recognisable. Cushions were scattered over the carpet, together with at least a dozen drink cans and several discarded food cartons. A discarded slice of pizza was balanced on the television cabinet; another lay on the rug before the fire.

By the light of a couple of reading lamps Lucy and a boy could be discerned entwined on the sofa. Philip switched on the main lights cruelly revealing the chaos and electrifying the young couple. Lucy sat up abruptly, pushing the boy away. 'Oh my God,' she exclaimed. 'It's you, Uncle Philip. I didn't think you would be back until ten o'clock.'

'That, I may say, is obvious,' Philip replied dryly.

Lucy jumped to her feet, trying to straighten her blouse and her dishevelled hair. 'You won't tell Mum, will you,' she pleaded. When Philip did not reply, she said, 'We haven't done anything much, really. We've just been messing about, haven't we, Tom?' She appealed to the boy, who looked completely bemused. He was, at least, still wearing his jeans, Philip noted. Lucy then looked appealingly at Magda, who could not think of anything to say.

'Honestly, Uncle Philip,' Lucy continued, 'we've just been stupid.' It was clear from the look she now gave him that, good-looking though he was, Tom had not been very satisfactory.

'I sincerely hope that is so,' Philip replied without any apparent emotion. 'It's not really my business but,' his voice became crisp and clear, 'in ten minutes I shall ring your father and ask him to collect you. If this room isn't completely tidy by then, I shall feel obliged to tell him the whole story. In any case, I advise you to tell your mother. You can't expect people to lie on your behalf. Understood?'

'Yes,' Lucy replied humbly, recognising the tone of command. 'Thank you.'

'Where is Isobel?' Magda asked slowly. She felt scarcely able to speak.

'She's in her room. I'll tell her you're here.' As Lucy moved towards the door, Magda gripped her arm. 'There's no need, I'll speak to her myself.' As she stood outside Isobel's room, Magda hesitated. Irrational though it might be, she was convinced that some life-changing event awaited her.

The room was in semi-darkness, lit only by the bedside lamp. But there was enough light to see that two people were making love on the bed. What ought I to do? Magda wondered. Isobel was eighteen, which was not an unreasonable age to have a lover. Immediately, however, other considerations flashed through her mind. Who was the youth? How had Isobel come to know him? Why had she not been more honest? Suddenly angry, she switched on the main light.

'For God's sake, Lucy, go away! Can't you see you're not wanted here?'

When there was no answer the boy who was on top raised his head. 'Holy Mother of God!' he exclaimed. 'It's your mother!'

'*Liam*!' Magda knew instantly who he was. There was no mistaking it. Only he could have said those words in that musical brogue. Only he would have looked arrogantly at her with brilliant eyes almost as bright as her own. 'How do you come to be here?' She sat down, suddenly feeling weak and faint.

After wrapping the duvet round him, Liam leaped out of bed, leaving Isobel to cover her nakedness with a sheet. 'Sure, and it's just a little fun and games, Mrs Peters,' he said mockingly, with a bright smile. 'Not anything that would really shock a beautiful woman like you.'

Turning to Isobel, Magda ignored him. 'But you've only met once before! Even to me that is somewhat shocking. I don't like to see my daughter behaving like this.'

'Oh, no, please don't think like that.' Isobel sat on the side of the bed, clutching the sheet round her. 'We've met lots of times since; I didn't say anything because I didn't want to upset Philip. But I was going to tell you because I was sure that you of all people would understand.'

'Understand what?'

'We love one another. We want to be together, that's all.'

'And why should I have particular understanding of that?' Magda still found it hard to speak.

'Because of Conrad. You've always loved each other, haven't you? I know you don't want to talk about it because of Philip. But Conrad made it quite clear when I spoke to him. Your horrible mother separated you, but I know you would never want to do that to me. I'm terribly sorry for what you've suffered and for what you must still suffer. I really am. Liam and I admire your courage. We've talked about it.'

It was at that moment that Magda realised that Liam was looking past her at the door behind her. Turning her head she saw Philip standing in the doorway. How long had he been standing there? she wondered. He looked pale and stern. Suddenly the possible implications of what Isobel had been saying overwhelmed her. No, it couldn't happen now, when she had just discovered that she loved him. Something seemed to snap in her.

Standing up quickly, she said loudly. 'Be quiet, Isobel! You don't know what you're talking about! It's just a romantic story you've invented. There's no truth in it at all!'

'But Conrad told me,' Isobel protested. 'How can you say that!'

'No!' Magda stopped her. 'He told you I was the only woman he's ever really cared about. That may be true but it doesn't mean a lot.'

'You can't blame him, Mrs Peters, can you?' Liam broke into the conversation with a wicked smile. 'You're magnificent! I meant those red roses, you know!'

Magda continued to ignore him. Philip remained pale and silent. 'The simple truth is,' Magda declared. 'I never loved Conrad in the slightest.' Everything suddenly seemed clearer to her than it had ever done. 'I did what I was expected to do and paid to do.'

'I don't understand? What do you mean?' Isobel was almost stammering.

'I mean,' Magda told her slowly and clearly, 'that my mother trained me to be a high-class prostitute – a mistress for wealthy men. She had done very well for herself in that way. She decided not only would it be a profitable profession for me, but that it would enable me to repay quickly the money she said I owed her.'

'How could you owe her money?' Isobel stared at her mother.

'She helped me out when I was a student. I thought it was a mother's gift but it certainly wasn't.' (How impossible it was to explain what she had felt then!) 'She demanded it back as soon as possible, and there was no one for me to turn to, so I did what she demanded. I chose Conrad because he was more intelligent and more pleasant. In the end, however, I came to dislike him because of his closeness to Lisa.'

'But you wanted me, didn't you?' Isobel raised imploring dark eyes to he mother. 'You wanted someone of your own to love, didn't you?'

For a few moments Magda hesitated. It would be easy to lie again and she would have preferred that, but now was the time for the complete truth. You can't build a house on sand, she reminded herself. 'No,' she said firmly. 'I didn't actually want you; I didn't decide to have you. I made a stupid mistake and forgot to take my pill. I'm sorry, but that's the truth.'

Isobel stared in horror at her mother. Her eyes were suddenly full of tears. 'Does that mean that you were glad when I apparently died? That everything else you have said was just lies?' She began to sob.

'No, that isn't true either,' Magda told her. 'Life is never as simple as the romantic stories make out. As you grew in my body I began to love you. It often happens, I believe. I would not agree to an abortion. Conrad supported me, so you must thank him, too. When I was told that you had died, I was heartbroken. But good came of it. Feeling that I had lost everything somehow gave me the courage to run away and to start life afresh.'

'And to end marrying a decent man like Philip,' Isobel's scorn was obvious. 'I suppose you think that was right! In the end, you did what your mother wanted, didn't you? How are you better than her?'

Philip interrupted suddenly. 'I asked no questions. I was content with the present and ready to forget the past.'

'Of course you were.' Liam too was scornful. 'It wouldn't have suited you to have the past investigated too closely, would it?' He turned towards Isobel, 'I'm afraid you've got the wrong idea about your hero – Philip.'

'Why are you saying that?' she asked him angrily. 'You shouldn't mock everything, Liam. Some people are actually good.'

'Perhaps, but not my Uncle Gerry, alias your stepfather, Philip. You can't deny it, can you,' he said, turning to Philip, 'that after telling my mam and me that you loved us, you went away and never gave us another thought? Of course, if we'd known that you'd killed Dad, we wouldn't have been surprised. But we didn't have any idea. You even gave us this address, but when Mother wrote after a few weeks and didn't get any reply, we thought you must have been killed, too.'

'If you believed that, why did you write again years later?' Magda asked him.

'I don't know. I was just desperate, I guess. But it's the truth, isn't it Uncle Gerry, that you deserted me – and worst of all my mam?'

After a pause, Philip answered slowly and wearily, 'It is a truth, but not the whole truth.'

A sudden thought struck Magda, *Why doesn't he tell the whole truth if he cares for me at all?* Unexpectedly, she found herself unwilling to voice her protest. She simply felt sick and weary and utterly tired of the whole affair. 'If you will excuse me,' was all she could say, 'I want to go.'

Clutching the sheet more tightly around her, Isobel jumped to feet and hurried towards her mother. 'You can't leave now, after what you've just said! Don't you care about me at all?'

For a moment, it seemed as if Magda would refuse to answer. Then she replied, slowly and wearily, 'Of course I care. I want you to have a home, a good education and a real chance in life. I've set aside money. You can ask Philip about it.' She turned once more to go.

'You don't understand!' Isobel tried once more. She was close to tears. 'I want your love. You're my mother! I've dreamed for years of meeting my mother and how wonderful it would be! It seemed like that at first, but now it's all gone wrong. Surely, you can love me like a mother?'

'I'm sorry,' Magda told her, 'but I don't know much about love, especially mother's love. When I was twenty-two I realised that my mother had probably never loved me. She had used me; even when I actually believed in her love, it was only part of her revenge. I thought you had died. There was no one. I decided, therefore to start life afresh. But I think something had died in me. I worked with people who had given up everything for the love of God. I admired them but I wasn't good enough. So I gave it up and accepted a comfortable life, as you have pointed out. You will have to make your own choice, as we all have to do. It's hard but that's all there is.'

As Philip moved from the doorway to let her pass, she stopped to speak to her daughter once more, 'Don't be too hasty, Isobel. Finish your A levels and go to university.' Magda was gone before anyone could reply.

After a moment Liam said scornfully, 'She's right, you know. She's just got the guts to say the truth. You've got to decide in the end. Do you want her or me or someone else? Lisa, perhaps?'

'Oh God!' Isobel cried out. 'I shouldn't have said those things! What shall I do?'

'Stop dreaming,' Liam suggested. 'Look at the truth.'

'That might be a good idea for you, too,' Philip said quietly. He turned towards Isobel. 'You should give Magda and yourself more time. You believe that you'll automatically love each, but in real life I don't think it often happens like that. You got to work on it.'

'He's right, you know,' Liam agreed.

'I'll leave you two to get dressed now,' Philip said. 'I'll go to my study to check my emails. I suggest you come along in about half an hour and make peace, Isobel.'

'I'll be there,' Isobel promised.

'I'm sorry, too, Uncle Gerry,' Liam said unexpectedly. 'What I said wasn't the whole truth, was it?'

'Not entirely.' Without more words, Philip went.

'Do you really care about me?' Isobel asked her boyfriend.

'Of course I do. You can move in, when you like, but be sure, I'm an awkward devil, like my dad. You might do better to take your time.'

'Perhaps I will,' she told him as she went towards the bathroom. As she stepped under the shower, a sudden thought struck her. Would Liam really make her happy? She had a comfortable home now, and perhaps she might one day meet someone like Philip. Perhaps even Lisa had been right after all...

Philip didn't check his emails, but simply sat there until he had the courage to look for Magda. He knew she was very upset, She was not, as he had expected, in their bedroom and the sitting room was empty and silent. Adam had obviously taken Lucy; but where was Magda?

He walked into the sitting room. Almost immediately, he saw the letter propped up on the mantelpiece. He read:

Dear Philip,

I have gone to Catherine's with Adam and Lucy. I have all I need for a few days. I'll be in touch. I need to think.

Magda

He stared at it; reread it; then threw it down. In his happiest moment he had, incredibly, lost everything. Walking across the room, he poured himself a strong whisky. What else was there now?

Chapter Twenty-four

For three days Philip makes no attempt to get in touch with Magda. She has left her mobile phone next to her letter. Making it quite clear that she does not intend to be accessible.

On the Wednesday evening Catherine rings just as he arrives home. She is, however, seeking news, not giving it. She can only tell him that Magda left her on the Monday morning, giving her no idea where she was going but promising to get in touch soon. She says finally, 'I'm hoping that she has at least rung you.'

'I'm afraid not,' he tells her. He does not want to say any more but Catherine does. She informs him that Lucy has told her the miserable story of the Sunday evening. 'I'm so glad,' she says, 'that you advised her to be truthful. It has made things a bit easier. But I'm terribly worried about Magda. She was obviously very upset and looked so dreadfully pale and weary. She was so distant, too. I've never seen her like that. Do you have any idea why?'

'Not really,' he replies after a pause. 'Please forgive me, Catherine, I'd rather not talk any more now. I promise to ring you if I have any news.'

Less than half an hour later when he is sipping his second whisky the phone rings again. To his disappointment it is not Magda, but a woman's voice which he does not recognise. In a pleasant voice, which inspires confidence, she announces that she is Margaret Vaughan, Magda's grandmother.

'Magda has spoken to me about you,' he tells her, feeling that here is hope at last. 'She stayed with you a few weeks ago, I believe?'

'Yes, and she is staying with me now.'

'Has she asked you to get in touch with me?'

'No, but she needs you very much and so I have decided to ring you.' Disappointed, he does not immediately reply. Undeterred, Margaret continues, 'Do you love her enough even to come on those terms?'

Now, Philip does not hesitate. 'I love her with all my heart. If you believe I can help her, I'll come.'

'I'm sure you can help. The trouble is that Magda herself doesn't know how to ask you. She needs help, however.'

'Is she ill?' He is suddenly afraid.

'No, she's not ill, but she needs help from you. Can you come by lunchtime tomorrow? Or is that too difficult?'

'I can come. I'll get my secretary to cancel my appointments for the next few days.'

'Good. I was sure you would be ready to respond.' She quickly gives him directions to her home and then rings off. 'Goodnight, Philip. God bless you.'

After throwing away the rest of his drink, he makes his way to his room, only pausing to tell Isobel and to ring Catherine briefly.

The instructions Margaret Vaughan has given him are very clear. Although the M6 is even more than usually crowded ten days before Christmas, he arrives on time and is lucky enough to find a parking place in front of her home. As he walks up the path to her front door he admits to himself that he has never felt so nervous and unsure since he was a small boy. Thoughts that he has tried to keep back on the journey rush into his mind.

What if this is not the opportunity Mrs Vaughan seems to think it is? Perhaps it is really the end? After the words spoken on Sunday evening, he is almost convinced that it must be. Has Magda realised that he is not the strong man she has always thought him to be? Does she now, therefore, believe that she can live without him? That she might, in fact, be happier without him?

This is useless, he decides. Squaring his shoulders, he rings the bell firmly. The door is opened quickly. Margaret Vaughan has obviously been waiting for him. 'You've made good time, Philip,' she greets him, smiling pleasantly. She is a small, white-haired woman, wearing a green housecoat. But what he notices most is the warmth in her smile and the genuine welcome in her voice. He takes little account of the shabby narrow hall. She is a good woman, he thinks. That is why Magda has come here. He is encouraged.

'Magda is expecting you,' she tells him as she leads him down the hall. 'She was pleased when I told her.'

She opens a door on the left. 'She is waiting to talk to you. I'll go and prepare some lunch for us.'

Before he can speak, Mrs Vaughan disappears into the kitchen. Philip enters the living room. It is large shabbily furnished and crowded with books. It is warm and welcoming too, like its owner, on this cold December day. He only has eyes for Magda, who is sitting by the fire in her favourite blue gown. As she hears him, she stands up and moves a step towards him. He hurries towards her and, as she says his name, he takes her in his arms and holds her close. She looks so pale and fragile that he can only think of protecting her.

After a moment, he leads her to the settee and they sit down together. 'You're not sorry I've come, are you?' he asks, taking her hands in his.

'No, of course not. I'm pleased. I'm sorry that I caused you so much anxiety again.' She pauses briefly then asks anxiously, 'I hope Isobel is all right?'

'I think so.' Philip tries to reassure her. 'She moved in two days ago with Liam. She said he was very insistent.'

'I'm sorry she has done that. I'm not at all sure about Liam.'

'I certainly am not.' He sounds very grim. 'But you shattered her dream and I think she felt compelled to make a gesture.'

She would like to placate him but refuses to compromise. 'I know it seems cruel but, if we don't speak the truth now, we can have no secure future. I gave her the information she needs to make the choice she has to make.'

'Why did you run away?' he asks almost angrily. 'I feel as if you want to reject me.'

'No, not that,' she replies firmly. 'I simply couldn't stand any more. I was too tired and weak. And, since you didn't tell the whole truth as well, it all seemed useless.'

'What do you mean?' He is afraid to admit that he understands her. 'The whole truth about what?'

'About Liam and his father. There is more to be told, isn't there? You must now tell me,' she insists. 'How can we stay together if you won't tell the whole truth, even now? I've told you all the worst things about me, so you have no need to be afraid.'

After a few moments of reflection, he replies firmly, 'You're right. It was a kind of fear. I told myself I was simply turning my back on the past but I was really unwilling to face up to it properly.'

'I understand,' she tells him softly.

'I did shoot Seamas,' he continues 'but the truth is rather more brutal than Liam thinks. Seamas had first tried to kill me. He had apparently discovered the truth about me because he came looking for me, shouting furiously, "I thought you were my friend but you're a fucking treacherous bastard!" Without a pause he levelled his gun at me and shot me. He missed, amazingly, by about a quarter of an inch. I was armed, of course, and almost without thinking, I shot back and killed him. Unlike him, I was a properly trained killer. I then went to warn Noreen and Liam. I told myself I was doing the decent thing! We have amazing powers of self-deception, don't you think?'

'Did you tell them you would come back?'

'I'm not sure but I probably did. I genuinely loved Liam, and Noreen and I had had a brief relationship. If I'd been capable of rational thought, I would have known it was impossible.'

'Was Liam speaking the truth when he said you gave them your address here?'

'Yes.' He gives no excuse or explanation.

'Why didn't you answer then when she wrote to you?' She still wants more truth.

'I never received the letter. I don't know what happened to it. It was over a year before I came back here.' She waits for what has never yet been said. Now he has to say it. He must reveal his whole self to her.

It is a terrible effort but at last he tells her what has not before been told. 'I was in hospital for several months suffering from severe post-traumatic stress disorder. I was struggling to retain my sanity. I was finally given a kindly discharge on family grounds because of my brother's death and my dying father's need of me. It saved me. It gave me something to live for; something new to tackle. I had some agonising times, however, when I was trying to avoid being sucked into that black hole again. It gradually seemed better not to speak of it; not even to think of it.'

'I'm very sorry.' She presses his hands gently.

'You were my salvation,' he says abruptly. 'You finally turned the light on. I suppose I haven't said this because I don't want to remember. Also I don't want Liam to know the whole truth about his father. I'm not sure he is able to accept it.'

'Have you the right to keep it from him? He has to make his choices, doesn't he?' she asks, thinking of herself and Isobel.

'Perhaps not, but it's very hard. Seamas wasn't just a hero; he was also a terrorist and a killer who sometimes enjoyed it.'

'I'm glad you've told me. I can now know you better and, therefore, it is possible for us to make a fresh start. I suppose –' she smiles at him – 'I tended to think of you as a superior Conrad who wanted to marry me.'

He smiles back at her. 'I played up to that because I wanted so much to be with you, and to be honest because I enjoyed the sex.'

'Why shouldn't you? I was excellently trained. But delightful though it may be, it's only the icing on the cake. It's the real, solid stuff that lasts. That's love, I think. Only I knew nothing much about love.'

'I know that it's love that matters,' he replies firmly. 'You didn't believe me but I loved you from the beginning because of your shining blue eyes, your smile and your courage. And when you told me what you had been doing during the previous two years I knew I was right. It needs courage and love to live among the desperately poor and help them.'

'Although I didn't understand it, I think perhaps I loved you for your strength and stability and because you gave me a home, which I'd never, had before. It seems, therefore, that we have a basis from which to start again if we want to.'

'I want to with all my heart! Life without you is an empty wilderness. But do you want to?'

'Of course I do! It's especially important now,' she tells him seriously. 'We really must start again. We can't fail now. We must make the right decisions this time.'

'Why do you say that?'

'Because,' she tells him abruptly, 'I'm pregnant. We are going to have a baby in less than seven months' time.'

He stares at her. For the moment he is shocked and bewildered. 'What do you mean?' This is totally unexpected.

'It's quite simple. I mean exactly what I say. Grannie guessed straightaway, and it was confirmed yesterday. I hope you're not upset.'

There are no words adequate to express what he feels. First, he lifts her hands and kisses them, then he pulls her close and kisses her tenderly on the lips. Finally, he sits up suddenly looking at her. 'But you said it was impossible?'

'Not impossible but improbable. When nothing happened I think we both decided it was impossible. I realised you actually need me, so I think I fell in love recently and that's why it happened.'

'It's about time you did fall in love!' he exclaims and kisses her again. 'Thank God you did!'

'You're happy to be a father, then?' Before he can answer, there is a discreet tap on the door. 'Send me away if you need more time,' Maggy says cheerfully, 'but soup, coffee and sandwiches are ready.'

Philip, after hurrying to open the door, takes the tray from Maggy and helps to serve the food. Smiling, Maggy comes in. 'All is well, I think,' she says as she sits down. When they agree, she adds warmly, 'That's good! That's how it should be. A child is one of God's greatest gifts, particularly when you've almost despaired of it!'

Magda says, 'It seems like a miracle.'

'It is a miracle,' Philip agrees firmly. 'A blessing I no longer expected to have.'

For a short time they are all happy living in the present. The past is forgotten; the future unknown; they rejoice in these golden moments. They are old enough and wise enough, however, to know that all happiness in this world is transitory. And so they glimpse dark shadows gathering. For Maggy it is the sadness of old age, which will gradually take away all familiar things. For Philip there is the growing realisation that he must continue now to be true to himself, leaving the greed and power-seeking of the financial world and start life once again, repudiating his earlier mistakes. Magda believes that she is at last learning to love but knows that she must nurture this gift if she is to keep it.

For Magda also there is the pain of knowing that Isobel has turned away from her in the moment when she loved her most and that, since her daughter is so like Lisa, she may have much yet to endure.

Wisely, however, they ignore these threatening clouds and rejoice in the light for the moment. 'I think,' Maggy suggests, 'it is the right time to get out my last precious bottle and drink to the happiness and health of the coming child.'

It is a blessed moment – one of those few which come in life; one which gives hope and banishes despair.

Epilogue

The storms of winter have long passed and it is late summer when Lisa goes at last to the clearing in the woods to meet her lover of long ago.

He is waiting for her in the place where they first consummated their love. The grove is saturated in midday stillness. The sun shines through the leaves making delicate patterns on the grass. Even the birds are silent as if holding their breath.

As he turns to meet her she sees that he is still a handsome, erect man in spite of his white hair and seventy-five years. 'You are as beautiful as ever!' he exclaims.

She smiles, but there is mockery in her voice as she tells him, 'It owes more to art than nature these days, I'm afraid.'

'Why have you taken so long? It is months since I wrote to you.'

'I was having treatment for my illness,' she tells him coolly.

'Have you recovered?' He is immediately anxious.

'I'm in remission – perhaps for many years, if I'm lucky.'

'Thank God for that!' He takes one of her hands and raises it to his lips.

'I was also waiting to see if Magda's child would be safely born. She deserves that after what I made her suffer.'

He has not expected this. 'Did you know about that, then?'

'Yes, she was generous and wrote to me twice. The first time was soon after she knew it was expected and the second time was recently when he was safely born – a healthy boy. But I suppose you know it all?'

'Yes, I have met them. Philip has partly retired and they are moving out of London soon, I believe.'

She smiles. 'So I suppose we may say that our story has had a happy ending.'

There is something in her voice and her smile which worries him. 'What do you mean?' he asks.

'I mean simply that our illicit relationship has finally resulted in a success. Our daughter is happily married and she has a legitimate child. Surely that pleases you and the family?' Her tone is light and casual.

'Of course, but can't we talk about us?'

'There's not much to say, is there? Do you mind if we walk back slowly to my car. I don't enjoy standing too long.'

'I had hoped we might sit on our log and talk,' he suggests.

She laughs. 'How romantic! But what have we to talk about?'

'I only want to tell you, Lisa, that I still love you and have always loved you. I was weak and wrong when I deserted you but I still loved you.' There is so much he has prepared to say but she does not let him.

'That is very sweet of you, Charles, but it's pointless now, isn't it?'

'Of course it isn't,' he declares firmly. 'If you can manage to forgive me, we can still spend a few happy years together.'

That is too much for her. She laughs. 'And you think after all that has happened we can have a happy ending. You amaze me, Charles. We both acted badly and others suffered. We suffered, too; we were changed. We can't just walk into the sunset together with an angelic chorus. This is life, not a movie.'

'You are very scornful,' he protests. 'I deserve it, I know. What you really mean, I suppose, is that you can't forgive me.'

'I'm not sure that forgiveness has much to do with it. When I was so ill, I finally saw things clearly for the first time. It's not a matter of forgiveness, Charles. It's a matter of repentance. You're supposed to be a Catholic, so you must have been taught that it involves not just saying one is sorry but having a change of heart. It also means that one should try to make reparation to the person one has injured.'

'Of course I understand that. It's exactly what I'm trying to do! Surely, that's obvious?'

'No,' she tells him firmly, 'it's not as simple as that. The evil is in ourselves. My mother recently told me that I was always tempted to be greedy and envious. You, I think, have always been self-indulgent and lustful. Following our inclinations, we sinned inevitably and injured not only ourselves but also our child. You wanted to ignore her and I made use of her. Unfortunately, the evil doesn't stop there but it affects *her* child, Isobel. It would be quite wrong for us to be together. You can't avoid your fate. You're wanting to live in a dreamworld again.'

He is overwhelmed; she is so changed. 'Magda said something like that,' he mutters.

'Naturally, because it's the truth. Don't, please, destroy her security. She is happy, at last, with her baby son and the security and love Philip gives her. Don't interfere! Your job is to put yourself right, if you can. Believe me, it isn't easy.' They are now standing by her car. She smiles at him. 'I must go now.'

She gives him her hand. He tries to hold on to it but she resists him. 'You're very cruel, Lisa,' he says sadly.

'I think I always was,' she replies lightly. 'I'm trying to reform, as you should while you have the time.'

'Is there nothing I can do for you?' he asks while she unlocks her car.

She pauses. 'There might be.' Opening the door, she sits down. 'If you have any faith left, pray that I resist the temptation to offer a home and guidance to Isobel.'

'To Isobel?' he questions her. 'I thought she was living happily with her boyfriend.'

'She was, but they've split up. She's lonely and bitter.'

'Then you're just the person to help her, surely?'

Lisa shudders as she puts in her key. 'Haven't you learned *anything*, Charles? That would be the worst happening for all of us! It is what I'm most afraid of! She is much more like me than Magda. I need your prayers.'

He isn't sure that he understands but he does his best. 'I think I see what you mean. She would be better with Philip and Magda. I'm sure they will have her. Philip is very generous.'

She looks pityingly at him. 'But people don't always choose what is best, do they? We know that. She and I have much in common. I'm afraid I will be tempted.' After shutting her door, she lets down the window. 'Goodbye, Charles, and pray that the story ends happily.'

Before he can answer, she has shut the door and has moved off. He watches until her car disappears round the bend, then turns to walk to his home, alone and suddenly old.

Lightning Source UK Ltd.
Milton Keynes UK
11 August 2010
158219UK00001B/14/P